ALBERT R. BROCCOLI

presents

TIMOTHY DALTON

as IAN FLEMING'S JAMES BOND 007

"LICENCE TO KILL"

starring
CAREY LOWELL   ROBERT DAVI
TALISA SOTO   ANTHONY ZERBE
Production Designer PETER LAMONT
Director of Photography ALEC MILLS
Music by MICHAEL KAMEN
Associate Producers TOM PEVSNER
and BARBARA BROCCOLI
Written by MICHAEL G. WILSON
and RICHARD MAIBAUM
Produced by ALBERT R. BROCCOLI
and MICHAEL G. WILSON
Directed by JOHN GLEN

Cover: Timothy Dalton as James Bond in
"Licence to Kill"
Photo by Keith Hamshere.
© 1989 Danjaq S.A and
United Artists Company

LICENCE TO KILL

There was another dreadful scream. The tank's water boiled and there were odd flashes of movement and what seemed to be light. It took Bond a moment to realize that the creatures in the tank directly below him were electric eels. What a way to go, Bond considered . . .

"Freeze. Then turn around very slowly."

Killifer stood only a few feet away, a large briefcase at his feet and a very large .357 Magnum held in the two-handed grip. "You perform any fancy business and you'll make my day, punk." Killifer smiled at the Clint Eastwood imitation.

Bond sighed. "I do wish you wouldn't refer to me as 'punk,'" he said . . .

Ian Fleming's
JAMES BOND
in
LICENCE TO KILL

By **JOHN GARDNER**
FROM THE MOTION PICTURE WRITTEN BY
MICHAEL G. WILSON AND RICHARD MAIBAUM

CHARTER BOOKS, NEW YORK

LICENCE TO KILL

A Charter Book / published by arrangement with
Glidrose Publications Limited

PRINTING HISTORY
Charter edition / June 1989

ISBN: 1-55773-192-6

PRINTED IN THE UNITED STATES OF AMERICA

10 9 8 7 6 5 4 3 2 1

Contents

− 1 −

Get Me to the Church on Time

To use Royal Navy slang, James Bond was *adrift*. His old friend Felix Leiter, onetime member of the CIA, and former Pinkerton agent, would have said he was playing hookey, while the big black man, known as Sharky, summed it up. "You just tell 'em you gone fishin', James," he said. "Lord, I wish I was goin' fishin' 'stead of bein' dressed up like a monkey." He ran his fingers under the stiff white collar, then turned up the air-conditioning of the Bentley.

All three men were dressed in morning suits: pinstripe pants, stiff collars with dove-grey cravats, grey waistcoats and black swallowtail coats. Top

hats rested on their laps, and three buttonholes—
white roses, wrapped in silver foil speared by
pins—sat in a container balanced on the ledge
above the polished burr walnut fascia of the dash-
board.

"When they teach you to drive these things,"
Bond had told the agent now at the wheel, "they say
you should always think of a glass of champagne
standing above the dash. The trick is never to spill a
drop . . . Whoops, there goes half a glass!"

"James, you have got . . . ?" Felix began, not
even smiling.

"The ring?" Bond smiled, producing the little
box and flicking it open to reveal the solid gold
band. "That's the fourth time you've asked me,
Felix. You're as nervous as a Victorian virgin and
you've been through all this before."

Leiter grunted. "They say it's worse the second
time." His face creased into a smile. "Anyway, I've
got other things on my mind."

"Other things?" Bond raised his eyebrows.
"You're marrying an old friend of mine, Felix.
Della Churchill and I go back a long way, so
beware."

"We go back a long way as well, James, so you
should know I get edgy when the job intrudes on
normal life."

"What could be more important than your wedding day?" They were cruising over Seven Mile
Bridge, part of the Overseas Highway that runs for
over one hundred miles from Miami right down the

Florida Keys to Key West, where Felix Leiter was now stationed with the Drug Enforcement Agency. In a little over two hours he would be standing next to the beautiful Della in front of the altar of St. Paul's Church on Duval Street, which was better known for its bars and restaurants than the church.

"Oh, nothing, I suppose." Leiter's voice did not carry any conviction.

"Come on, Felix, what is it?"

"Well, I guess it's Sanchez."

"Franz Sanchez? The drug king?"

Leiter nodded. "For the past five years, I've been waiting for him to set foot on soil or sand where U.S. law can deal with him. But the callous SOB rarely moves out of Central America."

"What's that got to do with today: with your wedding?"

Leiter scratched his head. "You remember the phone call I got during that toxic stag party you threw for me last night?"

"Only vaguely." Bond smiled again. "I think I got bitten by a swarm of insects of the Pommery variety."

"Well, just take my word for it, I got a call."

"And?" Bond was quietly dragging the London file on Franz Sanchez into the forefront of his mind. The British Secret Intelligence Service felt it necessary to keep files on all kinds of villains: particularly those connected with terrorism or drugs, for large-scale drug dealers could easily be used to finance terrorism. Franz Sanchez, so named because of a supposed conjunction between a Fascist German woman and a wealthy Panamanian businessman.

"There's a chance that he'll be lured into the open anytime now."

In his head, Bond saw the photographs of the man. Tall, dark, undoubtedly handsome in a brutal sort of way and, it was said, one of the wealthiest men in the world, all his money and power emanating from the huge drug distributing market he controlled from his hideout in the Central American city of Isthmus. He recalled one note in the file which said, *Sanchez is a man who believes that anyone who opposes him can either be bought or killed.* In other words, he possessed that most dangerous of psychological defects, *folie de grandeur,* fueled by the power he wielded through drugs and money.

"Why lured now?"

"You've read his file?"

Bond nodded.

"Then you know of his lady friend."

"Miss Thing . . . Not Miss World . . . Miss . . ."

"Miss Galaxy. Star beauty queen. The delectable Ms. Lupe Lamora, though I don't believe *that* name for a moment."

"Quite a lady."

"Yes, and darned stupid as well. She's left him. Gone off with one of his former business partners. Guy called Alvarez."

"That figures." Bond shrugged.

"They're a dangerous mix, and Lupe's elopement with Alvarez is enough to flush Sanchez out."

Bond laughed. "I know what I'd rather be doing, Felix. I'd prefer a honeymoon with Della to the hurly-burly of the Sanchez-Alvarez-Lamora triangle. This is dull talk on your wedding day." He glanced out to the left and the Old Seven Mile Bridge which ran almost parallel with the structure over which they travelled: the longest stretch of the highway to run directly over the ocean on this hundred-mile-plus highway, which was the beginning, or end, of U.S. Route One.

It all looked tranquil enough, though Bond had reason to remember the dangers that could lurk along the Florida Keys. For no particular reason he twisted, glancing back, and there, almost on cue, he saw the white predatory shape of a helicopter approaching them fast from behind.

A second later they all heard the clatter of the engine, and within seconds the beast was flying alongside to their right—a big S-61B with U.S. Coast Guard in black against the white side of the machine. The door was open and a figure smiled down, waving and holding a printed "Follow Me" notice.

Felix Leiter waved back.

"Friend of yours?" Bond asked.

Leiter was sitting bolt upright. "Yeah, my DEA partner at Key West. Hawkins."

Quietly Sharky muttered an "Uh-oh."

They drove on for about a mile, watching the helicopter which had moved forward, speeding low over the bridge, then hovering and landing. By the time the Bentley arrived Hawkins was out of the door clutching a pile of papers.

Felix Leiter made a quick movement with his gloved left hand, expertly adjusting the mechanism of his artificial leg. Bond felt a wave of bleakness as he always did when he saw his old friend manipulate the false limbs, for the shark that had so mutilated Leiter a long time ago had been meant for him, and, in a strange way, Bond felt responsible.

The mood passed as he saw how nimbly Felix moved towards Hawkins. The disabilities were not apparent unless you knew about them.

Both Hawkins, a lean, tall and tanned man, and Leiter were already in animated conversation by the time Bond and Sharky reached them.

"He's out." Leiter laughed with pleasure. "The bastard's left his lair." His finger stabbed towards the map held by Hawkins. "There," he said with undisguised glee, the finger hovering over the tiny island of Cray Cay in the northern Bahamas. "Not far as these things fly. If we hustle we can catch him."

Bond flinched. "Felix, your bride . . ."

But Leiter was not even listening. "You got everything?" You could feel the anxiety and static.

"You betcha." Hawkins grinned. "Green light from Nassau; Indictment; Arrest Warrant; Extradi-

tion Request; and Mullins here for extra muscle."
Mullins, a very large black agent, nodded, smiling
down from the chopper's door.

"You're leaving nothing to chance, then?"
Bond's prepared sarcasm was lost on Leiter, who
was obviously in a very serious mood and merely
shook his head violently.

"Damned right I'm not. Sanchez is the prize and
we're going to get him at last."

"And Della?" Bond put a hand on Leiter's arm,
feeling the hard metal of the artificial wrist under
his fingers.

"Oh, James, for God's sake explain it to her. Just
ask her to hang on. With luck and a prevailing wind
we'll be back. You'll get me to the church on time."

"No way, Felix. You're going to be two hours late
at best."

"Well, just tell her to wait." Leiter was adamant.
"She'll understand. She knows about duty."

Bond shook his head. "I wouldn't bank on it. Nor
am I going to face Della. I'd rather come along with
you. Just for the ride, of course."

Sharky shrugged and began to walk back to the
Bentley. Over his shoulder he mouthed, "I'll tell
her. But, for pity's sake, you move your asses.
Right?"

Leiter was already climbing into the helicopter.
He looked down at Bond following him. "You're
only coming as an observer, you got that?"

"Naturally." Bond's face was a mask. "Would I
try to interfere?"

Within seconds the helicopter was lifting off, setting course, flying at full stretch. Below, Sharky looked up unhappily as he drove on towards Key West. He knew Della's temper and, like Bond, would rather face the ruthless and violent danger of Franz Sanchez than the scalding tongue of Della Churchill.

Cray Cay supported a small resort community, one airstrip and a few scattered clapboard houses. The nearest, and largest, of these stood only a few hundred yards from the end of the airstrip where Franz Sanchez's white-liveried Gates Learjet landed, then taxied back to the threshold, turning in readiness for a quick takeoff. Several light aircraft stood, unmanned, around the threshold, and there was a little red Piper Cub parked near the house.

The S-61B Coast Guard helicopter was only thirty miles away as Sanchez unhurriedly climbed from the jet, looked around and sniffed the air like a man savouring a new and delightful morning. He was followed down the deployed steps by his close henchman, known to everyone simply as Perez, and a pair of well-chosen hoods: Braun, a German who had a price on his head back in his native Berlin, and Dario: squat, greasy and generally unpleasant.

The two pilots made their way back from the flight deck and Sanchez signalled for them to stay close to the aircraft as a jeep rumbled to a halt nearby. The driver, a short man built in the same mould as the other heavies, addressed Sanchez with deference. "They're in the house over there, patron," pointing at the large single-storey construction. "The woman and Alvarez're inside. They have one guard, but he's usually drunk or asleep."

"And which is it at the moment?" Sanchez spoke quietly, radiating calm. To hear him you would not have thought of him as a man of violence.

"Asleep, patron. On the steps: you can see him from here. And I think the others are asleep also. They were up until four this morning. At least lights were burning until then. I stayed on watch as you ordered."

"You've done well. It won't be forgotten. Follow us after we go in." He nodded at the man in the jeep. Then, to the others, "It's a short walk, and a pity to wake them. However . . ." He jerked his head in the direction of the house.

A few yards from the steps Sanchez motioned to Perez, nodding towards the sleeping guard and sliding a finger across his own throat. Perez smiled and moved ahead, his hand going to the inside of his jacket from which he extracted a short length of cord.

The sleeping man neither heard nor felt a thing. Perez looped the cord around the guard's neck in the classic garotting motion, pulling quickly and hard. It was so well done that the man's neck was broken before he suffered any pain from a slow strangulation.

Quietly, with Sanchez in the lead, they went up the steps and into the house. For a moment, Sanchez stood in the cool of the hallway, as though instinctively seeking out his prey, finally jerking his head towards a door to the left. Silently he opened it and entered the room.

Alvarez slept on the far side of the bed, his hair tousled and his face in repose. Sanchez prided himself on his knowledge of human frailty, and he understood the younger man's motives. Women had always been Alvarez's weak point. Often Franz Sanchez had told him they would lead to his death. As for the beautiful Lupe, whose long dark hair spread across the pillow like a thick question mark, well, she could be forgiven. After all she was only a woman, and women had a habit of falling for younger men with glib tongues, and a good line of chat. Sanchez had often remarked to Alvarez that he should not promise his women so much. "Your problem, my friend," he had said, "is that you always have to tell them you love them. It is a great folly this, because they all have a tendency to believe you. One day you will say this to the wrong woman."

That day, he thought, had now come.

His eyes moved back to the sleeping man. There was a pistol within reach on the bedside table.

Quietly Sanchez drew his own automatic and began to whisper. "Alvarez . . . Wake up . . . Alvarez . . . time to start work." Then, louder, "Alvarez!"

The sleeping man's eyes popped open, fear crossing his face as he locked eyes with Sanchez. Then he moved, grabbing out towards the night table.

Sanchez fired twice and the table leaped into the air, sending the weapon skittering across the room. Perez and Braun, taking their cue from their chief, hauled the young man from the bed, holding him in an armlock, so that he stood naked between them, his eyes full of the terror reflected by the screams coming from the now wide-awake Lupe.

"Hush, pretty one. Shush." Sanchez put away his pistol and stepped towards her. "Don't be afraid. It's me, Franz. I wouldn't harm you. You know that. Punish you, perhaps, but never harm you." Then his eyes flicked up towards Alvarez, who, in spite of the warmth of the room, was shivering between Dario and Braun.

"What did he promise you, honey?" he asked Lupe. "Did he promise you his heart?"

The silence was unbearable: the group frozen like some waxwork tableau. Then Sanchez spoke again, harsh and commanding. "Give the lady what our friend Alvarez promised her."

Dario and Braun looked at him blankly.

"Give her this fool's heart."

Dario's eyes widened, seeming to plead for a moment.

"Do it! Now!" snapped Sanchez.

From under his jacket Dario produced a long serrated hunting knife.

"Out there!" Sanchez nodded towards the door through which his two hoodlums hustled the now whimpering Alvarez.

Taking three steps away from the bed, Sanchez closed the door, then returned to Lupe, who also shook with terror, sitting bolt upright with only the flimsy sheet held in front of her to cover her breasts, which showed clearly through the material: her nipples erect as though the terror and violence aroused her.

"Franz . . ." she managed to say, her voice cracked, the throat dry with terror. "Franz, I didn't mean . . ."

Sanchez smiled down at her, ruffling her thick hair with his hand. "It's okay, baby, we all make mistakes," his voice soothing.

"I only . . ." she began again.

"Sssssh, my dear. Not a word. Not another word." His hand twisted on her head, so that she turned her whole body to relieve the pressure. The sheet fell away exposing the wonderful shoulders and the slim curve of her back. Her skin, Sanchez often thought, looked to have the texture of silk.

Sanchez slid his right hand inside his jacket again, drawing a whip from his belt. It had been fashioned from the long tail of a stingray and he laid it, almost lovingly, across Lupe's naked back before lifting it and bringing it down with a terrible crack. The girl shuddered and screamed, again and again, as Sanchez brought the whip down covering her smooth back with ugly bloody stripes, painting a picture of surrealist violence on the canvas of her skin. Yet, even as she sobbed and screamed with pain, Lupe's voice was drowned by the bloodcurdling shrieks of Alvarez in the hallway.

A few seconds later, the screaming stopped and the unmistakable sound of a helicopter's engine, growing louder, rumbled and clattered from the sky.

Sanchez flung the girl away from him across the bed. "Get some clothes on. Quick. We must move."

The Coast Guard chopper came in low over the beaches, then crossed the airstrip, the pilot juggling with the cyclic and collective controls, his feet moving on the rudder bars like a dancer so that the large machine seemed to stand on its aft rotor, then turned to sweep back across the area.

"There," yelled Hawkins above the chattering din of the rotors, his hand outstretched. They could all see the jeep in front of the low house and, as they passed, something was thrown from one of the far windows.

"Jesus." Leiter swallowed hard. "That looked like a mutilated body. Head for the Learjet."

Hawkins made signals to the pilot, who turned again and brought his machine hovering in to block any attempted take-off by the jet.

As they reached the ground, Leiter, Hawkins and the agent called Mullins, who had done nothing but smile amiably since the takeoff from Seven Mile Bridge, grabbed at the rack of weapons fitted to the starboard side of the cabin, each selecting an M16 carbine. Leiter saw the look in Bond's eyes and, smiling, passed him an automatic pistol. "Only if absolutely necessary," he cautioned.

Bond shrugged and checked the magazine and action of the Browning 9mm.

Mullins was first out of the door, followed by Leiter, who shouted that he wanted Sanchez alive. "I have to take him back breathing," he called after Mullins, whose bulk was already in the doorway of the jet. Hawkins covered the two pilots, who quietly raised their hands, showing they were neither armed nor looking for trouble.

"Nobody in the airplane." Mullins returned, and in the breath of silence that followed, they all heard the noise of the jeep, audible above the slowly turning rotors.

"That'll be them!" Bond pointed to a dust cloud moving fast from the direction of the house.

"Upstairs!" Leiter was already scrabbling back into the chopper, which was hovering as Bond, bringing up the rear, eased himself into the door.

The jeep was a couple of hundred yards away, weaving through the dusty ground between patches of dark green undergrowth. The vehicle swung, skidding dangerously from side to side as the chopper, nose down, approached low, trying to block its escape.

They could see several men aboard, and Felix put

a few rounds from his M16 in front of the vehicle. Instead of stopping the jeep, the shots brought a hail of fire from its occupants. Inside the helicopter, the agents flinched as the thuds and metallic whines battered at the fuselage. The pilot spun the machine on its axis and began to hover, descending in front of the jeep. At the height of the firefight, nobody saw Sanchez roll free of the jeep into the scrub, turning, crouching and running, bent close to the ground, back towards the house.

As the chopper came to about ten feet from the ground, Bond, who had been standing in the doorway, leaped out, rolled and brought the pistol up in a one-handed grip, loosing off three sets of double shots, aimed at the wheels.

Two of the tyres exploded and the jeep went into a long uncontrolled skid, slamming sideways, starting to roll, then ending up on its side.

As the jeep came to a standstill with a grinding crunch, so Bond moved forwards, both arms outstretched and the pistol a simple extension of his hands. He fired another couple of shots as he glimpsed figures flitting into the undergrowth, shouting a "Come on! This way!" to the others.

There was a girl in the jeep. Alive, conscious but looking shocked and with tearstains damp on her cheeks. Bond rested his hands on her shoulders, asking if she needed help. But the girl simply glanced towards the undergrowth into which the men had disappeared, and shook her head.

"You need a doctor," he said, looking closer.

There was something very wrong with this beautiful young woman.

At that moment Hawkins reached the jeep.

"They're in the bushes somewhere." Bond let go of the girl and took two steps towards the undergrowth.

"Stop!" The shout was from Leiter, who was signalling the helicopter forwards. "There! There!" He pointed, and, for the first time they saw, and heard, the little Piper Cub which had been parked near the house. It was gathering speed and the pilot raised his hand in a salute.

"Sanchez!" Leiter was white with anger. "We've lost him. He can be in Cuban airspace in twenty minutes."

The helicopter reached them just as the Cub became airborne.

"We can outrun him in this." Bond was already clambering back into the helicopter. To the pilot he shouted, "Can you keep up with that Piper?"

The pilot nodded and the machine began to rise again.

"You're supposed to be an observer, James. What're you trying to do, get yourself killed?"

"If I don't get you to the church within a reasonable margin of time, Della's going to kill me anyway," he said with an almost studied nonchalance. "And in twenty minutes you'll be right on time, only it's going to take us at least an hour and a half, not counting stopping time to pick up

Sanchez. Prepare for squalls, Felix."

Leiter's brow creased as he saw Bond reach out for the winching gear, complete with hook and line.

"What the hell're you doing?"

"Just what Sharky advised. I'm going fishing. Sanchez's just below us now. I'm going to give you a wedding present. Operate the winch, Felix, and instruct the pilot." With a smile, Bond swung out on the line, wrapping it around his leg with a practised flick.

The airflow caught his body and he swung backwards in a stomach-rolling twist. Glancing down, the world twirled, spinning, and Bond wondered what in heaven's name he thought he was doing. This was not only damned uncomfortable but also bloody dangerous. Some forty feet below him was the Cub's red tail fin, and he motioned to Felix, who started to winch him down.

Slowly the light aircraft grew larger and Bond began to be caught in both its slipstream and the downdraft of the rotors. Below the aircraft there was the best part of a thousand-foot drop into the sea. He felt his hair being blown around, and it was necessary to close his eyes because of the forces eddying about his face.

Bond grabbed towards the airplane's tail, missed, swung sideways, grabbed again and missed again.

Behind him there was a flapping noise which distracted him until he realised it was simply the tails of his morning coat blowing and cracking in the wind. In spite of the fear that engulfed him, Bond began to laugh. He was thinking that he must look a ludicrous sight, like some movie stuntman doing a particularly daring act for the cameras.

Suddenly the chopper seemed to put on speed and Bond threw his arms around the top of the tail fin, his body crashing painfully into the rudder.

In the cockpit, Sanchez felt the weight and fought the controls, deftly tinkering with the trim tabs to restore the airplane's balance.

But Bond had begun to inch himself down the rudder, making the plane yaw to and fro, his body swinging from side to side as Sanchez made sharp corrections. Bond traversed lower, feeling for the towing ring set behind the tail wheel.

His hands were sore, burning with pain, and he fought desperately to pull at the line which hung below his foot, trailing backwards in the wind with the hook jerking at the rope. It seemed to take hours, a few minutes in reality, to draw the line upwards and grasp the hook, one arm wrapped around the tail, the other hand on the hook, fighting the pressure until he had brought it up and around the Piper Cub's tow ring. But at last it was done. Bond hung on, his head straining upwards trying to see if Felix and the pilot had the right idea.

They had. The big helicopter slowed and the rope took the strain. Bond, clinging on like the proverbial grim death, prayed that there had been no parachute in the Cub's cockpit. Not that it would have mattered much. Jumping into the sea in these waters would almost certainly mean a blowout for the sharks.

Sanchez would have been a fool if he had not worked out what the helicopter and its crew were attempting. He had bucked the aircraft from side to side, tried reducing power and then slamming the little Lycoming engine through the gate. Nobody, he thought, could possibly remain on the tail, but he continued to feel the drag increasing. Then, to his horror, he found the aircraft was beginning to wallow. Even with the engine at full throttle, the controls had become mushy and the airspeed began to bleed off steadily.

At stalling point, Sanchez, who was not known for fear, cried out. The controls went slack and the horizon began to rise above him as the airplane's nose dropped sickeningly, then stopped, the ground below swinging and spinning, yet the force of gravity having no effect.

It took Sanchez a full minute to realize that he was sitting in an airplane suspended from a helicopter's winch which was slowly being drawn upwards.

The latter action was only to allow Bond to get back inside the helicopter to the jubilant trio of Leiter, Hawkins and Mullins.

Once he was through the door, they let the line out a little so that, when they returned to the Coast Guard helipad, on the northwest side of the town, they could dump the plane softly onto the tarmac.

When they did arrive back, people poured out of

hotels and shops to watch this strange sight of a light aircraft swinging, suspended, under the helicopter.

People drinking in Sloppy Joe's and Captain Tony's came out onto the sidewalks; folks who had been patiently waiting in church for the wedding stampeded for the door as the news passed through St. Paul's like a brush fire; the good ole boys sitting around Garrison Bight, and the smart young people around the modern Marina, watched, hardly believing their eyes.

"Airplane wreck, I guess," said one of the good ole boys.

"If'n God had meant us to fly he'd've given us jet engines 'stead of assholes," another good ole boy spat accurately into the gutter.

Outside St. Paul's Church, Sharky pleaded with the beautiful Ms. Della Churchill, who had, only minutes before, called the whole wedding off.

"They're here, Della. Just twice more around the block and they'll be sitting up front there, with the preacher, ready to go."

Della took a deep breath, then relented. "Okay, only twice more though."

Sharky leaped into the Bentley, over his shoulder he shouted back at Della, "Twice more. Slowly, though. Very slowly."

As it was, the future Mrs. Leiter went around four times at a crawl. Only then were Felix Leiter and his best man, James Bond, in place, their white roses pinned correctly, though the morning clothes looked decidedly worse for wear.

So, almost three hours late, the strains of the Bridal Chorus from *Lohengrin* piped out and Della, an irritated glint in her eyes behind the veil, came beautifully down the aisle to go through the wedding ceremony at last.

"Well, they got me to the church almost on time," Felix said later on their way back to his delightful gingerbread house which had cost him a fortune, his entire CIA kiss-off money together with the accrued interest.

— 2 —

Unwanted Guests

JAMES BOND FOUND himself a quiet corner in the main room of Felix Leiter's house, nursing a glass of champagne, running his eyes over the guests, looking for what he thought of as "likely winners." He had spotted one earlier, outside the church. A tall and striking brunette dressed in a crisp pink suit. Yet, somehow the suit looked wrong, as though the girl preferred to slouch about in jeans and a T-shirt. It was only a quick impression that Bond could never have explained, but, as lovely as she was, the girl seemed out of place and, in his constant inquisitive hunt for the secret of women, he was anxious to talk with her.

His eyes searched the room, but the girl was missing so he began to review possible second choices. It was not as though he had all the time in the world, for he was already late on site for an assignment his chief, M, had authorised a week ago.

Around him the wedding party shrieked, laughed, babbled and appeared to be going true to form. He wandered over to the buffet, where white-coated waiters assisted in dispensing platefuls of jumbo prawns, accompanied by the usual hot red sauce; salmon, both cold and smoked, and a great assortment of salads. Bond saw there were puddings also and eyed the local Key lime pie which, if not a gourmet dish, he always found cleared the palate wonderfully.

Two girls, talking animatedly about diets and what they dared eat, stood together on his left, so Bond quietly intruded with a remark about the millions of calories that lay in front of them. They seemed happy enough after he had introduced himself and they, in turn, announced themselves to be Lizzie Owen, a short and bubbly attractive young woman who turned out to be an artist, and a shy blonde who simply gave her name as Pat. Bond marked the latter as possibly his best chance for the evening and began the tedious business of small talk, leading gently to more serious matters. Half an hour later he had discovered that Pat had come to Key West for a week, en route for Australia. That had been nine years ago.

"Some people regard this place as the really tacky end of Florida," she told him, "but it has a strange sense of unreality. It's a place of escape. Mind you, I really don't know how people like Hemingway ever managed to get any creative work done here."

Bond was about to make some light remark about Key West being different in Hemingway's time when he saw Della, looking radiant and very happy, heading in his direction. As she approached she raised her right hand displaying a long and lethal cake knife.

"James!"

Bond thought he had rarely seen her so happy. He put his hands up in mock surrender, looking at the knife. "Take whatever you want. Just don't do your Anthony Perkins imitation."

She wrapped her arms around his neck and kissed him hard on the lips.

"Hey, hey. You're a happily married woman now."

"Just claiming my rights. Bride gets to kiss the best man." She was the tiniest bit tipsy.

Bond held her away from him, his arms resting on her shoulders. "I thought it was the other way around; but no matter. Anything goes."

"It certainly does." She brandished the knife. "It's time to cut the cake, but where's the groom? I'll tell you where the groom is: he's closeted in his study, and with another woman."

"The cad. Want me to get him?"

"Seriously, James, could you? We really should cut the cake."

"Anything for a lady, especially if she's got a knife." He told Lizzie and Pat not to go away, quietly took the cake knife from Della, then went up the stairs to Felix's study. Reaching the door he tapped and walked straight in.

Felix was sitting at his desk in the centre of the room, operating his computer. Next to him, leaning over his shoulder to look at the screen, was the delightful brunette he had seen outside the church.

They both looked up in surprise, but neither showed any sign of guilt.

"I'm sorry, I didn't know you had . . ." Bond began.

"Come on in, James, we're almost finished." He turned to the girl and handed her a sealed envelope. "There you go, Pam." Then, turning to Bond, "James, meet Pam."

Pam gave him an almost curt, utterly disinterested nod. She touched Leiter on the shoulder and said, "Goodbye, then, Felix. See you around," and went to the door without another look at Bond, who gave his old friend a quizzical look.

Leiter smiled. "Strictly in the line of duty, James. Nice girl but business only."

"Business or not, you've got a houseful of guests and they're waiting to cut the cake and make lame speeches with slightly risqué jokes. In other words, Della's on the warpath and sent me to get you."

Leiter turned to his computer and performed one

keystroke. "Okay, let me just save this and I'll be ready to face anyone. Take a seat, I'm afraid the DEA never sleeps and they want a full report yesterday."

Bond sat, knowing that, even on a wedding day, people like Felix, and himself come to that, had to put their jobs and duty first. Leiter was still talking. "I've a great deal to thank you for, my old friend. Without you, we wouldn't have got Sanchez. I think I told you he hasn't been out of his home base in a long time."

Bond grunted. "You couldn't extradite him from Central America?"

Leiter shook his head. "No way. That guy's intimidated, killed or bribed most of the government officials from here to Chile. Down there, they have only one law. Sanchez's Law—*Plomo o Plata.*"

"Lead or silver," Bond quietly translated.

"Right." Leiter closed down the computer and was about to get up when the door burst open and a tough-looking, grey-haired man came barging in, a big cigar clamped between his teeth.

"Ed!" Leiter greeted the newcomer with surprised delight. "James, meet Ed Killifer, our senior agent down here."

Killifer seemed to have hardly heard the introduction, for he spoke directly to Felix. "Double congratulations, old buddy. Great job you did. Now, just you take your time over the honeymoon." Then he turned to Bond. "Guess you must be James Bond, the guy who went along for the ride?"

Bond made a modest gesture.

"Some ride, huh? A great job. Don't know how to thank you, James."

"Give the credit to Felix. Between the three of us I'd rather have my name left out of this." He warmed to Killifer, mentally summing him up as one of those hardworking, dedicated, salt-of-the earth agents. A fast-disappearing breed from most intelligence, security and drug enforcement organizations.

"You'll never credit what that bastard did when we started to interrogate him."

"I'd believe anything of Sanchez." Felix's smile had disappeared.

"The son-of-a-bitch actually said he'd never come to trial. That he had too many people in his pocket. I told him he was facing at least a hundred and thirty-nine felony counts, and none of his famous million-dollar bribes would get him out of this. You know what he said? Two million's what he said. Cool as an iced beer. Hawkins looked like his socks had been blown off. That scumbag was offering *us* two million U.S."

Bond frowned as Killifer continued, "I told him. 'None of your filthy money's gonna get you out of this one, Sanchez. You're hooked.'" Turning to Bond, "Hooked! Good huh? I told him straight that he wasn't in some banana republic now. He just looked at me. Funny kinda look he has. Then he said, 'Very righteous, Mr. Killifer, but I think I'll be home very soon.' Some hope. They've got a cell all set up for him in the high-security block at Quantico and they're gonna ring the place with marines. No way is he gonna get out."

"Come on, Ed, come and have a drink. We're just going to cut the cake." Leiter was now standing.

"No. Sorry, pal, but I just came over to kiss the bride and wish you luck. I'm still on duty, we're leaving in half an hour. Everything's set to take *Mr.* Sanchez to Quantico. We go all the way to Virginia, and I won't rest till I've handed him over." He thrust out his hand to Leiter, pumping his arm as though trying to dislodge it from its socket. "See you around, buddy, and you take care of that bride." He turned and gave Bond a firm, dry handshake. "Nice to have met you, Bond. Hope there'll be another time. See you around, okay?" He gave an expansive wave with his right hand, the big cigar tucked between his fingers, and left the room.

"One of the best men in the business." Leiter slid out the disk and tapped it with his forefinger. "First rule when you're working with micros. Always keep a backup safely stored away. You never know. If something happens, you lose all the data." He then tucked it away behind a framed photograph of Della which stood next to a nice little plaster repro of one of the soldiers from the famous Qin

Shiuang's terra-cotta army. He took the cake knife from Bond. "Let's face the music. Della should be just about ready to kill me." At the door he stopped, placing the gloved false hand on Bond's arm. "I don't have to tell you how grateful I am—for everything."

"What are friends for?" Bond asked, realising that he really wanted to quiz Felix about the lovely young dark-haired beauty who had been in the study, but holding his tongue. He would look for her later, and maybe . . . Well, who knew?

At the Drug Enforcement Headquarters across the Key, they were ready to move Sanchez out for the journey to Quantico, and they were taking no chances. An armoured van stood near the doors, and the prisoner, looking quite unconcerned, was led from the building in chains which ran from his wrists to his ankles, which were also shackled with just enough chain to allow him an undignified shuffle. He was flanked by a pair of marshals, each armed with a shotgun, while another two marshals' cars stood by. On the helipad a police chopper stood, its rotors at idle.

Ed Killifer, having made his appearance at the wedding reception, brought his car to a halt in his marked parking slot, got out and walked over to Sanchez and the marshals, the eternal cigar clamped between his lips. He smiled grimly at Sanchez. "All ready for the joyride?"

"They didn't even give me time to pack an overnight case." Sanchez was infuriatingly confident.

"Where you're going, you'll need a couple of million night cases." Killifer was near to sneering. "Okay, boys, let's hit the road."

They helped Sanchez into the back of the armoured van where other chains were padlocked to steel rings on either side of the uncomfortable bench which ran along one wall of the van. With a nod, Killifer slammed the doors and one of the marshals inside pulled the locking mechanism.

"Have to be a Houdini to get out of that," Killifer muttered as he walked to the front of the van, picked up a shotgun and climbed in next to the driver. "Okay," he shouted boisterously, "wagons, ho!"

Slowly the convoy pulled away, a marshal's car in front of the armoured van, another behind and the police helicopter patrolling the sky overhead.

Once on Route One, they picked up speed: everyone, from the police in the chopper to Killifer beside the armoured van driver, alert, and ready for anything.

About a mile out of Key West, on a small stretch of bridge, the lead car signalled the convoy to slow down. Ahead a sign read, *Caution! Bridge Under Repair.* A section of the metal guardrail on the right had been removed and coned off to mark a stretch of temporary wooden fencing.

The police, high above, watched the first mar-

shal's car pass the spot, but as the armoured van
came abreast of the coned wooden fence, the van
suddenly seemed to speed up and slew sideways.

The bonnet hit the fence, which shattered under
impact. For a second the van appeared to leap
outwards and hang in space. Then, as though in
slow motion, it dipped and plunged into the muddy
water below.

Both the marshals' cars screamed to a halt and
the chopper descended, turning low over the spot
where the van had hit the water. The air was full of
the crackle of radios calling for special backup.

The armoured van sank almost lazily in the deep
water. In the rear, next to Sanchez, the two armed
marshals struggled in the last-remaining air. As the
interior filled, one of them managed to get the door
open, and, leaving Sanchez to his certain death, the
marshals were sucked out, exploding on the surface
with the last big air bubble. The first thing they saw
was the police chopper dangling its winch line to
help them.

Far below, the van came to rest on the bottom,
throwing up a cloud of sand, and sending a shoal of
snapper skimming off for the shelter of a labyrinth
of rocks. From under the bridge came what at first
seemed to be larger fish, making the sponges and
trailing flora of the sea wave gently as though in a
light breeze. But these were not fish. Figures in wet
suits, with breathing masks, air bottles and flippers,
moved swiftly along the ocean floor. They came in
two sets of three, the first trio heading directly for

the van, the others remaining as though on guard, spear guns at the ready, because more dangerous things than red snapper inhabited these waters. The first diver swam quickly into the rear of the van. He carried a spare breathing pack and mouthpiece, which he rammed into Sanchez's mouth until the man began to suck in air and open his eyes.

Meanwhile, the second frogman was busy dealing with the chains, using a heavy-duty bolt-cutter. When they had Sanchez free, they fitted the air bottle around his shoulders and helped him to swim clear.

At the front, in the van's cabin, the other frogman was fitting a mouthpiece and air bottle to Killifer, dragging him out as though taking a hostage.

Within seconds a large Plexiglas-domed undersea sledge appeared, its motors slowing so that the pilot could hover close to the van. The three divers almost lazily brought Sanchez and the captive Killifer over to the sledge and helped them aboard, while the guards snaked away, moving through the busy and beautiful world, with its own brand of flowers and strange-shaped rocks, at a surprising speed. A minute later, the pilot of the sledge opened the throttle and the long, shark-like vehicle moved away, back in the direction of Key West, clinging low near the ocean floor as it built up speed.

* * *

Bond had been unable to find the dark girl in the pink suit whom Felix had introduced as Pam, so he settled for the blonde Pat, whose shyness had almost completely disappeared. Night had come, as usual in Key West, with a spectacular sunset, and the wedding party had wound down.

"Time to go," Bond said to the blonde. "Fancy dinner? I'm staying at the Pier House."

"Oh, I couldn't eat another thing, Mr. Bond." She looked up at him with sloe eyes. "Except, perhaps, you."

Bond smiled. "Good, I rather fancy a light snack in my room." They headed for the door where Felix and Della waited, saying goodbye to their guests.

"Just one little thing before you go, James." Della gave Pat a rather wickedly jealous smile.

"Not another knife?"

"No." Felix stepped forwards, his good hand moving to his pocket. "The best man always gets a gift." He withdrew a small velvet box which he handed to Bond. "A small mark of thanks"—he paused—"from the Leiters."

Inside the box, nestling in a velvet tray, lay a solid gold Dupont cigarette lighter. Bond smiled as he took it out to see the engraved words *James, With love ever, Della & Felix*.

"It's the thought that counts," Bond said. "You're both tempting me now that I'm down to five a day." He flicked the lighter on and they jumped back as the butane flame leaped skywards.

"Jeeerusalem!" Bond mouthed, capping the flame quickly.

Della giggled. "It does need some adjustment. But the thought was there."

Bond thanked them and they embraced. "Look after her, Felix. Look after her well." He held Leiter's eyes with his, still thinking of the strange girl in pink he had encountered in his friend's study.

Della leaned forward to kiss him, whispering, "I don't have to tell you to have a good night."

Bond helped Pat into the Six-Sixes cab that waited for them and was still waving as the cab turned the corner out of sight.

"Well, Mrs. Leiter, how about me carrying you across the threshold?"

"Watch it, Felix, you're no good to me with a strained back."

They were both laughing as they reached the bedroom. But there the hilarity stopped. Felix froze inside the door, Della still in his arms, head thrown back as the laughter died.

Leiter recognised the two men who stood in the window, the drapes softly moving around them. He had seen the pair among Sanchez's men at Cray Cay and now they were here, unwelcome guests at his wedding.

One of the men, the Germanic-looking of the two, had a pistol in his hand. Slowly Leiter put his bride down on her feet and stepped in front of her. "Leave her out of this," he said quietly. "I'm a different matter, but she has nothing to do with my work."

"Sure." The man called Dario moved forwards. "Sure, Mr. Leiter, we'll leave her here. Don't worry about it." As he spoke a short-barrelled shotgun seemed to appear suddenly in his hands, and with one movement he clubbed Leiter to his knees.

Braun had to push in and grab Della, jamming a hand over her mouth to stop her screams.

— 3 —

Lightning Sometimes Strikes Twice

KEY WEST INTERNATIONAL Airport always struck Bond as a somewhat pretentious title, for the major number of scheduled flights were made by twin-engined Pipers, Beechcrafts or, if you were really lucky, those wonderful old DC-3s (C-47s as the Americans called them) which had seen sterling service prior to Big Two, a euphemism for World War II which Bond rather liked. The main international destination of ninety percent of these flights was Miami.

On the day after Felix Leiter's wedding, Bond made his way into the relatively small departures building of Key West Airport. He had breakfasted well, paid his bill at the Pier House, asking them to give the lady in his room anything she required and charge it to his Amex card, and now, walking from the cab to the tiny departures lounge, he realised two things. First, he felt much fitter than he had any right to feel; second, the lounge was unusually crowded. People were actually still outside the door, standing in line for the one check-in counter. There were no first-class check-ins at Key West. As someone once remarked, "You're rather lucky to get a check-in at all."

Bond stood in line for fifteen minutes before he reached the harassed young lady who took his ticket. "What's going on here this morning?" he asked pleasantly. There were a large number of police, marshals and security men around, which was most unusual.

"Oh, some big-wheel drug dealer got arrested yesterday, then escaped," the girl said, still looking down at the ticket." She looked up, but her Mr. Bond had vanished and an elderly lady stood in front of her tapping a ticket on the counter.

"Oh, gee." The check-in girl looked anxious. "I hope it wasn't anything I said."

Bond paid off the cab he had grabbed outside the airport. He was within fifty yards of Felix's house and he must have beaten some records getting to the front door. Far away inside, the telephone was ringing. He tried the door and it opened easily into a home which seemed to have been almost syste-

matically wrecked. He looked around for the phone
but it had stopped ringing, another sound taking its
place, a buzzing in Bond's head, accompanied by a
terrible churning in his stomach. No, he thought,
no, it could never have happened twice, and his
mind began to spin into an horrific nightmare.
Taking a few paces into the large main room, he
saw the bedroom door was open. There was a
blurred glimpse of white. Something on the bed. A
dozen steps took him to the door and Della.

She had been arranged on her back, still in the
wedding dress in which he last saw her, hair neatly
spread on the pillow and her hands clasped together on her chest: clasped in a terrible red stain.

"No!" Bond said aloud. "No! No! Della! No."
But it was not a nightmare. He was alive and
standing here in this room, close to the bed. At first
his mind refused to accept the truth that the
obscene thing sticking in the centre of the great red
stain was the haft of a dagger and someone had
placed her hands neatly around the weapon. He
also saw now that there was more blood, higher up
around her neck.

Bond reached out to feel for a pulse, knowing he
would not find one, and as his fingers touched flesh,
Della Leiter's head rolled to one side displaying the
vicious slash that had sundered her throat. He
actually recoiled, as though the cold flesh would
have stung his fingers, and he was aware of his
mouth twisted in grief.

He raised his head, feeling so shocked that he

could hardly take anything in. Yet facts were forcing their way to his brain. He saw other stains running from the bedroom window and realised that he stood in damp splatters of blood that formed a trail through the room and out into the body of the house.

"Not again!" Bond heard his own voice and knew exactly what he meant. His near total recall of that terrible time in Miami, when Felix lost half a leg and an arm to Mr. Big's shark, came scurrying, like a pack of tarantulas, into his head. This time, Felix had already lost his new bride and Bond began to face the probability of his old friend being dead also.

He followed the trail of blood up the stairs, and experienced a number of horrifying sensations: Felix' gloved false hand on his own arm; the man's laugh; memories of a girl called Solitaire, the scent she used—Vent Vert—and the sick message Leiter's torturers had left. *He disagreed with something that ate him.* Strangest of all, his mouth and taste buds brought back the flavour of Key lime pie which he had eaten during the wedding reception. Was it only yesterday?

Walking into Leiter's study was like stepping into the past. In a way, he had known what was there before opening the door, but when he saw it, the whole of his being shrank back. The room had been ransacked, but there, on the leather couch, lay the bundle wrapped in a rubber sheet, blood dripping from it onto the floor.

Bond gritted his teeth. The whole thing had a doom-laden sense of *déjà vu*. Quickly he unwrapped the sheet. The only question now was whether Felix was alive.

What was left of his clothing was bloody and torn, the false limbs were gone, and with them a lot of flesh and some bone around the stump of his leg, together with jagged rips in the shoulder to which he once fitted the artificial arm.

Leiter moved his head, took a deep breath and groaned—"Della?"

Before Bond had a chance to quiet his old friend the telephone shrilled out. It took over a minute to find the instrument.

"Felix, where the hell you been . . . ?" The voice at the distant end was Hawkins.

"It's not Felix." Bond was struggling for control. It was almost impossible that this kind of thing could happen to a man a second time. "It's Bond, Hawkins. You'd best get over here pretty fast and send an ambulance ahead. And the cops. Something pretty dreadful's happened." He slammed down the phone and ran from the room. There was a guest room down the hall and Bond dashed to it, tearing the sheets from the bed, returning to Leiter, using the torn sheeting, trying to staunch the flow of blood from leg and shoulder. He had no doubt as to what had done this, just as he had quickly known on that other occasion years before. The tearing gashes had been made by a shark, or some other razor-toothed predator. Bond would have bet considerable funds on it being a great white.

The ambulance and paramedics arrived, and Hawkins came with the police. They took Felix away after working on him for the best part of half an hour, tying off veins and generally making him as comfortable as they could with injections which dropped him into merciful oblivion.

The police saw to Della, taking photographs first and doing all things normal in this abnormal situation. A scene-of-crime squad worked in the main bedroom while the officer in charge, a leathery-skinned captain, went through everything with Bond and Hawkins.

"Well," the captain said at last, "I have no doubt this is somehow related to the Sanchez thing."

"I only found out about it at the airport this morning," Bond said grimly, his mind on what might be happening to Felix, and whether they could possibly do anything for him. "What actually happened?"

Briefly the captain and Hawkins went through the scenario of the escape.

"We thought the bastard'd bought the farm until divers went down. Somehow it was a rescue operation. People got to the van, and Sanchez had been cut free from the shackles." The captain scowled. "It was a very well mounted operation, considering the time element."

"They took Killifer with them," Hawkins added.

"We're expecting him back in a body bag, or some kind of ransom note."

They talked for a further ten minutes, and the captain was about to leave when raised voices came from downstairs.

Sharky was attempting to get into the house and becoming very belligerent with the police guarding the door.

"You can let him in," Bond said. "He's a close family friend."

The captain nodded. "Okay. Keep in touch, Mr. Bond. I might well have a few more questions."

Hawkins added that he would also be in touch, and the pair left the house.

"What in hell happened?" Sharky looked angry, his eyes showing a mixture of desperation and fury. "I know about Della, but Felix . . . ?"

"Someone fed him to the sharks."

"But . . . ?"

"Yes, I know, Sharky. Lightning isn't supposed to strike twice, but it has. My guess is that they didn't know about his arm and leg. The shark, or sharks, chewed up the artificial limbs and just sliced the flesh off the stumps. I imagine he's going to be okay, but the trouble'll begin when they tell him about Della."

Sharky nodded. "Know what you mean. This down to Sanchez? I heard he's gone missing."

"Sanchez is the best bet."

"What we gonna do, James?"

"Well, I, for one, am going shark hunting. Know

any good spots where someone might keep an untamed pet?"

"They got some small ones in the aquarium. Right on the ocean at the bottom of Duval. But that wouldn't be any good to Sanchez. The . . ." He stopped abruptly as a sudden thought struck him. "Hey, wait a minute. There's this place on the other side of the Key. What the hell's it called? Ocean something. Ocean Exotica, that's it. They have this big warehouse, built out on a pier. All kinds of fish there. They're also into some kind of special breeding. Some guy told me they have pumps or something for fattening up fish. Large place, and there'd be plenty of room under the pier to keep a shark cage."

"What're we waiting for, then?"

The Ocean Exotica Warehouse was sited within a small cove on the eastern side of the Key. Sharky said that his father, who had lived around the Florida Keys all his life, maintained that the area had been a favourite beach party and swimming place until it was bought up by some firm in Miami in the early 1970s. Certainly whoever owned the company had a great strategic advantage, for the pier on which the large building stood could be approached only from one road. Anyone watching from the place would spot visitors a long way off.

Using Sharky's car they drove almost to the door. Bond got out and looked around. There was a light breeze but the afternoon had turned hot, the air clear and pleasant. The first thing that Bond took in was the camouflage.

From a distance, the warehouse looked as though it was built in a clapboard style which had become decayed and even crumbling over the years. Close to, however, you could see it was a stout two-storey stone building with a rough clapboard overlay which seemed almost to have been antiqued by human hand.

From the metalled roadway there was a walk of fifty yards or so to the gable end of the place which towered above, built on a very solid pier, the piles of which had no trace of decay about them. A metal catwalk, complete with guardrails, ran around the outside, and the entire area must have taken up at least fifteen thousand cubic feet.

There was one door in the gable end, and next to it a polished brass plaque which read, *Ocean Exotica Inc.*

Alone by the door, with Sharky in the car, Bond composed himself, allowing his face to take on the look of a man who was a little out of his depth. He reached for the little metal silver card case he usually carried and selected a business card with care. Only then did he press the bell push set next to the plaque.

It was several minutes before someone slid back bolts on the other side of the door, which opened to reveal a man in shirt and blue jeans, carrying a shotgun in the crook of his arm. "Yeah?" he asked, as though he did not care a damn about what the caller wanted.

"This is the Ocean Exotica Warehouse?" Bond asked, pitching his voice high and using an exaggerated and affected English accent.

"Yeah," the guard said. This time the word was an answer, last time it had been a question. Bond, with Felix Leiter very much to the forefront of his mind, recalled the early days of their friendship when Leiter had cautioned him about American language. You could get by with three words, Leiter said—"Yeah," "Nope" and "Sure." But that was long ago and very far away.

Bond burst into rapid speech. "I'm from Universal Exports, Marine Branch, of course. You've corresponded with us and I'm here on behalf of the Regent's Park Zoological Gardens Aquarium Department. I have to arrange for the shipment of a *Charcharodon carcharias.*"

"A what?" The guard moved a little further towards him. Bond had already glimpsed the inside of the warehouse, which was well lit, the walls filled with huge glass tanks—very much like the London Regent's Park Zoo Aquarium but on a much larger scale. He also took in a humming noise, as though some electrical engine was at work.

"Charcharodon carcharias," Bond repeated. "Great white shark."

The man made as though to close the door, but Bond put his foot inside. "We're closed," said the guard firmly, then a hand appeared on his shoulder, quietly pushing him to one side and opening the door a little wider. The man who had appeared was dressed in smart leisure clothes. Apart from that he was distinctly unsavoury. He was short, running to fat and with the florid complexion of a heavy drinker. He stood, legs apart, trying to stare Bond down. A bully if ever there was one.

"I've come all the way from London," Bond pleaded, still using his English yuppy accent. "I understood . . ."

"I heard you. The name's Krest. Milton Krest." He still tried to stare Bond down and a small smile of superiority played around his lips.

"Oh, how d'you do . . ." Bond began, edging his way forwards so that he was now just inside the door.

"Our sharks were sold off years ago." The smile had gone from Krest's lips, and his eyes glazed over as though made of ice. He jerked his thumb over his shoulder. In the centre of this forward part of the building stood a strange machine which reminded Bond of some unpleasant piece of sci-fi equipment. It looked as though it was made of grey plastic, cone-shaped with long tubes running from its main body, snaking everywhere, like giant tendrils, across the floor and into the tanks. There must have been sixty or seventy of these tubes, and the whole thing shook gently from side to side.

"We only do research here now," Krest continued. "The company's working on a project which will help to feed the Third World."

"Oh, how jolly interesting," Bond gushed, almost ashamed of himself. Then any other thoughts were removed from his mind, for behind the strange, pulsating piece of equipment he spotted a large undersea sledge with a smooth Plexiglas dome. The sledge would probably take ten people, including its crew, and while it would not be any use at great depths, it was certainly just the thing for inshore work—even for pulling people out of armoured security vans.

Krest was still talking. "That's a maggot incubator. Dispenses the right kind and right number of maggots to the tanks. From that, we feed a special breed of genetically engineered fish."

"How very interesting."

"Yeah, ain't it? We use hormones to make them all males. Sex changes're our speciality here. Makes 'em grow." He had allowed Bond to come a few feet into the warehouse now. Red fish, some of them fat and up to five feet in length, were crowded into the tanks along the wall to the right. Other species swam in even larger tanks to the left. Behind both sets of tanks there were long walkways, and Bond could see other walkways higher, above the larger tanks.

"Yes, very interesting indeed." Bond gestured towards the long underwater sledge. "That from your shark-hunting days?"

The guard with the shotgun moved slightly, as though about to become threatening.

Krest smiled thinly. "Why are you so interested in sharks?"

"Because I was sent from London to . . ."

"Nuts. Nobody here has been in touch with London. I bet you're one of those busybody ecology people who don't approve of our kind of fish farming."

"I do assure you, sir . . ."

"Time you left, buddy." Krest motioned to the guard.

"Well, if you really haven't . . . I mean my instructions were quite explicit . . ."

"I don't care if the Queen Mother sent you. On your way, brother. Now. Okay?"

As Bond turned in the doorway a flash of white caught his eye, low down among a pile of swept dirt near the tanks to his left. Even in that brief moment he had a chance to see the object clearly. It was a white rose, with silver paper around the stem. One of the white roses they had worn at the wedding. He had no doubt that it was Felix Leiter's rose.

"Well?" Sharky asked when Bond was back in the car.

"Sent packing with a flea in my ear." He paused. "Though I suppose I'm lucky it wasn't a bullet. Felix was there, Sharky, and we've got to get in and find out what happened."

They had driven back onto the main road again. "Tonight?" Sharky asked.

"How?"

"I got a dinghy. Quiet enough. Looks like the only way in is from the sea."

Bond thought for a full minute. "Let's hit them at a good strategic time. About an hour before dawn. Now, I suppose I'd better go and reregister at the Pier House."

"Okay. Just before dawn." Sharky thought he had a great deal to do before then.

— 4 —

What a Terrible Waste

ONCE IN THE small bay where the Ocean Exotica Warehouse was situated they were guided by a single red warning light at the far end of the pier, and dim lights which burned within the warehouse itself.

It had taken Sharky over an hour to row, close inshore, to the spot, and now he brought the dinghy silently in around the pier on which the warehouse stood. In the half-light of dawn they could see that it was a very solid structure indeed. Not only had the piles been sunk into great stone foundations, but also a whole solid concrete wall had been erected around, and between, the piles.

They became aware of tunnel-like gaps within the walls, each one leading deep into the area directly below the warehouse. Slowly and silently they traversed the entire structure, in an attempt to find an acceptable entrance—one which would afford them access to the building above.

Finally they came to rest in an area which did not appear to have any direct entrance, but was one to which boats could be tied. The concrete came up to their shoulders if they stood in the dinghy which bumped against old tyres which hung down from this area and were obviously used as fenders for docking craft.

Sharky motioned to Bond and they both took short wooden gaffs from the bottom of the boat, hauling the dinghy in close to the pier. Bond was just about to tell his friend that he would climb onto the wall and explore when they were both frozen into immobility by the whir of running engines from some point near at hand.

Without further warning, a section of the tyres to their left was thrust apart by the bows of the underwater sledge Bond had seen in the warehouse earlier in the day. Light streamed out for a moment from the area behind them. Three men crouched within the Plexiglas dome, and Bond glimpsed the legend *Wavekrest* on the stern of the craft which slid under the water as soon as it had cleared the pier.

Far away, from under the pier they could hear the mutter of voices, receding, and Bond nodded, gesturing towards the point where the tyres had parted. They waited a few more minutes, then, using the gaffs, pulled the dinghy through.

They were in a lighted tunnel which ran, it appeared, to a larger docking bay and a high wall which could be climbed using a firm-looking metal ladder.

Bond checked that his automatic was in the holster he had attached to his belt so that it would lie snugly against the rear of his right hip. Using the gaff he pulled himself up onto the dock, then went down on one knee to speak low to Sharky. "Just stay and listen out. If there's trouble I want you to get away as quickly as possible and warn someone like Felix's partner."

"No way," the black man whispered back. "If you've got problems up there, I'm coming to give you a hand."

Bond did not argue. He turned away with a brisk nod, stuck the gaff in his belt and slowly climbed the steel ladder which took him to a bare concrete walkway. On the left was a strong wire-mesh cage, three or four layers deep, which protruded from water, going on above the ladder. To the right a plain wall rose to what seemed to be the wooden floor of the warehouse, while ahead another ladder rose to a closed trapdoor. Silently he prayed there were no bolts or locks on the upper side.

Quietly he began to move towards the ladder, and was nearly there when the gaff sticking from his belt hit the wire mesh with a rasping bump. The entire caged area seemed to rattle and thud, as though something enormous had hit the side, and the next moment he recoiled, almost in terror—he was looking at three sets of razor-sharp teeth, and the ugly snout of a huge shark.

Flattening himself against the wall, Bond watched. The massive creature made another run at the side of the cage, its mouth once more coming from the water, biting the air as though frustrated that it could not attack. So, he thought, that beast was probably Felix Leiter's last enemy. He drew the gaff from his belt, and holding it in his left hand, began to climb slowly up the final ladder until he was able to gently push at the trapdoor, which moved.

He climbed the last few rungs, levering the trapdoor open quietly. A few moments later he was able to peer into the warehouse.

The area in which Bond now found himself had been hidden from his view when he was visiting the place during the previous afternoon. As he eased himself through the trapdoor he could see there were a couple of large tanks on thick stands, in front and to the right. Directly to the left there was a large sunken area, around fifteen feet square. He crept towards the left and saw that the sunken section was protected by four very strong sheets of steel mesh, in the centre of which was a firm-looking, large steel hinged trapdoor. About ten feet down, the water glinted, motionless.

Forwards, to the left, were the huge tanks he had seen before—a walkway running directly behind them, and a steel ladder leading to a kind of viewing platform, which he had taken as another walkway, running the length of the building.

In the centre of the main floor, the obscene-looking grey object, with its many tubes, hummed away, sending food into the main tanks. But from this angle, Bond could see a further piece of the machine: a long, high container from which lights blinked and glowed.

There was no sign of any human being; no movement or the sound of conversation. The warehouse was pleasantly warm, and smelled slightly of seawater and fish. Bond decided he would investigate the two big tanks to his right. The first one appeared to be empty. There was a sand bottom—which he presumed went below the bottom of the tank—and a cluster of rocks in the far left corner. From where he stood, he could reach in with the gaff to probe the sand. His hand brushed the surface of the water as he stirred. Nothing.

He was about to withdraw the gaff when a shape moved, at speed from the rocks, lashing out, a yellow-brown-patterned snake-like creature. Bond felt the strike on the gaff and had the impression of a mouth with sharp teeth. He whipped his hand back, to find the gaff neatly cut through as though a chain saw had ripped it apart.

The suddenness of the strike shook him, and he reflected that he had never seen a moray eel that close, or that big, before. He wondered what other hellish creatures were being bred, normally or genetically, in this place.

There was still no sign of human life, so he now set off to examine the automatic feeding device, with its many tubes and pulsing throb. Climbing carefully over the tubes, Bond made his way behind the ugly machine, to the oblong box he had spotted. It was attached to the cone-like body of the machine and stood about six feet high, projecting around twelve feet. At the far end he could make out what seemed to be a sliding drawer, about four feet by four. Small red lights glowed next to it, and, beside the lights, a small on/off button. Through ventilation grilles, the interior of the box glowed with what looked like high-density light.

As he searched, Bond noticed a logo and legend embossed into the top of the coffin-like structure. The legend read, *Krestfeed Maggot Incubator, Patent Pending.* Feeling like a naughty child, Bond gently pressed the button near the drawer. There was a slight whirring noise and the drawer slid out towards him.

At first he shrank back at the unpleasant sight of thousands of white maggots, a seething, squirming mess which filled the entire box. Well, you eventually got to know maggots pretty well, he thought. In a way they were a symbol of death, for it was the squirming maggot that fed on your putrefying flesh. It was still a revolting sight, and Bond, not usually so squeamish, had to screw his face into an idiot grimace before plunging his hand into this moving mass of tiny living predators. He scooped around, searching with his hand for anything that might have been hidden. Within a minute his fingers struck paydirt and he pulled out a clear heavy plastic bag. It was obviously waterproof, and he did not think the white powder which weighed heavy in his hand was a detergent. Most likely what had been hidden here was cocaine.

He was about to lift the bag out of the live coffin of maggots when instinct suddenly signalled to his brain that he was not alone. He dropped the bag back among the maggots, where it had been hidden, but too late. The cold muzzle of a pistol pressed against the back of his neck, and a voice—he thought it was the guard who had greeted him on his previous visit—whispered, "Just hold it right there, friend." At the same moment Bond felt his automatic being removed from its holster.

An entire scenario of thoughts cracked through Bond's mind in the fraction of a second. Like all trained men in his profession, tactical movements in this kind of situation assembled themselves almost instinctively, and were acted upon with the same precise speed. He lowered his hands into the boiling sea of maggots.

"Can I take my hands out?" he asked, his voice cool, but heart and brain racing.

"As long as you do it real slow, friend."

Bond cupped his hands and began to withdraw them, just like the man said, real slow. Then, at the last minute, he quickened the upward movement, and fast as the moray eel, swung the handfuls of maggots over his left shoulder, whirling upright, his body turning away from the pistol at his neck.

The guard—it was the one he had seen earlier—gave a little cry of disgust, both of his hands moving towards his face, which had taken the pile of wet maggots smack in the eyes. Bond closed in with a series of blurred moves. The hard edge of his right hand, outstretched with the thumb pulled back, chopped at the guard's right wrist, sending the pistol clattering to the wooden floor. But before the gun hit the ground, Bond had both hands around the man's wrist in a vice-like grip, pulling down hard, so that, for a moment, the subclavian artery was pinched between muscle, cutting the flow to the jugular. The result, as always, was a fractional blackout, and in this eye blink, Bond whipped the arm behind the guard's back, moving behind him and pushing upwards. The movement was enough to flip the man's body off balance and upwards. With one last jerk he toppled his attacker into the long drawer of seething maggots.

The man must have regained control of his brain as he hit the undulating live brew, for he screamed with terror. The scream came to an abrupt end as Bond threw himself forwards and banged at the on/off button in the main framework of the incubator. Silently the drawer, with its struggling occupant, slid into the closed position.

"Enjoy," Bond muttered to the unhearing maggots as he leaped for his automatic, which was a few feet behind the tank. As he swept it from the boards, a high-powered rifle bullet splintered the woodwork only inches from his hand. He wheeled, the pistol up in the two-handed grip, getting off two shots in the direction of the rifle fire. He caught a blur as the marksman dropped to the ground, firing again.

Bond rolled onto his feet, diving for cover behind the first of the huge main tanks and, crouching, began to move to the left. As he reached the third of these, another shot cannoned out in the relatively enclosed space of the warehouse, shattering the tank and covering Bond with water. A fish leaped out and he found himself skidding among a whole waterfall of fish running from the broken tank.

Another shot clanged against the metal of the catwalk high above, and Bond rolled to his right, behind the second tank, mind racing. The shot had come from his far left, which meant the rifleman was trying to position himself in a line with Bond. Thinking of the many movies he had seen where the hero races upwards during pursuit, he made a grab at the metal ladder leading to the upper catwalk. As he reached the top he could hear his adversary clanking up the ladder at the far end. If he did not move quickly, they would be facing each other along the metal walk. He ran half a dozen paces, fired another two shots to discourage the rifleman from getting onto the catwalk too quickly, then, vaulting over the guardrail, he grabbed the edge of the catwalk and hung there with one hand, the other still clutching the automatic.

He had jumped at a point where a shaft of tubular steel led under the catwalk, strengthening it, and holding it to the wall with around two inches to spare between it and the metal slats of the walkway. Like a monkey, Bond swung under the catwalk, holding the shaft of steel with one hand, taking all his weight.

He could hear the rifleman pounding above him, firing shot after shot as he ran towards where he thought Bond would be standing. The man was almost certainly firing from the hip. Bond, now feeling agonising strain on his left arm, raised his automatic, so that it pointed directly upwards in one of the gaps.

The catwalk juddered as the man came at a run. The shot had to be perfect, not too soon, but just as the rifleman was above him. Almost by instinct, Bond judged the moment. He felt, rather than saw, the shape getting nearer, and as it loomed directly above him, he fired off two rounds. There was a shriek of pain, and he heard the rifle go flying, while the man, doubled up, still conscious but screaming in agony, clutched at his loins.

Bond withdrew the pistol from the gap in the metal. "Right between the slats," he murmured, holstering the gun, then clinging on to the steel support, mercifully taking the strain on both arms.

He felt a sticky wet splatter of blood fall onto his forehead, and as he looked upwards, the rifleman fell against the guardrail. He was a big man, tall and heavy, breathing in short rattling gulps. As he hit the guardrail he seemed to stand up. But all control had gone, and the man fell again onto the side of the rail and pitched over into the tank below.

There was another dreadful scream. The tank's water boiled and there were odd flashes of movement and what seemed to be light. It took Bond a moment to realise that the creatures in the tank directly below him were electric eels. What a way to go, Bond considered. Shot through the loins and then shot through with high voltage.

Bond swung himself towards the edge of the catwalk, and with great care, knowing what lay beneath him, climbed back onto the catwalk, slippery with blood.

He walked slowly back to the ladder and finally went down the steps again, automatic at the ready, even though he could hear no other movement inside the warehouse. It was time, he thought, to get back to Sharky.

Walking forwards he paused by the tank holding the moray eel, then went closer to the edge of the great sunken cage. The water remained placid, though he knew now what horror waited below. The shark he had seen on his way up was a simple and very effective killing machine. Holstering his pistol, Bond saw for the first time that, directly above the trap in the steel mesh which covered the cage, a rope hung from a pulley on a beam high in the rafters. There was a large hook, roughly at shoulder level. He could imagine what pleasure some of these men must have had, lowering meat through the trap and into the water below. But it was time to go. He would have to make some kind of report to Hawkins.

He was just about to move towards the trapdoor leading down to the jetty when another voice, once more quite recognisable, came out of the shadows behind him.

"Freeze. Then turn around very slowly."

Killifer stood only a few feet away, a large briefcase at his feet and a very large .357 Magnum held in the two-handed grip. "You perform any fancy business and you'll make my day, punk." Killifer smiled at the Clint Eastwood imitation.

Bond sighed. "I do wish you wouldn't refer to me as 'punk,' " he said. "If anyone's a punk, it's you, Killifer. You sold out, uhu?" nodding towards the briefcase.

"Two million is an awful lot of dollars to refuse, Mr. Bond. Fact is I really had no option. Now, if you'll just move over to the trapdoor in the middle of the cage, we'll finish the day's work and I can get on my way."

Bond moved out into the centre of the mesh covering. You did not have to possess much experience to know it was not a good idea to argue with the kind of revolver Killifer was holding. It flashed through Bond's mind that, if it came to it, he *would* make a wrong move. Rather a Magnum bullet than the slightly slower horror of the shark.

"Now you can open the trapdoor."

Bond did as he was told. "I suppose this is where you put your 'old buddy' Felix Leiter."

"Not me, Bond. Chalk that up to Sanchez and Krest. I found it rather revolting. They hung the best part of a steer on that hook there. It was heavier than poor old Felix. The steer went down and Felix dangled at the other end of the rope. Sanchez and Krest had a name for that damned shark. Called it the Tooth Fairy. How d'you like that?"

"Bizarre." Bond was thinking of his next move. There really wasn't one.

"Well, that's what they called him. As he bit at the steer, it got lighter and, no pun intended, Leiter started to go down. That Tooth Fairy got real frustrated when he couldn't reach the steer. Eventually he reached Felix, though; and he'll reach you, Mr. Bond."

"Don't be too sure of that." The voice came from behind Bond, from the trapdoor leading down to the jetty. Sharky had arrived.

For a second, Killifer turned sideways and fired two shots. In the moment of distraction and firing, Bond grabbed the hook and rope, swinging it with full force at Killifer, who dropped to his knees, his Magnum clattering down. Bond stepped in and to one side, kicking with full force. Killifer opened his mouth and was projected along the mesh until his body was half in and half out of the trapdoor meant for Bond.

"Bad shot, Mr. Killifer." Sharky came bounding up from the other trapdoor.

"For God's sake help me." Killifer sounded short of breath and terrified. He was off balance, half his body through the trap, his hands scrabbling at the steel mesh. "For God's sake, Bond." His eyes went to the large briefcase. "I'll share the money with you. Split it even. That's a million each. Please. A million each."

Slowly Bond went over to the briefcase and picked it up, weighing it in his hand as though thinking about it. Then he lifted the case and flung it at Killifer. "I think you should take the lot, Ed. It's all yours."

In a reflex action, Killifer took his hands off the mesh to grab at the case. Almost in slow motion his body slid through the trapdoor and down into the water, accompanied by a scream of sheer terror.

They saw the shark's head and jaws rear up once, then the briefcase hit the beast on the nose and exploded money across the water. Killifer's head appeared twice more, screaming hysterically, the water around him becoming red, and the money settled across it, like a scarlet oil slick.

"What a terrible waste," said Sharky, his voice quivering with shock. "What a terrible waste—of money."

"Come on." Bond put a hand on his shoulder.

"Let's get moving. We've got a lot to do and it's getting light. By the way, thanks for the nick-of-time rescue. You could have made it a little sooner."

"Oh, I wanted the man to have a bit of fun in his last minutes." Sharky smiled. "But what a damned waste of dollars."

They went down, back to the dinghy.

"What now?" Sharky asked.

"Find Sanchez, what else?"

"How we do that? Put an ad in the paper?"

"No, but I think Felix had a way. You find out about that underwater sledge. It must be registered somewhere, and it belongs to Krest, if the name's anything to go by."

Sharky began rowing away, down the tunnel, then out into the bay. "And while I do that?"

"I shall be risking life and limb, trying to get at Felix's little secret. I'm pretty sure I know where it is."

— 5 —

For Whom the Bell Tolls

THEY HAD AGREED to meet in Mallory Square to watch the sunset. This, as any visitor to Key West knows, is a must ritual for tourists and even for some residents.

"Let's lie low today," Bond had said. "You find out what you can. As for me, well, the things I have in mind can only really be done after dark." He did not know then that with the darkness would come other unplanned events.

About an hour before sunset, the worshippers begin to gather in Mallory Square, and with them, the showmen, travelling magicians, jugglers, fire-eaters, acrobats, painters and the purveyors of handmade baubles. It is a fun occasion, harmless, and certainly beautiful on clear nights when the sun produces a spectacular crimson sky, the colour reflecting on the whole town.

Sharky and Bond met just as the sun went down and the hundreds of people in the square began to applaud God for the special effects.

"Okay, I got what you want." Sharky spoke without even looking at Bond.

"Tell me."

"Wavekrest is really a big marine research ship, owned by your good friend Milton Krest."

"Who else?" Bond said to the sunset. "So that undersea sledge is an adjunct of the big ship?"

"You got it. They're out collecting specimens off Coy Sol Bank."

"What kind of specimens?"

"Nobody knows, except maybe the Shadow." Sharky laughed. "But if you want to find out, we can get there in my fishing boat. Take around six hours."

Bond walked a few paces. Then—"Can we leave in an hour or so? I've got to try and do my little bit of work, then pick up a few things."

"Why not? I'll be ready and waiting, at the charter boat dock."

"About an hour, then." Bond turned away abruptly, quickly putting distance between Sharky and himself. His first priority was Felix Leiter's house.

He had done nothing but lie on his bed in the Pier House all day, calling room service for food. The telephone rang twice, but he did not pick up, except to make one call out, to the hospital. Felix was doing well, they told him. The rest of his time was spent thinking: trying to work out the next move. His conscience pricked, knowing that he should really be elsewhere on business for London. But Felix Leiter was a special friend—a man who had saved his life many times over.

When he had eventually left the hotel, to keep his appointment with Sharky, Bond had done what was known in the trade as a "round-the-houses," or "dry cleaning"—in plain language watching his own back, checking that he was not under any surveillance.

On his devious way to Mallory Square he picked up no indicators, yet there was this odd intuition that he was, in fact, being watched. In the end he doubled back to the hotel shop and loitered there for a few minutes. Still no result, so he set out again, and was forced to dodge a Conch Train as he crossed the road. Conch Trains ply the whole street system of Key West all day—motorised vehicles made to look like engines, drawing a series of coaches filled with rubbernecking tourists. It was a good and colourful way of seeing the sights.

Now, having left Sharky, Bond again got the familiar feeling that somebody was on his back. This, he thought, could turn out to be a time-waster. He had an hour to get over to Sharky's fishing boat and he wanted to fit in the clandestine visit to Felix's house before then if possible.

He turned into Duval and was aware of someone coming up fast behind him. His muscles tightened as he prepared himself for anything, slipping the button on his lightweight jacket to be sure he could get at his automatic, now oiled, cleaned and resting in a shoulder holster.

"Hi, James Bond. Got time for a word?" It was Hawkins, Leiter's former partner, now walking beside him, just a shade too close, as though he was leading a blind man.

"Sure, but I haven't got long."

"I'll walk with you." Hawkins smiled.

"Okay. What do we talk about? Felix?"

"Something connected."

"Such as?"

"Well . . ." Hawkins was taking his time. "I'd best tell you. The local cops got an anonymous tip first thing this morning—very early. Some old guy called in to say he had heard shots."

"So?"

"So, he *had* heard shots. The cops turned up five hundred keys of Colombian pure in the warehouse."

"Cottage industry around here, isn't it?"

"Maybe. But they also put their hands on a pair of stiffs, and some pieces of what used to be Ed Killifer."

"I'm sorry about that."

"It just so happens that the warehouse is owned by a company belonging to a Mr. Milton Krest, who, in turn, is a very close friend of Sanchez. I've no need to tell you that Sanchez is still missing, and so is the ignoble Mr. Krest."

"Looks like someone's on the job, then."

"I just hope it isn't you, James."

"Never heard of this fellow Krest. Don't know any warehouses."

"I wonder. We know you came into the charter boat dock in a dinghy with Leiter's friend Sharky. The information indicates you could have just made it from that warehouse if Sharky rowed fast enough."

Bond smiled pleasantly. "Mr. Hawkins, you've a vivid imagination. Why don't you ask Sharky?"

"Oh, they're going to—the cops, I mean. You see, the DA's tearing his hair out and yelling blue murder. He wants the truth, and fast. We've got laws in this country, you know."

With a sigh, Bond realised he would have to get over to the charter boat dock as quickly as possible. Leiter's house could wait.

"Laws," repeated Hawkins.

"You got a law against what they did to Felix?"

They walked on in silence for a few minutes: Bond trying to think of a way to dodge Hawkins, and Hawkins obviously becoming more and more tense. Finally Hawkins turned and stopped directly in front of Bond, his voice now harsh and completely unsympathetic. "Look, Mr. Bond, you're in over your head. This is where it ends as far as you're concerned."

Bond cursed himself. He had been so intent on trying to get away from Hawkins that he had not even noticed the appearance of anyone else. Now he was flanked by two young, and very fit, men. They were dressed in lightweight suits: one grey and the other blue. Bond thought he vaguely recognised the one in the grey suit.

Bond looked at each in turn, and then at Hawkins. He was blocked in, unless he did something violent, not a good idea in streets that were already filling up with cars and people making their way on foot to the many good restaurants in the area.

He looked up and realised where he was. A gate which led into a pleasantly laid-out garden, and behind this a house, with a balcony surrounding the whole of the second floor. There was a bust of Ernest Hemingway above the gate, and a sign which said, *Historical Monument. Hemingway House. CLOSED.* So, he was at the famous place. On his previous visit to Key West he had planned to visit this house where Ernest Hemingway had lived from the early thirties until 1961, and where he wrote *For Whom the Bell Tolls, Green Hills of Africa* and *The Snows of Kilimanjaro,* among many others. Someone had once told him that the Hemingway house had the saddest atmosphere he had ever encountered in any home.

"Take no notice of the sign, sir. Just go straight

in." The one in the grey suit was firm-voiced, and Bond now knew where he had seen him before. He even remembered the man's name. The accent was very English.

He nodded and walked inside the garden, the newcomers flanking him, directing him around to the right. There were cats everywhere. Hemingway had loved cats and had some hybrid variety with extra toes.

They led him past the swimming pool, where Hemingway had thrown down his last quarter into the wet cement, saying that was all he had left. They had left the quarter for all to see—though the infant son of an English author had secretly prized out the quarter on a visit. It turned out to have been minted in 1970.

Very gently the pair of bodyguards—for that is what they were—led Bond up the flight of steps to the veranda. Even on this structure, Bond could feel the sorrow. Someone had been very unhappy here. He hoped he was not about to join in with the sense of despair which permeated the place.

His guards shouldered him to that part of the veranda which looked out onto the street— Whitehead Street. The man who stood there had not been so positioned when they entered the garden, but he was certainly there now, his back immediately recognisable.

From somewhere, maybe the church where Felix and Della had so happily married, a bell tolled once. Bond shrugged. He did not believe in omens.

"Sir?" he said to the man, who now turned to look at him with cold grey eyes. The two bodyguards seemed to nudge closer to Bond.

"Well, Commander Bond, what have you got to say for yourself?" M—the CSS, or Chief of the Secret Service—asked. He looked furious, and his hands clenched and unclenched as though he was trying to keep his anger in check.

Bond opened his mouth to speak, but M spoke for him. "You were supposed to be in Istanbul two days ago. It was important to your Queen, your country and the Service. That's why I've bothered to spend Lord knows how many hours on aircraft, to come to this tacky little showplace. Instead of dealing with matters in Turkey, I understand you took time off to attend a wedding, which ended up in carnage."

"It was Leiter, sir. I've worked with him before . . ."

"And not scheduled to work with him in Istanbul, Bond. I've been here for almost a day and heard some most unsavoury things. The local police suspect you of mayhem, if not murder. I know Leiter was a friend, but from where I stand it looks as though the whole business had clouded your judgement. You have a job to do and I want it doing. Now. Got it? I want you on a plane out of here tonight and whatever connections you can make to Istanbul as quickly as possible." All this was said with the stabbing of M's right forefinger, the body language for killing.

"I'm afraid I haven't quite finished here, sir."
Bond was not going to be bullied. The Istanbul
business, as he knew only too well, had been on and
off the boil for months.

"You are to leave it to the Americans, Bond. It's
their mess. You will let them clear it up." M took a
pace back. His two bodyguards seemed to have
relaxed and were not crowding Bond so closely.

"With respect, sir, the Americans just won't do
anything. *You* know that Leiter put his life on the
line for me many times . . ."

"Enough sentiment," M snapped. "He knew the
risks he was taking. Just as you always know the
risks."

"And his wife?"

M made a pshawing sound. "Do you not realise
the other dangers, man? You're running a private
vendetta, and that could compromise Her
Majesty's government. Now, you have an assignment. I expect you to carry out that assignment
objectively and professionally as you have many
times before."

There was a long pause, filled only by a laugh
from somewhere out in the street. Then Bond
clenched his teeth. This was one of the most
difficult decisions he had ever had to make. "Then
you can have my resignation, sir."

"This isn't some country club, Bond. Nor your
London club."

Bond took a deep breath and waited, staring out
his old chief.

"All right," M snapped at last. "All right. Your resignation. Effective immediately, your licence within the Service, and all that entails, is revoked. I need hardly remind you that you're still bound by the Official Secrets Act . . ."

"As is every British citizen, sir. That's sometimes forgotten."

M took no notice. "I require your personal weapon now." He held out his hand.

After a pause, Bond shrugged and removed his automatic from its holster. "I suppose it's a farewell to arms, then." As he said it he felt the bodyguards relax once more. Making as though to hand over the pistol to M, Bond whipped around without warning. The grey-suited man caught the full force of the pistol butt under his chin, while his partner received Bond's knee in the traditional street fighter's target and doubled up with a sharp cry of pain.

"Sorry, sir." Bond shouldered past M, jarring him to one side, and vaulted over the veranda railings. It was a longer drop than he had reckoned, but he rolled and came up, pistol at the ready, making his way to the gate. As he reached it, a Conch Train passed by. The driver/conductor was saying, "And on our right we have the most famous house in Key West, if you don't count the Audubon House and President Truman's Little White House . . ."

On the veranda, the bodyguard with a stabbing pain in his groin had risen, gun out and ready to fire into the garden. M stepped forward and stayed his hand. "Too many people. Don't they teach you anything these days?"

From the veranda, M looked out into the night. "God help you, Commander Bond," he said aloud, and the bodyguard could not tell if it was anger, sorrow or humour on the old man's face. Then M turned and walked inside. He could not get out of this place quickly enough, for he had also found it deeply depressing.

Through binoculars, at a range of two miles, *Wavekrest* gave the impression of being very much a working ship. She was about 150 feet long, broad in the beam, with a strange overhang on the stern, which also sported a pair of booms, port and starboard. There were small cranes on the booms, and men scurried around. There were obviously divers in the water. Behind the ship, Coy Sol Bay made a beautiful backdrop. A pair of catamarans bobbed nearby, and there were diving flags in the water.

Bond had watched dawn come up as they rode at anchor about six miles from Coy Sol Bay, and shielded from *Wavekrest* by the headland. "We don't want to get there until late morning," he had told Sharky. "It might look a little odd if they all woke up and just found us sitting watching them."

Sharky grinned, "Like we would have woke up and found the cops sitting on my boat."

After his leap from the veranda of the Heming-

way house, Bond had slipped onto the Conch Train.
It was evening and this was probably the last ride
any of the tourists would get. The end two coaches
were empty, and Bond rode the short distance back
to the train offices, then had speedily made his way
to Sharky's boat.

They were a mile out of Key West when the
sound of police sirens came floating from the
charter boat dock. For an hour or so, both men
scanned the night for the blinking lights of a police
helicopter, but they had obviously either been
called off or called it a day.

Now it was eleven o'clock on a beautiful calm
morning. Sharky had dropped nets over the side
and Bond lay hidden near the bows, watching
Wavekrest on binoculars supplied by Sharky.

He scanned the superstructure which did not fit
into the rest of the picture of *Wavekrest* as a marine
research ship. Certainly they appeared to have all
the technology, radar and sonar dishes turned lazily
from behind the bridge, but towards the rear there
was a somewhat luxury area. He could pick out
very smart cabin doors and what could well be a
small pool abaft the main superstructure. Bond
also spotted something more sinister. Set for'ard,
below the bridge, was a long rack of spear guns.
Most of them were the normal things, high stan-
dard and the kind of things carried by scuba divers.
But towards the end were another kind altogether,
the type that fired small harpoons, often fitted with
small explosive charges.

He swept the ship again with the binoculars, and this time caught a flash of something else, a sight which made him swing the glasses back towards the first cabin door for'ard—the one that appeared to have a brass plate on it.

The door had opened, and a pleasant sight emerged. A young, dark girl dressed in a one-piece swimsuit which covered her, both front and back. She carried a towel and beach bag, and walked as though the world was watching her, towards the place where Bond thought he had spotted a pool. He recognised her immediately.

"Well, well, well." His lips creased into a smile. "Lookee here, me hearties."

"What you found, James?" from Sharky on the bridge.

"The girl."

"What girl?"

"The one I last saw when Sanchez made his visit to Cray Cay. Sanchez's girlfriend. Miss Galaxy, the flamboyantly named Lupe Lamora."

"That mean Sanchez's aboard."

"It could very well mean that. Could we move in a little closer?"

"Sure thing, James. Anything. You enjoying yourself?"

"Inordinately, Sharky my old shipmate." Indeed, Lupe was a sight for eyes infected by the most severe conjunctivitis. As the fishing boat moved closer, Bond watched the girl stretch in the sun and begin to cover her body with some kind of lotion.

"Careful, Lupe," Bond muttered. "Too much sun can be as harmful as too much tobacco and too much booze."

Sharky must have heard him, for he laughed and asked since when had Bond let that kind of thing worry him?

Bond smiled again and murmured back, "You'd be surprised, Shark. I've cut down massively on my cigarette intake, and I've really never been all that heavy on the drink. Good wines, yes; good whisky, the odd martini, if it's made properly. I fear Felix has been libelling my reputation."

They had come in quite close now, and Bond saw someone else he recognised, coming down from the bridge. Milton Krest himself. The man who was partly responsible for Della's death and Felix Leiter's injuries.

"That bastard Krest's aboard," Bond whispered loud enough for Sharky to hear above their engine noise and the whine coming from *Wavekrest*.

"Then we might be in luck." As Sharky said it, Bond saw one of the men on deck, wearing a wet suit, shout something to Krest, who turned and looked straight at the fishing boat.

A minute later, Krest had a loud-hailer in his hand. His voice echoed across the water, as the hailer was pointed directly at Sharky's boat— "Ahoy! D'you hear there! Fishing vessel stand off. We have divers in the water. I say again. Divers in the water. You are a danger!"

Bond pressed himself down among the bits of

rope and other junk piled in the bows. "Better make for the headland, Sharky, and wave nicely, just to please the man."

"Aye-aye, Cap'n." There was a hint of sarcasm in Sharky's voice.

"Run away, Sharky. Live to fight another day— or I should say another night."

When they were out of the immediate vicinity of *Wavekrest,* Bond shifted his position, crawling back towards the stern and refocusing the glasses. As he did so, there was another flash, low in the water, on the periphery of his vision. He refocused again. There, moving fast, just above the surface, water pluming behind it, was a short, stubby periscope.

"They have a submersible in the water," he told Sharky. "Powerful and fast by the look of it. Could be an unmanned probe. But I reckon we'll get the answer to that, and all the other questions, tonight. Do you happen to have any spare tarpaulin aboard?"

"Yep, sure do."

"Good. Any odd bits of wood or metal?"

"The whole of this tub's made of old bits of wood. Yeah, I got some metal. Two old aerials that got broke off in the winds we had last winter. Why?"

"I'm going to a fancy-dress party. On board *Wavekrest.* Give them all a nice surprise. We might find Sanchez into the bargain."

"A fancy-dress party?" Sharky screwed up his face.

"Why not? Just get behind that headland and anchor. I think this is a job for tonight."

There was a long pause. Then Sharky said, "Might I ask what you're going to this fancy-dress party as? Long John Silver?"

"You must learn not to be so inquisitive, Sharky. I'll tell you one thing, though. I'll get first prize in the grand parade."

— 6 —

The Journey of the Manta

THE MANTA BIROSTRIS, usually known simply as the manta ray, is the largest of the *Manta* genus. Its name originates from the huge wing-like fins— capes, or mantles—and they come in one size: very large; sometimes seventeen feet long and twenty-two feet wide. They move through the water like massive ocean birds, and though they look both graceful and sinister, the manta ray is not danger-ous to man—except for the fact that a swipe from one of the fins can send a diver out of control, doing a great deal of damage.

This one swam low, almost skimming over the coral and sand in the entrance to Coy Sol Bay. In the darkness, a couple of hours before dawn, it changed direction slightly, seeing pinpoints of light moving towards it, then continued on its stately way, passing four scuba divers, torches lit to guide themselves, heading in the direction from which the manta had come.

A little further on, the manta saw a very bright light, slicing through the water, as though searching. The light held on the huge fish for almost a minute, then began to turn away.

Aboard *Wavekrest* the crewmen on duty had spotted the shape in the water. They had the probe, *Sentinel,* out in a matter of minutes, guided by a specialised operator and attached to *Wavekrest* by an umbilical cord of electronics and wires. When *Sentinel* spotted the manta its powerful light sought out the big fish, and the cameras sent back pictures to the mother ship, *Wavekrest.* It was the periscope of *Sentinel* that Bond had spotted before he and Sharky had run for the cover of the headland, that very morning.

"Only a manta," the senior man on the bridge said as he watched the creature on his monitor, fascinated, and a little repulsed by the protruding horns of flesh, like a beetle's antennae, curving out from its head. The officer in charge of the bridge picked up a telephone and called the probe operator. "Bring *Sentinel* back in," he said.

Sentinel looked like some futuristic model submarine, about four feet in length and three feet high, with an oblong rising higher above the centre line of the fish-shaped hull. The oblong was a watertight compartment which contained the thing's eyes—its merciless searchlight, cameras and stubby periscope. Behind the oblong compartment, another watertight box slanted back towards the stern. This was obviously some kind of storage container, for its flat top clearly showed hinges and a securing lock.

Now it turned away from the giant manta ray and began to move swiftly back towards *Wavekrest*. James Bond put out his hands and hitched a ride on *Sentinel*—the name was clearly embossed on the rear, above a U-shaped handle to which he could cling.

The black tarpaulin, fashioned over a wire-and-bamboo frame that had been the manta, fell away and drifted to the bottom. Bond and Sharky had worked for several hours to make the manta: bending wire and some of Sharky's fishing poles; sewing with line, tying down and cutting the tarpaulin, to make James Bond's "fancy dress." It was a job well done, for when Bond put on a wet suit and scuba pack the tarpaulin mantle covered him, even allowing him to move his arms, and so imitate the action of the fins.

"Very lifelike," Sharky had said. "Just hope you don't meet a male manta down there who takes you for a likely mate."

"Or an amorous female." Bond laughed. He had roughly an hour's supply of air, and considered he could reach *Wavekrest* well within that time.

Now, as he clung to the rear of *Sentinel,* his fancy-dress party was over, and the real job would be getting on board *Wavekrest.* If Sanchez *was* aboard, the security would be very tight, but he had abandoned the camouflage in favour of speed.

Sentinel began to slow in the water and Bond, still clinging on, allowed his body to sink from view. He could see they were being drawn towards the stern of the ship, and realised why there was such an overhang. A pair of doors, big enough to take at least three men, opened up just below the waterline. *Sentinel* was gradually being pulled into what was virtually a dock within the mother ship, *Wavekrest.* He still hung on, remaining underwater as the doors closed and the probe started to move upwards, presumably lifted by an electronic winch.

Sentinel broke surface, but Bond stayed below water and behind the craft. There was plenty of bright light in the dock, and, just above the waterline, he could see the refracted image of a man leaning over the probe, attaching other lines to it. As he came to the rear, the rippling figure bent down, as though to examine something towards the stern.

Bond prayed the man was working alone. As he bent really low above Bond, the agent lashed out with his feet, to give an upward momentum, fist clenched and his arm rigid, breaching the water like a small missile.

More by luck than judgement, he felt his knuckles crunch onto the side of the operator's jaw, and saw him reel back against the metal wall of the dock, his head hitting the metal with a nasty thud.

With as much agility as he could manage in a wet suit and the heavy scuba pack, Bond pulled himself up onto the narrow metal strip which ran around the probe's docking area. The man was wearing a boiler suit, and he now looked like a pile of dirty laundry, crumpled in a heap, head sagging forwards and one arm outstretched towards *Sentinel* and the water in which it still floated, hanging on chains.

The probe operator was alive but out for the count, the force of his head hitting the metal having done the real damage. Bond saw that the probe's control mechanism was still switched on—a box, set in the bulkhead, with an array of dials and two levers, like computer joysticks, with which the speed and direction were remotely controlled. Above the box a monitor flickered, busy with "snow," which meant all picture signals from the probe had been cut off.

Bond leaned against the bulkhead for a moment, looking around. On the far side, near a companion-way ladder leading to the decks above, was a solid metal door, inset with thick glass. To one side, tubing connected to a high boxed-in control with a small, lightning-flash sticker and danger sign on it. Above the box was a big dial. A pressure gauge. A divers' decompression chamber, Bond thought.

He dragged the sagging body of the probe operator over to the chamber, pulled down on the heavy lever that controlled the door's locking device and pushed the body inside. Stacks of neat oblongs, shrink-wrapped in blue plastic, were piled inside the chamber, but he had no time to examine these now. Stripping off his scuba gear, retaining his knife in its sheath attached to a belt, Bond left the chamber and reactivated the door lock. It was time to see if Sanchez was on board.

Barefoot, and wearing only the dark slacks and T-shirt that had been under his wet suit, Bond slowly climbed the companionway ladder, leading to the main deck, abaft the main superstructure. The noises were normal for a ship at anchor during the dog watch: the light slapping of water as *Wavekrest* rode the slight sea; murmurs from for'ard, above, on the bridge. All the companionways would be open on such a warm night, he thought. Riding lights burned, green and red, with a few low deck lights so that crew could find their way around.

Bond moved to the port side, where he had spotted the luxurious cabin door through the binoculars on Sharky's fishing boat. In the far corner of his mind there was slight concern about Sharky, for the divers he had seen when disguised as the manta ray had been heading in the general direction of the fishing boat. He scrubbed the worry from his mind. Sharky was big enough to look after himself.

From where he stood, in the darkness, Bond could make out the lines of a small lifeboat, swung in on its davits. The lifeboat would, he figured, be almost opposite the cabin from which he had seen Lupe—tall, slim, dark and with a figure that would tempt a saint—emerge during the previous morning. If Sanchez was aboard, that would be where Bond would find him.

Almost silently he padded across the deck into the shadow and relative safety of the lifeboat. It was as he crossed the strip of deck that he realised the cabin door he had seen through the binoculars stood slightly ajar, and lights shone brightly through the ports. Now there was even more. Voices. Milton Krest's, slurred and aggressive, combined with Lupe Lamora's angry, fiery accented English.

"You'd better know you caused us a whole mess of trouble, girl." Krest's voice was not only slurred with drink but hard and bitter.

"You're *borracho*. I told you, I was trying to sleep. Why you keep bothering me like this? Get yourself to bed."

There was a scraping noise, as though Krest had risen from a chair. "You know, when Sanchez heard you'd run off with that idiot, he went nuts. Never seen him so angry."

"This is none of your business, Krest. Go, and let me get some sleep."

"Oh, none of my business, eh? None—of—my —business. You gotta understand, kiddie, it *is* my business when your playing around gets Sanchez arrested and leaves me to mount an escape operation. That escape put my own people at risk. Not just my people either. You realise the Key West warehouse got raided by the DEA. Cost me a whole load of money."

"He'll get your money back."

Krest gave an unpleasant laugh. "Sanchez doesn't work like that. You haven't figured that out for yourself yet? I've known him the hell of a sight longer than you, you bimbo. I've seen girls like you come and go . . ."

Lupe snapped, "Get out, Krest. You're drunk, and you're annoying me. So get out. Now. Or I'll make certain Sanchez won't give you a red cent."

Krest's shadow filled the door. "We've got a serious operation running out here, Lupe. So you just keep in your cabin." Bond could see him clearly now, dressed in old slacks and a shirt. "What're you so damned stuck-up for? He fixed that beauty contest for you. You know that? He fixed it. He . . ." Something hit the wall near the door which Krest closed, giving a little laugh. "Stupid little cow," he muttered under his breath. "Doesn't know when she's well off." He was unsteady on his feet as he made his way to a cabin door nearer the aft end of the superstructure.

The lights in Lupe's cabin went out, just as those in Krest's came on. Half an hour later both cabins were in darkness.

Bond waited a further half hour, looking at the open ports in both cabins. Then, as the first light began to show from the east, he slipped from his hiding place to the door of the cabin occupied by Lupe. He could see the brass plaque now. It read, *Owner's Stateroom.* Carefully he tried the handle. It was shut tightly, so he reached for the wallet, zipped and watertight, which he kept in his back pocket. He was about to make his next move when the lights came on in Krest's cabin.

Bond flattened himself against the metal wall, edging towards the first open port of Krest's cabin. He heard the quick *beep-beep* of a telephone number being punched out. Then Krest's voice.

"Any sign of Clive yet?" There was a pause as he listened. Then—"Okay. He should be back soon. It's nearly first light and the plane'll be here before we know it. Best send a couple of men down to load the stuff into *Sentinel.* I want the exchange to go like clockwork. It's always risky. I don't like that damned plane on the water for too long. Okay, get on with it."

So, the blue shrink-wrapped packages were to be loaded onto *Sentinel.* Drugs, Bond guessed, and if a couple of men were going down to the decompression chamber, they would soon report that an intruder was on board.

He pulled his knife from his belt, then unzipped the wallet, taking out a credit card and inserting it carefully into the space between door and lock on Lupe's cabin. "Hope it takes MasterCard," he almost said aloud. There was a slight click and the door opened. Quickly he returned the credit card, zipped up his wallet, returned it to his pocket, then took the knife in his right hand.

He made no sound getting into the cabin, closing and locking the door behind him, then standing for a minute so that his eyes could adjust, though the darkness outside was starting to dissolve into the pearly wash of day.

Lupe Lamora lay on her back, sprawled across the bed, dressed only in a small, lacy bikini. No wonder she won the beauty contest, he thought. Sanchez would never have had to rig it. Her body, seen at close quarters, was superb.

Gently he approached the bed, knelt down, then moved fast, slamming his hand down on her mouth, the knife at her throat.

Lupe came out of whatever she was dreaming into a nightmare that showed in the fear of her wide-eyed look.

"Make a sound; call for help, and I'll kill you. Got it?" Bond snarled.

She nodded vigorously, and he slowly removed his hand. He could see the recognition in her face. The last time had been out at the little airstrip when Sanchez had made his escape.

"You?" she mouthed.

He nodded. "Krest's in his cabin. I gather you two don't get on so well. Now, where's Sanchez?"

"Not here," she whispered. "Not on board. I suppose he's back home—or what passes for home. Back in Isthmus City."

"You're his girlfriend, so you should know."

"That's *probably* where he is. He doesn't tell me a thing. Only do this and do that and do the other thing. Usually it's the other thing."

"Well . . ." Bond began, but was interrupted by sounds from Krest's cabin next door. Raised voices, then the noise of feet on the deck and a hammering at Lupe's door.

Bond motioned with his knife, "Answer it."

She paused for a second, then grabbed a robe from the foot of the bed, holding it against her as she went over to the door. Bond, knife ready, put his back against the cabin wall on the hinge side of the door as Lupe called out, "Who is it?"

Krest answered loudly, "Open up, bimbo. I gotta talk to you."

"Not again. I'm trying to get some sleep."

"Open it!"

Gingerly she pulled back the door. Through the slit, Bond could see Krest, who looked anxious, full of panic, backed up by two heavy-looking seamen, both armed.

"We've got an intruder. Someone slipped aboard. Probably rode in on the probe."

"You waken me up for . . ."

"To warn you, bimbo. You seen anybody?"

"I've been asleep."

"Okay. Lock your door and stay out of sight. There's work to be done and I don't want the crew distracted."

"And I want to get back to sleep." She pulled the door closed, clicked the lock and looked at Bond, whispering, "I did okay, yes?"

He nodded and smiled as she walked across the cabin, the light from the sun's first rays catching her back. Bond saw the marks with horror, a crisscross pattern of deep welts, only just starting to heal. "Who whipped you like that?" he asked.

She shrugged into her robe, not answering. In the background Bond was aware of another boat's engine which sounded all too familiar.

"Who whipped you?" he asked again. "Was it Sanchez?"

Another pause. Then—"It was my own fault. I know Sanchez and what he does to people who cross him. I crossed him, and I'm lucky to be alive."

Outside, the engine noise grew louder, and she crossed the cabin, back to the port through which they both looked.

They heard the voice from somewhere outside, shouting—

"Clive's back, Mr. Krest."

Then the boat came into view, the engine note dipping as she prepared to tie up next to *Wavekrest.*

Lupe gave a little moan, and Bond felt anger and horror rise in equal portions. He put an arm around Lupe's shoulder and turned her head from the sight. Sharky's fishing boat was abreast *Wavekrest,* the three scuba divers he had passed underwater standing on deck. The fishing boat's "catch" hung netted from the side. There were two young sharks and, between them, the terribly mutilated body of Sharky.

"Well done, Clive." It was Krest's voice, probably from the bridge.

The diver in the centre of the three, a short, pugnacious-looking man, waved back. "Thank you, Mr. Krest," he shouted. "But guess what? His name was Sharky. Neat, eh?"

There was laughter, broken by another engine note, further away. Then Krest's voice again, "Best get aboard, Clive. Here comes the plane. We got work to do."

Bond turned to Lupe, knowing his face was contorted in anger and grief. "I want Sanchez," he said, grabbing hold of the girl's shoulders.

"Your name. Please. Your name."

"Bond," he said. "James Bond."

"Mr. Bond, I'd truly like to help you. Please believe that. But you must go now . . ."

"Oh, I am. We've all got work to do. You heard what Krest said . . ."

". . . If you don't go now, we'll both be killed."

"I'm going. But, like the man said, keep your door locked." Cautiously he opened the cabin door and squeezed out onto the deck. Two of the men who had been with the infamous Clive were disappearing down a hatch, while Krest, followed by other men, climbed an external ladder towards the bridge. Bond ran to the lifeboat and looked down over the side of *Wavekrest*. Sharky's boat, with its grim cargo, had been tied up for'ard while the two catamarans rode in station, about three hundred yards off the port beam.

The man called Clive had started to climb the gangway. Bond looked to his right, remembering the spear guns racked against the superstructure. The guns were there, and the rack stood almost opposite the gate leading to the gangway, up which Clive was plodding in his scuba kit.

He ran forwards, glancing at the guns. Some were normal undersea CO_2-powered spear guns, but there were also three loaded, high-powered harpoon guns. Bond had one out of the rack and pointing at Clive just as he reached the deck.

Krest's lieutenant, his mask and air mouthpiece hanging around his neck, stopped stock-still, face registering surprise more than fear. He smiled, slowly raising his hands, and as he did so his eyes drifted upwards towards the bridge. The smile widened slightly, and in that fraction of a second, Bond, knowing he had just been spotted from the bridge, spoke, "Compliments of Sharky, Clive." He pressed the trigger as he spoke, and the little harpoon hit Clive in the centre of his chest. Everything seemed to stand still for a second, then the harpoon's small explosive charge went off, leaving the harpoon buried in a large hole of blood, bone and flesh.

With a half scream, Clive pitched backwards. The harpoon line tightened in Bond's hands, and, still clinging to the gun, he found himself lifted off his feet and pulled towards the gangway, hurtling through space into the sea below.

As he fell, he was vaguely aware of shots buzzing past him, and shouts from all around. Then the sea came up and hit him full in the face. The harpoon line had become wrapped around his wrist, so that he was dragged down and down until his lungs began to feel the strain and pain as Clive's dead body acted as a plummet. It seemed to go on forever, and Bond could think of only one thing: was this to be the end of the manta ray's journey? Then his brain cleared and he realised there was one hope. Stretching his body into a diving position, he caught hold of the taut line with both hands and began to pull himself down towards Clive's body, which, as he hauled, came up to meet him.

There was a bloom of blood around Clive's chest where the harpoon had struck, exploded and left a great gaping wound. Bond's lungs were almost at bursting point when he reached the man, splayed out like a huge starfish. He hoped there were no sharks near, for the place would be full of them in minutes if they sensed the blood.

With Clive's mouthpiece, clutched from the corpse's neck, in his own mouth, Bond was now able to breathe. Carefully, and with difficulty in the water, he managed to unbuckle the air bottle, get Clive's mask around his face and strap the whole scuba pack onto himself.

Above, he thought, they were probably searching for him. Maybe they thought he was dead, either from the shots fired as he had gone overboard, or drowned as he was pulled down by the harpoon line.

He was aware of the catamarans ploughing up and down above, and of another thrumming noise, the aircraft, he supposed.

For a few moments, Bond waited, taking deep breaths, unsure of which way he should now move. Up, he considered, was the only way, so he allowed himself to rise slowly, surprised when he discovered himself to be almost directly under *Wavekrest.* The next thing he saw was *Sentinel,* obviously just leaving its dock. He kicked, then grabbed the umbilical cord, hanging on as the probe dragged him through the water.

He recalled what he had heard. There was to be some kind of exchange between *Wavekrest* and the plane. Drugs for cash, he thought, hanging on more tightly than ever as the probe skimmed the surface of the water just above him. Below, tendrils of weed and undersea flora waved in the probe's wake. Twice he nearly had to allow himself to surface in order to avoid outcrops of rock and coral.

Then there was another noise, the unmistakable chugging of one of the catamarans' engines. Turning he saw the floats coming directly towards him, and thought he could glimpse another spear-armed diver swimming below and behind.

He let go and swam down to an overhang of coral, pressing himself against the rocks, praying the diver would not see him.

The catamaran and its diver passed overhead, and Bond wondered how long he could hold out. He had not checked the scuba pack he had taken from Clive's body. There might be an hour's supply of air, or five minutes'.

He swam out from the overhang of rock, then slowly in the direction the catamaran had been going. It might just be possible to ambush the diver and make certain he had enough air. In readiness he drew the knife from its sheath, pacing himself, swimming gently, listening and ready.

The next thing he saw was the sub-like shape of *Sentinel* making its return journey. Well, he could do some damage there. If he had been correct, and the exchange was drugs from *Wavekrest* and money from the plane—a seaplane, he presumed—then he could at least try to spread the money out among the fishes.

Grabbing at the umbilical cord, Bond pulled himself to the stern of *Sentinel*, then, staying as far into the water as possible, climbed up to the watertight compartment and wrestled with the locking lever on top, knowing that some of his body would inevitably be showing above water, even though the compartment was still submerged, but near the surface.

He forced back the lock, the doors sprang open, and he found himself looking down at a store of large clear plastic bags, like the one he had seen at the warehouse. Better still, the money was in the plane, and the drugs were here. Of course, they were en route to the warehouse, and then all stations north, south, east or west.

As though fighting some deadly beast, for that was exactly what Bond felt these drugs were, he started to slash at the packets which exploded their white repulsive powder into the sea.

Like a man on a crusade, he ripped the bags apart with knife and fingers. Then, just as he was completing the job, down to the last three packets, he heard a mechanism whir inside the for'ard compartment. Looking up, he saw the periscope turned towards him like an evil eye. Bond looked straight into the eye, smiled, then waved as he pushed himself away from *Sentinel,* knowing he would have to go deep and hide, gambling on the amount of air left to him.

But, already, one of the catamarans was near. He could hear the engines, and then saw the floats almost above him. Within seconds, they were on him. Four of them, in wet suits and scuba gear, moving very fast indeed.

He tried to turn and make a run for it, but they were fresh and faster. The first diver came straight at him from the front. Bond lifted his knife, but the man was already through his guard, his knife finding a target first—Bond's air hose, which he neatly sliced in two. As he struck, so Bond slammed his hand through the water pressure, grabbing at his assailant's face mask, which he ripped away. The diver struggled for a second, then went shooting upwards towards the surface.

But it was far from over. As the first diver was still on his upward journey, a second crashed into Bond's back, hanging on to the air tanks, forcing Bond, now struggling for air, onto his back, slashing the empty water with his knife.

In a last desperate bid, Bond slipped from the scuba harness and the diver floated away with the tanks.

Bond kicked, trying to make for the surface and air, but before he had even managed to get within yards, another man was behind him, slipping a spear gun around Bond's neck and pressing backwards, capturing 007 in a choke hold. His vision was beginning to blur and he knew there was little time left. He could just see a fourth diver moving in front of him, coming in for the kill.

One last effort. Bond grappled with the spear gun, found the trigger and pulled, hoping somehow that the fourth diver would be impaled. But the spear shot away, projected by the CO_2, the line running out behind it.

There was an almighty jerk, and Bond thought he could just see the underside of one of the catamaran's floats. But the jerk was final and very strong. Still hanging on to the spear gun, Bond felt himself being ripped away from the divers. For one horrific moment, he thought he had perhaps hit a shark. Then he broke surface, a wall of water spouting out around him as he was dragged along.

The spear had not hit the catamaran's float, but the float of what looked like a Beaver 1 seaplane, its big radial AN-14B Wasp Junior, Pratt & Whitney engine roaring into full takeoff power.

James Bond was being towed behind the seaplane like a rag doll on the end of a string, bouncing on his back, slapping into the water heavily every few seconds.

Common sense told him to let go of the spear gun, but something in his brain countermanded the orders. Heaving with all his strength he pulled himself upwards, his eyes stinging with wind and spray. By now he had managed to get both hands together, on either side of the line, and with one last effort he found himself in the ideal position to water-ski on his bare feet.

The plane towing him was gradually increasing speed, but he now had control of his body. As an expert skier, on snow or water, his feet were correctly placed and he found he could even skid from side to side, sending up walls of spray, hoping these would confuse the men on the catamarans who were shooting at him. He had heard the crack and thump of bullets passing near too many times in his life not to recognise them now.

But his main problem was the seaplane, which was already beginning to bounce prior to its lift-off from the sea.

There was noise, excitement, the spray and wind blowing in his face, coupled with the almost burning sensation from the soles of his feet. Anything he did now was purely intuitive, and he did the one thing possible.

Dragging in on the line, Bond swung wide, in the classic waterskiing manoeuvre, then pulled in close. The first time brought him within a couple of yards of the seaplane's float. Too far.

He hauled in again, and went through the wide swing again. This time, as he came back along the line of the swing, he pulled harder. The float flashed up, and he let go of the spear gun, throwing himself onto the float with a thump that almost winded him. But he was there, clinging on to the port float, reaching for the struts and hanging on, the wind and spray still hitting him. Then it was just the wind. The Beaver had lifted off, and was in a shallow climb. He took a deep breath, for the pilot was obviously aware of the added weight, desperately trimming the aircraft to climb with its wings straight and level.

Bond had to hold on with all the power left to him. He was looking forwards, and saw the small door on the port side begin to open. Fighting the slipstream, he ducked down, reaching for the forward strut on the starboard float. Whoever had looked out of the port doorway must have thought the danger over.

Still forcing himself against the slipstream, he made his way under the floats, then onto the starboard float, along it, at a painfully slow speed. The door was on the port side, but on the fuselage's other side was an emergency escape hatch, just behind the small flight deck and almost opposite the main door.

Being an emergency hatch, this one could be opened from inside or out, and he smiled against the pressure of the slipstream as he reached it and saw the little recessed lever marked in red, with a warning sign beside it. Bond put up his hand and pulled hard.

The hatch flew off, like something fired from the aircraft, and with huge effort he swung into the plane.

The initial moments seemed to happen in slow motion: a long freeze-frame in his mind. He saw the pilot, in the left-hand seat, turn his head, surprise painted over his face. But there was a second pilot who stood near the door immediately opposite Bond. The door was still partially open, and the copilot had almost certainly been telling the pilot that their uninvited guest had disappeared. He held a gun in his right hand, and Bond lunged as it came up. The main door swung fully open.

Bond closed, twisted the copilot's wrist and pulled down hard. The gun dropped from his hand. There was a grunt and the man went backwards out of the aircraft, clutching at the flapping door and finding a grip so that he was spreadeagled on it as it swung, almost lazily, to and fro.

The pilot was trimming the aircraft prior to putting it on automatic so that he could help his partner. But the copilot was beyond help now, for Bond reached up to pull the emergency release which shot the entire doorframe away from the aircraft, and with it the screaming copilot.

The act threw Bond himself into the doorway, and he only just managed to grab at the inside of the hole, spreading himself across the opening, his feet locked around the interior and his hands white-knuckled towards the top of where the door had been.

The pilot must have seen what had happened, for the engine note changed and the nose dipped, then raised slightly as the whole world went mad and the seaplane barrel-rolled.

The G-force built up and Bond just managed to remain in the doorway, then, as the plane righted itself, he flung himself into the flight deck to grapple with the pilot.

The man was quick enough to react, for a second later Bond found himself being thrown back into the main body of the aircraft, the pilot's hands around his throat. There was another change in the engine note, and the aircraft's nose dipped again. In a moment they would be out of control, streaking down to smash into fragments in the sea.

Bond threw a hand back, trying to feel for a weapon, but his fingers only grasped one of the shrink-wrapped oblongs. It seemed heavy and solid, though, so with a tremendous effort he brought it down on the pilot's head. He heard the grunt, felt the hands let go of his throat, saw the cabin suddenly fill with hundred-dollar bills as the packet broke open, then felt the plane begin to wing over and drop into its final dive. The pilot gave a yell of alarm as the fuselage tilted and he slid towards the doorway, hands scrabbling for some kind of hold as he fell, turning over and plunging towards the sea below.

Bond dragged himself into the left-hand seat. The aircraft tilted almost at right angles, while the nose was down, sea filling his vision and the horizon way above him.

He throttled back, easing the stick to the right to level the wings and control the aircraft in its dive. The wings straightened with ease—it was a very forgiving airplane—and as he gently pulled back on the stick, the nose obediently came up.

Not too soon either, for *Wavekrest* now filled Bond's forward vision. He increased power, still pulling back, and the Beaver climbed away perfectly. He did not even see the men, including Krest, flatten themselves on *Wavekrest's* deck, thinking their last hour had come.

He climbed to around a thousand feet, trying to make up his mind what to do. He was there, in a seaplane full of money—there must have been hundreds and thousands of dollars in those blue packets—with no registered flight plan and, by now, both Sanchez's men, the Drug Enforcement Agency and quite probably the IRS looking for him. He turned the aircraft out to sea. What he needed was some landing place away from shipping or aircraft lanes, and just far enough away from *Wavekrest* so that they would not come looking. He also needed time: time to pack away the cash, and time to get back into Key West undetected.

Bond allowed the Beaver to lose height in order to get under any radar that might be operating in the area. He slowed his speed and began to think. The DEA people combed the waters around Key West for smugglers, so he could not just fly in and say, "Look what I've got. A heap of money from a drug operation." That would never work because he had already destroyed the evidence.

One thing was sure: whatever he did now, the journey of the manta was definitely nearly over.

The Beaver flew on as Bond cudgelled his brains to think of some way back in without alerting anybody. About twenty minutes later, he smiled, looked at the compass and turned the plane onto a new heading. There was only one way, and he would need a lot of luck.

— 7 —

Final Contact

THE TELEVISION NEWSCAST came via CNN-TV direct from Isthmus City. Lights twinkled in the background as the attractive lady commentator stood in front of the sumptuous casino. Every few seconds, limos discharged suave men and svelte women who walked into the casino as though they owned it.

James Bond, in his hotel room, was particularly interested. He had turned the TV on while he ate dinner provided by room service, and the CNN-TV commentator had immediately caught his attention with her opening lines—

"Isthmus City is aglitter tonight." She looked

confidently at the camera. "And very much aglitter as Franz Sanchez arrives at this luminous party which some people are saying is being held to celebrate his recent escape from custody in the United States . . ."

At that moment Bond had stopped eating, the fresh salmon on his fork hovering between plate and mouth. He saw all the glitter, and he also saw Sanchez in close-up for the first time. He had descended from a limo with Lupe on his arm and surrounded by a whole phalanx of bodyguards.

The commentator approached him, and Sanchez smiled, relaxed and looking very much at ease.

"Señor Sanchez," the commentator began, as her name—Anna Rack—came up at the bottom of the screen. "Señor Sanchez. Recently a leading American newspaper described you as a drug lord . . ."

Sanchez turned directly towards the camera. The smile had gone from his face as he interrupted the unhappy Ms. Rack. "I know nothing about drugs. The United States should look elsewhere and not blame me for its drug problems. I am a businessman who runs this gambling casino. I love the American people. They're welcome here. Most welcome, and they should come; after all we have better odds than the U.S. Only one zero on the roulette wheel . . ." As he spoke, a limo flying official state flags arrived behind him. The limo was surrounded by a motorcycle escort of military police.

"Looks as if they came straight from Ruritania," Bond muttered to himself.

"You will excuse me." Sanchez smiled once more. "I have to greet my guests." He turned away abruptly to embrace the stout man who climbed from the official limo. The military police seemed to surge forwards, making the camera back off. Off screen there was a little squeal from Ms. Rack. A moment later, she was there, composed once more—

"Well, as you see, Franz Sanchez is escorting his guest of honour, President Hector Lopez of Isthmus, into his casino's Gala Evening. This is Anna Rack for CNN News, live from Isthmus City."

Bond sighed. Well, he's there, he thought. Where you lead, Franz Sanchez, I must follow. He had a lot to do before then, though, and it had been a tiring day.

He had flown the Beaver 1 out to sea, around thirty to forty miles out, praying the weather would hold. The sea was calm, and finally he put the plane down, hoping he would not be called upon to take off and make a run for it in a hurry. He needed until nightfall at least, and spent the rest of the day dealing with the packets of shrink-wrapped money.

The pilots had obviously made careful preparations, for there were two large suitcases in the body of the plane. It took Bond over an hour to pack the cases. Then all he had to do was wait. By an hour before sunset, Bond was a very hungry and thirsty man, but he knew that if he was going to put himself, and the money, to good use, he had to keep going. He started up the engine, turned into what little wind there was and took off, not climbing but setting course very low above the sea.

He had set his altimeter to zero, and his memory of the entire area was that sea level did not rise much around the Florida Keys. In the darkness he relied wholly on the magnetic course he had set, the altimeter and the clock, which he had also set on takeoff. He kept up a steady speed, flying for over an hour, without lights. At last, in the very far distance he could see a glow in the sky, so he landed the plane and taxied it over the water very slowly and carefully. In all he must have taxied for almost ten miles.

He checked the course again, knowing that this would be the really difficult part. He was heading for one particular island off Key West and it was important that, in the darkness, he made a correct approach from the west, as the water to the east— between the island known as Ballast Key, and Key West itself—was shallow with a narrow marked lane for small motorised craft which did not draw more than a few feet. One false move now and the Beaver 1 seaplane could crunch its way onto a sandbank, from which it would be almost impossible for him to extricate it.

With the engine at idle, Bond stared into the darkness ahead, occasionally flashing the plane's landing lights on and off. It took almost two hours and, even then, the hump of land which was Ballast Key came up very quickly. There was a fifty-yard wooden landing stage on the south side of the island, with enough depth to bring in the seaplane. Gently, Bond manoeuvred it right up to the dock, climbed out and tied up.

The island was in darkness, so he knew its owner would be at one of two numbers, his house on Key West itself or his New York apartment. Ballast Key had a house, built with great ingenuity, by an old friend.

Like all field agents, Bond had documents stashed in most of the major cities throughout the world, and he was also careful to cultivate friends and acquaintances wherever he went. Some had an inkling of his arcane work; others just got on with him, liked him for his company and conversation. David Wolkowsky, a man who had changed the Gulf side of Key West, by restoration and rebuilding, was among the latter, and Bond was unhappy about using him in this side of his life, but there was no other way. It was David who owned Ballast Key and the house he had built on it.

Before anything else, the money had to be removed. Three times he moved between the plane and the wooden pier. Twice to bring the heavy suitcases onto dry land, then one more time to check the cabin and storage compartment with a torch from the cockpit. The last time proved worthwhile, as he discovered two more of the blue shrink-wrapped packages, hidden away under the copilot's seat. The money was drug money, so he felt no moral conscience about it, for this loot would be used to bring Franz Sanchez to his final destiny—either death or a long spell of imprisonment.

Once the money was on the pier, he returned to the seaplane one last time, his torch on a lanyard around his neck. Rummaging in the storage compartment, he had discovered a set of tools, including a soft mallet and chisel. Starting the engine again, he taxied out into deep water, cut the motor and climbed down onto the floats. It took fifteen minutes to rip metal from the starboard float, and the airplane was already taking in water and listing badly when he got to the second float, which he treated in the same way. He was in the water now, with the plane gently sinking. To make certain, he punctured the fuselage in four different places, then kicked himself away, lying on his back, to watch the Beaver 1 guzzle water and slowly go down. Tomorrow it might well be seen from the air, but by then he hoped to be far away.

He swam back to the island, using a lazy but fast crawl, his nerve ends tingling, for these were waters where sharks came inshore. Luck held, and, soaking wet, he once more checked the cases on the pier and made his way up to the deserted house. Using the torch, he found the main door, dealt with the

lock and went inside. In a couple of minutes he had
found the telephone and was punching out a local,
Key West, number. After four rings a languid voice
answered.

"David, it's James. James Bond."

"Oh, how nice of you to call, James. Where are
you?"

"On your island. I've just broken into your
house."

"My, how ingenious of you. Shall I send the local
cops?"

"I rather think it would be better if you didn't
know about it."

"About what?"

"Me breaking into your house."

"What break-in?" David replied with no hint of
humour in his voice. "Now, what can I do for you?
I suppose it's some woman. Usually is."

"I need to be brought in, and deposited at the
Casa Marina."

"Really? I thought you always stayed at the Pier
House."

"So does the husband," Bond lied.

"Oh, then the Casa would be better. I'll get Steve
to pop over and pick you up." Steve was also an old
friend. A tall, fine-looking young man, and an
excellent sailor.

"Will he make it through the channel?"

"Steve can take a boat anywhere. He knows the
channel like the proverbial back of his hand. Anything else?"

"If he could pick up a couple of cases of mine from the Pier House . . ."

"Of course, James. Lovely to talk to you. We really must have lunch when you've finished deceiving husbands. Bye."

And so it was. Steve already had the two cases, collected from the Pier House, aboard the light speedboat. "What in heaven's name have you got in these, gold bars?" he asked, picking up the cases of money.

Bond smiled in the darkness. "Almost."

The journey, from Ballast Key to Garrison Bight, had taken twice as long as usual, with Steve peering into the darkness, using a small floodlight to follow the twisting narrow channel, marked with red flags. But they eventually made it. There was a small bar at Garrison Bight, but it was frequented by fishermen who could not have cared what was being brought in from Ballast Key. Half an hour later, Bond was settled into the renovated Casa Marina Hotel, with its huge airy lobby, the smooth polished floorboards, great whirling fans and strange pedigree—for it had been originally built by the legendary Henry Flagler, who constructed the Overseas Railroad and chose one of the most beautiful locations for the hotel, set between County and South beaches, shaded by palms and backed by elegant lawns. The Casa Marina, like the Overseas Railroad, had not been one of Flagler's successes. Between the wars it began to fail, and during Big Two was used by the Navy before returning to private ownership, apart from being taken over by the military during the Cuba Crisis, after which it fell into disrepair, to be renovated again in 1977.

Now this pleasant hotel was a haven of peace for Bond. What was better, nobody knew he was there. He had only partially unpacked, making certain the money was secure in the two big cases, and taking a look in the special secret compartment in the briefcase Q Branch had prepared for the Istanbul trip. Peeling away the false bottom, which was shielded from any airport X-ray eyes, he found, among other things, a spare automatic and holster.

He grunted, seeing they had given him a Walther PPK—not his favourite weapon, since it had been taken out of use with the SIS several years before. But, on closer inspection, he saw that it was not the old PPK, but the P38K, the shorter and more effective version.

Changing into dark slacks and a black rollneck, and with comfortable black doeskin moccasins on his feet, he slipped the pistol into a specially tailored holster pocket, out of sight on his hip, placing a small zippered wallet into his normal hip pocket on the left side. The time had come to return to the Leiter house, scene of disaster and tragedy.

He went on foot, as he wanted no record of this visit, even from a cabdriver's memory. The house was still cordoned off with white tape, and there was a light, discouraging police presence—one car containing two officers outside the main entrance, from which, Bond had figured out, the room that interested him could not be seen.

Stealthily Bond made his way through the trees, climbing the wall, taking care that there were no alarm devices or electronic eyes to trigger. Silently he moved towards the back of the house, and the door which led directly to the kitchen. He knelt down, removed the wallet from his hip pocket and extracted, first, a pinlight torch, and second, that simplest of lockpicking devices known in the trade as a rake.

The lock was easy enough. Old and well used. He inserted the rake into the keyhole and moved it slowly back and forth in a gentle, steady sawing movement, listening for the moment when the curves in the tool made contact with the pins and drivers inside the lock's cylinder. Gradually Bond increased speed and, within a minute, heard the pins snap up and the driver disengage. There was a click and the lock gave way, the door opening slightly.

If he went out the same way, Bond knew he could close the door and the lock would click back into place, leaving no trace that it had been forced. He stepped inside and made his way through the kitchen and main rooms, up the stairs, moving by feel and with no torch, for this could have been detected by the two cops outside.

At last he reached Leiter's study. He had wanted to visit it sooner, but M's sudden arrival had prevented it. He stepped inside and switched on the light. This could not be seen from the street, and he had to gamble on there being no guards on the rear of the house.

The last time he had been in the room it was a shambles, drawers turned over, books pulled from place and—the screaming horror still made his flesh creep and the back of his neck tingle—Felix dumped on the couch.

Since that incident, though, he had thought of his penultimate visit, during the wedding when he had walked in to find the tall brunette called Pam leaning over Felix's shoulder as he tapped in something on his computer which still stood on the desk. He faithfully recalled everything Felix did at the time, and knew that whoever had turned over the room had left what he had been searching for. Bond knew, because Felix had hidden it in plain sight.

He walked over to the shelves near the desk and reached up to the lovely photograph of Della. There, in a small holder behind the picture, was a 3.5 computer disk. It had been there since Felix put it in place while Bond had waited to take him down for the cake-cutting ceremony.

He moved to the desk, sat down and touched the power switch on the extended keyboard. The drive and fan began to whir slightly and the screen gave out its little message, *Welcome,* with a small drawing of the computer to one side. Then the screen cleared, leaving the lozenge-shaped icon of a hard disk drive in the top right-hand corner, and a small menu line across the top.

Bond slipped the 3.5 disk into the external drive. A moment later the icon of the disk came up below the hard drive icon. Two clicks, with the mouse, on the image of the disk and the entire thing began to open up, the screen blacking out, then turning to grey, the application programmed on the hard drive taking over whatever had been saved on the disk.

Then, almost before he realised it had happened, the screen filled with data. A list of files spread themselves over the screen, each in a little folder icon. The folder icons each had a name—*Sanchez: U.S. Assets. Sanchez: Swiss Bank Accounts. Sanchez: Isthmus Accounts;* and finally, *Sanchez: Informants.*

Bond clicked on the last file. Eight names scrolled down the screen. Against each of the names there were details, but one word, *Deceased,* completed the data. Except for the final name. Bond peered at the screen and read, *Lexington Contact—P. Bouvier, CIA. Maximum support and protection plus technical backup. Next meeting: 2100 hrs. Thursday. Barrelhead. Bimini W.I.*

Bond nodded, as though he knew exactly what was supposed to happen. Indeed he did know that the Barrelhead Saloon was in one of the worst areas of Bimini's West Island. Tomorrow was Thursday, so P. Bouvier would be waiting there for Felix.

There was only one thing he could do. Take Felix's place. He did not even think about who the contact Bouvier might possibly be. But he would know by tomorrow night. What worried him now was that this had only been a backup disk. He opened up the machine's hard drive and checked through the programs. The data was there also. He would bet a hundred to one that Sanchez's people had read everything here. They did not need the backup. It would be interesting to see if the Bouvier contact actually turned up.

Back at the hotel, he checked that no intruders had found their way into his room—he had left the usual little traps: a matchstick here and a piece of cotton there. Nobody had searched the place.

He put the Walther under his pillow, secured the door, stripped off, performed his nightly toilet and slid into bed. He could do nothing until the morning—there was no point in worrying about things now—so he blanked everything from his mind, dropping into a deep, dreamless sleep.

At eight forty-five on the following evening, Bond drove the sleek powerboat alongside other light craft tied up at the dock in front of the Barrelhead Saloon.

There had been fun in buying the craft that morning, and Bond reflected that, with the many thousands of dollars at his disposal, much more fun was in store. After breakfasting, he had informed the hotel that he would be away for a day or two and asked them if they would put his luggage in their secure baggage area. They were delighted, and after removing what amounted to a great deal of cash from one of the suitcases, he saw the baggage stowed, then left to walk down to the Key West Marina, thinking that a likely craft might be for sale.

In the event, there was nothing and the only likely target was a slim and sleek powerboat.

A rather unpleasant-looking young man was tinkering with the engines and Bond called to him.

"I rent your boat?" he asked.

The young man did not even look up. "Not a chance," he mouthed.

"What's up? Engines faulty?"

"No way. This baby'll outstrip anything else in her class."

"Okay." Bond smiled. "How much to buy her from you?"

This time the man did look up, his lips twisting in a condescending smile. "More than you could afford, wise ass."

Bond smiled again. "Name your price."

The boat owner looked at him steadily. The look said, "What have I done to deserve meeting a nut this morning?" Aloud he sneered, "To you? Two hundred K."

"That include a full tank of petrol?" Bond began to pull cash from his pockets in ten-thousand-dollar packets. Carefully he counted out twenty of the packets, revelling in the shocked look on the man's face.

But now it was night and in fifteen minutes he would be meeting Bouvier, Leiter's final contact.

Right on time, he climbed from the boat and walked the few paces towards the saloon, thinking that it certainly was not the Ritz Grill. Inside it was even worse than he had expected. The decor was by chance, and faded at that. The clientele looked to be the dregs of humanity. Some looked to be downright dangerously wicked as well. On a small stage, in the far corner, just about visible, a tired-looking stripper performed in a manner that would make it fun to watch paint dry. Cigarette smoke clogged the air and the noise level would have worried anyone who lived near the edge of a major airport's runway.

A pair of men in outdated and slightly mouldy dinner jackets stood inside the door. You did not have to be brain of the year to mark them down as bouncers. Bond approached them with caution. "Looking for someone called Bouvier," he said.

The larger of the two men, who, at a guess, had suffered from a broken nose at least six times, give or take a break, gestured, pointing into the darkest recesses of the room. Bond could just make out a shadowy silhouette sitting alone at a table at the far end of the long bar which reached from the stripper's stage to the wall.

He made his way through the room with as much

caution as he had approached the bouncers. There were only a few women in the place, and he would not have trusted them very far, while the men could not be trusted at all. They obviously did not like strangers, and were affronted by anyone trying to push through the crowd, for the tables were crammed into the place; chairback touched chairback, and Bond added extra courtesy into his journey.

At last, he shouldered his way to the lone figure.

She looked up, surprised to see it was him. Bond had first seen her outside the church before Felix' ill-fated wedding; then again in the study. It was Pam, the beautiful brunette in the crisp pink suit. The one with the legs that went on for ever.

"This is an unexpected pleasure," he said, noticing that she now looked very different. Her hair was slicked back and tied with a headband; she wore grubby white pants and a padded jacket. Also, she did not look pleased to see him.

"Where's Leiter?" she snapped as he took the chair next to her.

"He's in intensive care. Where we're likely to be if we don't get out of here fast. I'm pretty sure Sanchez has all of Leiter's files, and your name's all over them, as you know."

"Hell!" she muttered. "I knew something was wrong. Don't look around but there're a couple of heavy guys right at the end of the bar. They're just Sanchez's speed and they've been there for some time. They're professional something-or-others, but they're not professional watchers. Probably been waiting to see who turns up to meet me." She stopped short as a waitress appeared at the table.

"Hi, y'all. What y'all havin'?" The waitress was chewing gum and the only word that came to Bond's mind was "buxom."

"Give me a Bud with lime." Pam did not even look up.

"The same." Bond did look up and caught a glimpse of some new arrivals in the doorway, which was raised above the room by plain planked steps. "I have a feeling trouble's just arrived," he said.

Pam turned her head. "Oh, shit!" she groaned. "That's one of Sanchez's personal men. Dario. Very bad news. Used to be with the Contras, but even they kicked him out. Just the nice kind of guy Sanchez would send. The other one's a run-of-the-mill hood. The kind that pulls wings off flies on a dull day. You carrying?"

Bond coughed, allowing his windbreaker to fall open, just enough for her to see the butt of the Walther P38K. Pam saw, but made a tutting sound, pushing herself back slightly. Across her lap lay a Handgrip Model .38, 20-gauge shotgun.

Out of the corner of his eye, Bond saw the bartender look across the room at the man called Dario, nodding in the direction of Pam and Bond.

"Is there a back way out?" he asked.

"At the far end of the bar. The place where those

two heavy guys have just been reinforced by another three." Pam seemed to be looking everywhere at once, planning some kind of escape. "Look," she said, "Dario's heading this way. If they start shooting just hit the deck and stay there."

"Well . . ." Bond began when Dario appeared out of the crowd, standing on Pam's right, while the other hood materialised beside Bond.

Dario smiled. Unaffably. *"Qué pasa, Señorita Bouvier?* Don' I know you from somewhere?"

Bond rose so that he was standing slightly behind Dario's stable mate as Pam gave an abrupt "No."

"Sure I know you." Dario came closer. "You used to fly special charters for some of my friends. Listen, I got a job for you." He reached down and took her arm. "Let's go outside. Talk about it, all private, eh?"

"The lady's with me," Bond said, very politely, but with a firmness that would have pleased a marine drill instructor.

Dario looked across the table. "Nobody ask you, gringo!" As he reached the last word it came out in a kind of gasp. Bond's eyes flicked down. Pam had shoved the barrel of her shotgun right into the man's crotch. He winced as Pam said, "He's with me."

The waitress, still chewing, arrived with the beers. "There you go. Three-fifty, unless your friends want something."

Dario's friend said, "Let me take care of it," reaching inside his coat, and nobody saw Bond's hand come up and chop the back of his neck. The hood slumped forwards and Bond caught him.

"He's had enough already." Bond slipped a ten-spot out of his pocket and dropped it on the waitress' tray. "Keep the change."

"My! Thank y'all," she pouted, mainly with her chest. "Anytime, hon."

"Now, let's all sit down quietly." Bond looked at Dario as he lowered the other man into a chair. "You, my friend, are going to get us all out of here in one piece. Right?"

Dario's eyes had lifted, to look past Bond's shoulders. Pam raised her eyes also. "Keep your hands on the table," she ordered Dario, pressing with the shotgun to make him sit down. Then, to Bond she said, "How did you get here?"

"Boat."

"Where is it?"

Bond nodded to the wall behind her. "On the other side of that." He was conscious of scuffling around the bar.

"Sanchez's other little friends are trying to push their way over. There're some other people who don't like being jostled." There was a crash and a shout. Bond glanced around to see quite a reasonable barroom brawl. One man was using another as a punchbag, and a further couple had started to slug it out, blow for blow. All they needed was a pianist who just continued to play.

"Let's go." Pam was on her feet, and, as she moved, Dario whipped around, grabbing a bottle.

Bond tapped him lightly on the head. "'Night, Dario," said Bond, following Pam towards the wall.

There was a shout of "Hold it," and he turned to see one of the other Sanchez hoodlums pulling a gun. He raised the Walther, and for a second there was a Mexican standoff.

In that small space of time, Pam turned to face the wall, brought up the shotgun and fired. The whole room seemed to stand still, and Bond saw that a four-foot hole had appeared in the wall. "If they will use cheap building materials," he said.

"Come on," Pam shouted. "Get the thing going. I'll hold them off," whirling towards the crowd, bringing the 20-gauge up. As Bond ducked through the hole and ran towards the powerboat, he thought that a weapon like the Handgrip Model .38 was quite a deterrent.

He made the edge of the dock in five seconds flat, and had the boat's engines going in another five.

Pam came through the wall, turning and firing in the air, then running full tilt towards the jetty. She had just reached the edge when Dario appeared out of the hole, his gun hand coming up. Bond fired and his target dodged back inside, but not without firing.

He heard Pam gasp as the shot threw her forwards into the boat. With an oath, Bond gunned the engine and began to put distance between himself and the jetty where another of Sanchez's men had appeared, a stubby Uzi in his hands.

There was one fast rip of bullets, and Bond felt the boat shudder from impact as he returned the fire and, to his pleasure, saw the gunman clutch at his stomach, dropping the Uzi into the water and following it with a cry.

He had to get right away from this place, and very fast. Pam almost certainly needed help. But as he bumped along at speed, Bond saw her move, then sit up. He slowed slightly and watched her unzip the padded jacket, grope around in the wadding and remove a bullet.

".357 Magnum." She threw it onto the deck.

"Kevlar?" asked Bond, knowing this was the new lightweight combination from which the best flak jackets were made these days.

"In my business you never leave home without it."

"Tough business you picked."

"Speak for yourself, James Bond. Felix told me who you were, and what you did. Me? Well, I was an army pilot. Put in two years with Air America. What can a girl do after that? Be an air hostess? I still fly a lot. Even got my own little Beechcraft Baron. Keep my hand in."

Under the jacket she wore only a pink silk camisole which gave Bond an admirable view. "I've got just the job for you." His voice carried an air of frivolity.

"Oh, yes?" she replied.

"Oh, definitely yes. A private charter to Isthmus City. Nobody must know I've left the U.S."

"You serious?"

"Deadly."

"Why?"

"To get Sanchez. I need a full briefing from you on the whole of his operation, everything you know. I'll pay good money."

"You're actually going after him?" She looked appalled; and when Bond did not reply she asked how many men he had.

This time Bond smiled at her. "Just you and me."

"You're crazy. That guy has a whole army down there. Everyone's in his pocket."

"Okay. Just drop me there and leave. Fifty thousand dollars."

She came towards him and laid a hand on his arm. "A job like that would cost you a hundred K."

Bond throttled back, his hand going to her shoulder, their eyes locking. "Seventy-five," he said.

"You pay the fuel."

"We use your plane."

"Deal." She looked happy as she said it, and in the next moment the engines gave a stutter, then a rumble. They were slowing down.

"Damn!" Bond moved aft and leaned over the side. "Several of that Uzi's bullets ended up in our gas tank." By now they had slowed to almost a stop. He turned back towards her. "You're not going to believe this . . ."

"You're out of gas? I haven't heard that one since high school."

"Did it work then?" He came back to her as she leaned against the wheel. "It should only take us a couple of hours to drift into Miami." He was very close now.

"And what will we do in the meantime? That was your next line, wasn't it?" She reached up and kissed him, open-mouthed, on the lips.

"Why don't you wait till you're asked?"

"So ask me." Pam was in his arms and they both slid towards the deck. Slowly, moving gently, the powerboat drifted on the calm sea.

"What a night to go sailing," Bond said.

— 8 —

Dollars and Dealers

IN LONDON ON the fifth floor of the building over-looking Regent's Park, which is the headquarters of the British Secret Service, M came out of his private office with a face like thunder.

His secretary, Miss Moneypenny, a legend in her own right, looked up from the word processor. She had obviously been daydreaming and not working. M's thunder, plus a little lightning, seemed to bring a major storm into her usually calm workstation.

M brandished a sheaf of papers, and spoke as though giving orders to a crew on an open deck in a force-ten gale. Nobody doubted, when he was in this mood, that M held a very high naval rank.

"What in the name of Drake, Nelson and Raleigh

are you up to?" He stood directly in front of her and noted that she looked ready to burst into tears. His mind registered that this was most unlike Moneypenny.

"What seems to be the trouble, sir?" She spoke in a "little" voice unlike the efficient secretary she was.

M brandished the papers again. "Five errors— typing errors—on the first page alone. Damn it, woman, I thought these new contraptions corrected things like that!"

"Oh. Oh, I'm sorry. I must have forgotten to run the spell-check over it." Even though she was looking M straight in the eyes, the Chief caught the small movement of her hand on the desk. His eyes flicked down, and he saw she was trying to cover a telex with some spare papers. "Let me see that." He whipped up the paper and began to read aloud, his voice rising into near fury as he read—

"U.S. Immigration has no reports of 007 leaving the United States as of 1500 hours today. By heaven, who authorised this?"

"I'm afraid I did, sir. I thought you'd be worried about James. He's gone missing."

M's voice softened. "You know better than that, Moneypenny. Much better, and it's you who's worried, isn't it?"

She bit her lip and nodded.

"Hrrumph! Well, think it through. You know what he'll be up to. On his way to get that blighter Sanchez. I'm afraid James's gone off the deep end, and he has to be stopped—or helped." He gave her a thin smile. "Look, I've already alerted our man in Isthmus." He drew out a smaller piece of paper from under the pile he carried. "Now, to put your mind at rest, I want this memo out now. This afternoon. Understand?" M turned and marched back into his office.

Moneypenny smiled as she read the memo, then, picking up the telephone, she said, "Get me Q Branch, please."

The approach to Isthmus City International Airport is straight in over the sea. You cross the harbour, and a mile further on there is the threshold to runway 33 Left. What you see of the city as you cover that final mile in the air is typical of what you see on the ground. Huddled, ugly and decayed buildings, almost cheek by jowl with modern highrise apartment blocks and hotels. Isthmus City has only four types of resident, not counting the quick and the dead. You are either very rich or very poor; or you either have work or, as in most cases, you have no work.

Pam flared the Beechcraft Baron neatly, right on the white bars of the threshold, then, as instructed from the tower, taxied towards the executive section, where other small aircraft were unloading or starting up.

From the right-hand seat of the flight deck, Bond saw an enormous poster on the side of one of the airport buildings. It showed a garish, toothy, smiling, highly cosmeticised painting of the President. Underneath, in Spanish, were the words *Presidente Hector Lopez—Profits for the People.*

Pam followed the instructions of a ground crewman, parked, applied the brakes and ran the two Continental IO-470-L engines down until the spinning disks that were the propellers assumed their normal shape again. "Welcome to Isthmus City, James. Home of the corrupt, the hungry and the biggest drug baron in the world."

A ground crew had arrived, and already their matching sets of Louis Vuitton luggage had been loaded onto a small truck. "Ah," Pam gave a little sign of interest as they came down the steps, nodding towards a Gulf Stream II that had parked nearby, the whine of its engines blotting out any other sound. "Interesting," she continued. The Gulf Stream was painted cream with a gold logo on the tailplane. The words *Isthmus Casino,* with a coin as the final "o." "Look at that reception committee."

Bond saw two men greeting a group of six Orientals who were disembarking. The first had light-coloured hair and a Wall Street taste in clothes. The other man was tall and built like a blockhouse. He had seen the latter, on television: Sanchez' arrival at the Casino Gala Evening.

"The blond guy's called William Truman-Lodge; Sanchez' financial whiz kid."

"Looks like a gecko to me." Bond gave an innocent smile, hoping that the little joke about the *Wall Street* movie was not lost on Pam.

"Oh, yes. He's just like on the movies. They'd very much like to see him back home. Wanted for insider trading on Wall Street."

"Figures." A customs official and an attractive hostess had joined the party and were shepherding them through a side entrance and a couple of stretch limos that waited for them. "The other guy?" Bond asked.

"The tall one. Name of Heller. Ex-Green Beret captain who went to the bad. Handles security for Sanchez, with the rank of colonel. The Bureau would like to get their hands on him as well."

"I believe it." Bond saw that they only rated a customs official, who stamped their passports after removing the five hundred-dollar bills Bond had folded into his. "How much for a limo?" he asked.

"For you, sir? Another hundred. To me." The note changed hands, and the wheels were oiled nicely. Ten minutes later they were being whisked through wide streets flanked by overcrowded and dilapidated buildings. Ragged children played in the streets, and men sat, disconsolate, on the kerbs.

From this squalour they passed into a more opulent area. No rags and no desperate-looking people inhabited this quarter. Shops glistened, bulging with luxuries, and there were a large number of security men around. Big fellows dressed in blue pants and shirts, with short leather jackets and baseball caps—flashy with a gold insignia. Each man had a pump-action shotgun. But even here, in the upmarket part of town, pictures of President Lopez could be seen everywhere.

They had called ahead, Bond ordering the best suite they could give him at the Hotel El Presidente, and they were greeted with much rubbing of hands, bowing, scraping and flashing teeth. It took three bellboys to bring the luggage, and they were accompanied by an unctuous assistant manager who showed them the considerable amenities and then asked if the suite was satisfactory.

It was more than satisfactory, but Bond looked around as though the place stank. "It's adequate," he said. "But I want fresh flowers in all the rooms, and some Bollinger—*récemment dégorgé*, if you have it . . ."

"But certainly, señor."

"A case, I think. Sent up straightaway. Oh, and could you hire a Rolls-Royce for me?"

"Of course, señor." The assistant manager bowed even lower. "With a chauffeur?"

"For now, yes. Later we'll see."

"Very good, señor. I wonder, señor . . ." He hesitated. "Could you sign the registration cards, señor?"

Bond looked at him as though he had crawled out from under a stone. He brought out a wad of notes and dispensed large tips to the bellboys. "My executive secretary, Miss Kennedy, will take care of that." He waved towards Pam, who gave him a laser look before smiling sweetly at the assistant manager and signing the cards.

"*Ms.* Kennedy, if you don't mind," she said when the door closed. "Anyway, I already told you,

I'm not related to *those* Bouviers. Why can't *you* be *my* executive secretary?"

"South of the border, Pam. Still a man's world down here." He went to one of the larger cases which lay on a luggage stand. Now he manipulated the combination locks and opened it. The case almost overflowed with bank notes, and Pam gave a little gasp.

He counted out several packets and handed them to her. "Thanks for everything, dear Pam. Your job's finished."

She took the money, looked at it and then at Bond again. "James, you can use some help here. I'd like to go the full distance."

"Dangerous, Pam. Said so yourself." He put his arms around her shoulders. "Enough people are dead. I'd like you waiting when I get back."

A very desirable lady, Bond thought. Intelligent, beautiful, courageous. These were the pluses. He bent down and kissed her hard on the lips, and felt her body react against his. More pluses. But he was aware of the minus signs also. Headstrong, her own woman with a very short fuse.

She drew away from him. "James, listen. They were already on to me in Bimini. They probably think they got me, but they're soon going to find out the truth. When that happens, when they figure out I'm still alive, I'm not going to be safe anywhere. My only chance is to help you get Sanchez before he gets me." She gave that irresistible grin. "Besides, I like the pay."

He looked at her for a full minute, then nodded, reaching down to take another packet of money from the case. "Okay. This is for expenses. If you're going to play at being my executive secretary, you'll have to look the part." He gave her his quizzical glance, raising one eyebrow. "So, get your hair done and buy some stylish clothes instead of the tomboy gear you're wearing."

Pam's fuse burned out and fired the detonator. She snatched the cash from his hand. "You bastard," she muttered, turning on her heel and heading for the door.

"Oh, Ms. Kennedy," he called after her. "I need to deposit this paper. Which bank does Sanchez use?"

She went on walking. "Which do you think?" she mouthed back over her shoulder. "The biggest in town. The Banco de Isthmus. He *owns* it." The door slammed behind her, like a pistol shot.

An hour later, Bond lolled, at ease, in the back of a silver Rolls. The suitcases were in the boot, and the chauffeur was of the silent variety. They drove two blocks, and before he knew it, there was an imposing classic façade with a huge carved *Banco de Isthmus* picked out in gold spreading across the entire building. Gold seemed to be Sanchez's favourite colour. Not surprising, Bond considered. Really it should be gold and white. White for the toxic powder from which he made the gold.

Almost before the door was opened, a bank porter appeared by the car, together with a couple of the ubiquitous leather-jacketed guards, complete with the pump-action shotguns. Bond had the boot unlocked and the two large suitcases were loaded onto the porter's handcart. Once more he had telephoned ahead, and the porter said the manager was expecting him.

They passed through the doors, snaking among the many well-dressed customers, and across a magnificent marbled Art Deco lobby. Sanchez certainly was not mean when it came to putting up a front, Bond thought as they entered a large, very spacious office.

"Hey, amigos!" The voice seemed to be directed at Bond's little procession, and his heart skipped a beat as he saw Sanchez, looking bronzed and fit, immaculate in a white suit, coming down the main staircase.

For a few seconds it looked as though Sanchez was coming straight towards him, but at the last minute he sidestepped and Bond saw he was really greeting the six Orientals who had arrived on the casino's jet. With them was the financial whiz kid. What had Pam called him? Yes, Truman-Lodge. The name sounded like a motel, Bond thought, smiling to himself as he passed into the manager's office, noting that Sanchez and company were heading up the wide marble staircase which would not have looked out of place in a First Empire palace.

The manager, tall, suave and as immaculately dressed as Sanchez, rose from a desk which could possibly just be used as a small helicopter landing pad. He smiled pleasantly and extended a hand—

"You are Mr. Bond, yes? Good. My name is Montolongo, and it has been my privilege to manage this bank for the last five years. It is good to meet you."

Bond had opened both suitcases. Now he gestured to the alarmingly large pile of money. "I've come to make a small deposit," he said.

Montolongo glanced at the cases. If Bond had expected any amazed reaction he was out of luck. The manager merely smiled, as if to say this was really a caring bank. He pressed a small button on his desk and, almost without warning, a door opened to admit a slim young woman who looked more like a model than a banker.

"One of my more attractive assistants, Mr. Bond." Then, turning to the girl, who had already greeted Bond with a dazzling smile, "Consuela, I wonder if you would have Mr. Bond's deposit counted."

"Of course." The girl spoke excellent American English, with no trace of an accent.

"There's exactly five million dollars there." Bond turned away to examine a mural which covered one wall.

"Then you needn't count it, my dear. Just make out the deposit receipt."

Consuela nodded, signalled to a porter, who brought in a handcart. The cases were loaded up and taken away. Bond tried to give the impression of a man waiting to speak privately, and Montolongo regarded him with eyes that seemed to show infinite understanding.

"There'll be additional monthly deposits in the same amount," Bond said, turning back to the mural, which depicted a street scene, circa 1920. It also gave the impression that everyone in the scene had great wealth: women rode in long cars smoking through what seemed to be even longer cigarette holders; men paid over large sums of money to banks, or were sitting in boardrooms, when they were not buying things.

Montolongo came up behind him. "It is a good piece of work, yes? Made by a talented local artist. It's called 'Prosperity Through Work.' "

"Very apt." Bond raised his eyebrows and continued to look at the mural.

"Mr. Bond," the manager continued. "Here at the Banco de Isthmus we understand about accounts such as yours. If you wish it, we can always put your money through our bank in the United States and from there into the U.S. Federal Reserve. We have a trading room, right here in the building. We do it all the time. Once the funds are in the Federal Reserve, we can use them for—how can I put it . . .?"

"Legitimate investments?" Bond turned to face the man, who smiled.

"Quite so, Mr. Bond. Legitimate investments. Our trading room is wired to all of the world's leading financial exchanges. We offer complete anonymity to our customers. One might say we operate the world's largest private investment fund."

Bond thought, "One might really say the Banco de Isthmus operates the world's largest laundry." Aloud, he said, "I'll give it some thought. You can never tell how useful a service such as that could be."

"I'm glad we understand one another. Good."

There was a discreet tap at the door, and another young woman entered. Bond did not immediately recognise her. A vision, beautifully turned out, coiffured, made up and wearing a lightweight white suit which could have borne the label of any really top designer.

"Señor Montolongo," she began, and Bond realised it was Pam. The change was dramatically effective. She gave Bond a sharp on-and-off smile. "Allow me to introduce myself. My name is Kennedy. *Ms.* Kennedy, and I am Mr. Bond's executive secretary."

Bond stepped in quickly. "Just one moment more, Ms. Kennedy." But Montolongo was already charmed out of his socks. "Mr. Bond, you did not tell me you had such charming staff."

"He doesn't talk to many people about the hired help." She said it straight-faced.

"Yes. Well." Bond stumbled for a second. "Sir, I wonder if you could arrange a credit for me at the casino? I fear that gambling is my besetting sin. Shall we say two million dollars?"

"No problem, Mr. Bond. No problem at all. You've excellent collateral and our chairman also owns the casino."

Pam gave off one of her brightest smiles. "What a convenient arrangement."

Montolongo returned the smile in kind. "We have always thought so, señorita."

"I shall have to ask Mr. Bond to take me along. He's often unlucky at the tables."

"Well, señorita, you know the old saying— unlucky in the Casino; lucky in the bedroom." He laughed as though this was a truly original piece of wit, but the laugh died when he saw the freezing looks given to him by both Bond and "Ms. Kennedy."

"Well, you've already been lucky in the bedroom. Let's see if you're unlucky at the tables." Pam spoke warmly, squeezing Bond's tuxedoed arm. The Rolls was just pulling up in front of the casino. "You look gorgeous, James."

Bond sat in silence, his thoughts elsewhere.

"Thank you, darling," Pam said. "Thank you so much. You look absolutely stunning as well. I've seldom seen a girl who looked so stunning. Hey, Bond? Hallo, anyone there?"

"Oh, I'm sorry, darling. A lot on my mind. Yes, you *do* look dazzling. The gown is just a shade daring, and there's one thing I really find attractive . . ."

"Yes?"

"You're one of the few women I've ever met who can get ready, and look like a fashion plate, in ten minutes flat."

She smiled. "Trick of the trade." The doorman was approaching the car. "Wish I could say the same thing about you. You were one hell of a time in the bathroom. What on earth were you up to?"

"Trick of the trade." Bond gave her a knowing look as he stepped out of the car and offered her his hand.

Indeed, he had been a long time, and it was certainly to do with the tricks of his trade. Tonight, he wanted to engineer a meeting with Sanchez. He also wanted to arrange a little sound stealing.

Inside, the casino was beautifully appointed, as indeed were its clientele. Marble floors in the wide lobby gave way to deep-pile carpet. "Monte Carlo with trimmings," Bond whispered as one of the many smooth young managers appeared.

"Welcome." He bowed. "Señor Bond. Señorita Kennedy."

"Word gets around." Bond's eyebrow rose.

"Here in Isthmus City, one thing is the key to all doors, señor."

"Of course, how silly of me. Money."

"Quite so, señor. If you would like to follow me. The Salon Privé is upstairs."

They climbed a marble staircase, passed through a wide archway and down three steps into a remarkable room. A lot of people were playing, and the casino obviously had every type of game to suit every taste.

A fair amount of buzzing conversation went on at the long fan-tan table set across the room, but those not playing that particularly noisy game were ranged around the other tables—baccarat, chemin de fer, roulette and blackjack. These were the serious players, and it showed in their concentration and on their faces.

Among the players, Bond immediately picked out the six Orientals whom he had seen first at the airport, and again at the bank. In particular he took note of one large and fine-looking Hong Kong Chinese. Very impressive, he thought, especially next to the smaller, fragile woman on his arm. She could easily be Japanese. "The Chinese gentleman over there." He turned to the manager. "I think I know him from somewhere."

"A personal friend of our owner, Señor Sanchez." The manager lowered his voice. "A very important man from Hong Kong. His name is Kwang. You know him?"

"I don't think it can be the man I was thinking of. His name was Lee Chin. Perhaps I might speak with Mr. Kwang later. And his charming . . . er . . . wife?"

"Friend," the manager corrected him. "Indeed, it is a case of East meets East. She is from Tokyo. A Miss Loti."

"Charming," said Bond. "Charming . . ." feeling Pam's fingers dig into his arm. "I wonder, could I have a private table? Blackjack?"

"But certainly, Señor Bond. I have your plaques here," handing over a package wrapped and sealed, letting Bond glimpse at a card on which a number was written.

Bond nodded. "That'll do for tonight, I think."

"Well, there's plenty more where they came from, señor." The manager led them across the room, snapping his fingers for a tall blonde dealer, and a pit boss who looked as though he had just stepped over from Caesar's Palace in Vegas.

The dealer greeted them with a smile that showed teeth as perfect as her hair. Her accent was unequivocally Texan, for the words came out as "Heidi yawl. Yawl Markin?"

"I'm American," Pam said sweetly. "My friend's from England."

"Oh! Ah bin to London once. Real suede that city of yahrs."

"Thank you." Bond laid a $5,000 plaque at each place at the table. "You don't mind if we raise the limit to five thousand a box, do you?"

The dealer almost blinded them with her smile and turned to the pit boss, holding up five fingers. He nodded laconically.

"That'll be fahn." She began to deal.

Twenty minutes later, the pile of plaques in front of Bond had dramatically decreased. With a deep sigh he said, "I'd like to double the limit. Ten grand a box."

The dealer looked at the pit boss, who picked up a telephone. Bond's eyes did not leave him, and the man spoke clearly enough so it was easy to lip-read, an art Bond had learned many years ago.

"Got a live one for ya, chief," the pit boss was saying. "British sucker who dropped five hundred grand. Now he wants to play the limit."

His lips were still while he listened. Then he said, "The English. Table one. Plays like a real jerk-off." Then, "Okay." He nodded to the dealer.

"Good." Bond slapped a large $10,000 plaque down on each of the empty places. The Texan dealer flipped the cards like the expert she was.

He had drawn a five and a six. Both spades. He slapped another $10,000 plaque onto the table. "Double down."

His next card was a ten. A straight twenty-one.

On the following deal he ended up with a pair of eights which he split, increasing his bet. And so it went on, the pile of plaques rising rapidly. From being half a million down he was now a quarter of a million ahead. A few people had gathered to watch the fun, and, out of the corner of his eye, Bond saw the pit boss pick up the phone again.

The dealer called for a virgin deck, and they waited a few moments. The big Chinese, Kwang, hovered on the edge of the crowd and Bond kept his eyes down. He was conscious that the Texan dealer had moved away. A new pair of hands beautifully manicured were stripping the wrapping off a deck of Bicycles. A superb emerald bracelet twinkled on a slim wrist. It bore the name *Lupe* in smaller stones.

"The new deck." Lupe skilfully discarded the jokers and score cards, riffle-shuffled the cards and offered them for Bond to cut. He looked full into Lupe's face, but she kept her eyes down, so, turning to Pam, he quietly asked, "Would you mind very much if I asked you to get me a vodka martini? You know how I like it."

"And how you like your martinis," she whispered with a wicked little smile. "Medium dry. Shaken not stirred."

"Right."

As Pam left his side, Lupe completed the deal. "Most professional."

"I used to work here," she said quietly.

"So? Am I going to win or lose?"

She did not answer, so he asked, "Is that why he sent you?"

"That, and to find out more about you."

Bond concentrated, playing all five hands simultaneously, standing on two of them, and busting on the other three. Lupe showed her house cards: a ten and a three. Flicking herself a third card she turned it over. An eight. "Twenty-one," she said. "House wins." Then, more quietly, "Looks like your luck changed."

"When that happens I usually quit for the night. It's the only way to stay ahead." He smiled at Lupe and walked from the table, conscious she was coming after him. He slowed, and when she reached his side she spoke fast, with great urgency. "You got to walk straight out. Go from here. Go to airport and never come back. You understand?"

"Where's Sanchez?"

"Upstairs. In his office. He has some people over from the East. Orientals. He's been here all day, planning a big party for them tomorrow night."

As she spoke, Bond saw a pair of waiters entering a service lift area, set back in an alcove. "What did you tell him about *Wavekrest?*" he asked.

"I told him nothing. Nothing at all. Please go."

"Take me to Sanchez, Lupe. Now."

"You crazy? You'll get us killed. Both of us. You want that?"

Bond took her by the elbow, propelling her towards the elevators. "We won't get killed. Just take me, and stay calm."

"Look, I know Sanchez, and he's got something big going down at the moment. He's setting up a big meeting with that crowd of Orientals for tomorrow night. Here, in his private boardroom."

As she led the way to Sanchez's private elevator he felt her shaking with fear. "Don't worry," he said, glancing back to see Pam, looking stunned and angry, holding his martini.

He looked at her, smiling and wondering if he would ever see her again. For all he knew, Lupe could be right. But it was necessary for him to come face-to-face with Sanchez if anything was to be done to avenge Della's death, Felix's injury and the untold misery this man was prepared to mete out in cities the world over.

He winked at Pam. She merely turned away and tilted her head as she swallowed his martini.

— 9 —

Face-to-Face

THERE WAS A reception committee of two waiting in the lobby beside Sanchez's private elevator when Bond stepped out, Lupe hanging back slightly.

He thought these men had been among the party at Cray Cay, on that first day, but there was no way in which they could have recognised Bond. In fact, the men were the two Sanchez henchmen, Perez and Braun, and it was the former who came up to Bond, a heavy .45 Colt in his hand, a nasty leer on his face and an even nastier stink to his breath.

"Whoever you are, my friend, I should get them to hold the garlic for a few days." Bond gently pushed the man's hand, including the Colt, to one side. "You should be careful of those things. They can be very dangerous."

For a moment he thought the thug was going to hit him, but the doorway facing the elevator opened and a third man stepped into the lobby. From the room came the sound of a television, a soft, pleasant voice talking with some eagerness. The man who came out was Heller, onetime Green Beret captain, now chief of Sanchez Security.

"Hands on your head, please." Heller had a convincing manner and Bond did as he asked. "I presume you wish to see Señor Sanchez?" Heller's eyes moved to Lupe for a second.

"I couldn't stop him. He says he must see Franz now." Lupe sounded frightened.

Heller smiled as he began to search Bond. "Lupe, my dear, there's no need for you to look so frightened. Franz' door is open to anyone who visits this casino. Particularly someone who has the sense to walk away when his luck changes. Our friend, here, will collect his original stake plus his winnings. An extra two hundred thousand is not to be sneezed at, is it, Mr. . . . ?" He took out Bond's passport. "Is it, Mr. Bond?"

"I've never suffered from hay fever, Mr. Heller. Or should I say, Captain Heller, or even *Colonel* Heller?"

"So. You seem to have a name for me."

"Good news travels fast in Isthmus City."

"So does bad news." He removed the Walther P38K from its shoulder holster. "This is bad news.

A nice little piece. Far better than the old, outdated
PPK." Bond could have sworn there was a half-
smile on the man's face as he gestured to Sanchez's
door. The room was ornate, though comfortable.
Sanchez sat, with the whiz kid Truman-Lodge,
engrossed in a TV programme. A kindly looking
man in strange robes was backed by what looked
like an Inca temple. He was asking for viewers to
continue sending donations to "the OMI," whatever that was.

Sanchez barely looked up, but waved them forwards, giving Bond a pleasant smile as he did so.
The man on TV referred to himself as Professor
Joe, and Bond took in the fact that the OMI was the
Olimpatec Meditation Institute, connected with
research, philosophy, life-style and the religion of
the old Olimpatec Indians.

"It's almost over," Sanchez said. "I wish to see
the end."

There was a large picture window which took up
the best part of the far wall, looking out over the
city. He went to it, noticing that Lupe had also
joined him. The most bizarre thing was a pillow,
near Sanchez, on which sat a medium-sized iguana,
which had a diamond collar around its neck. Occasionally, Sanchez put out a hand to stroke the
reptile. Out of the corner of his eye he saw Lupe
give a little shudder when she looked at the iguana.

He stood for some time looking out of the large
window, examining what he could see of the roofs
and buildings across the street from the casino.

Slightly to the right, a decrepit block of houses was in the process of demolition, and the thought struck Bond that this might well be a good place for a sniper. With the right rifle and scope he could take out Sanchez with ease.

Then he spotted a tiny logo engraved into the glass of the picture window. The wording on the logo said *Armourlite-III*. Ah, well, bang went that idea. Or rather, it did not go bang at all. This glass was as tough as the metal on a light tank.

He turned to Lupe. "A lovely view, isn't it, señorita . . . I didn't catch your name."

"Lamora." She did not even look up at him. "Lupe Lamora." And, as she said it, music came up from the TV, signalling the end of this Professor Joe's programme which seemed to be part genuine interest in an old, almost forgotten culture, and part fund-raiser. Behind him, Sanchez spoke to Truman-Lodge. "Send Professor Joe an anonymous donation. Say, ten thousand bucks. Those people do wonderful work. Now . . ."

Bond began to walk towards him. Lupe moved in quickly. "Franz, this is . . ."

"Bond," 007 cut in. "James Bond. But I suspect you already know that." He reached out to shake Sanchez's hand, but Heller moved between them and Sanchez went on stroking the iguana, which looked suspiciously towards Bond.

"Sit!" Heller commanded, pointing to a chair on the other side of an occasional table set before Sanchez. The hood who had been careless with the

Colt .45 stood directly behind Bond's chair, and Heller sat down to their left.

Lupe sounded frightened. "He insisted on seeing you, Franz!"

Sanchez raised his eyes lazily towards her. Dark, coal-black eyes, bright and bearing the look of a man obsessed by something, though all his mannerisms were slow and calculated.

"It's okay, baby." He gestured for Truman-Lodge to leave them, while Heller placed the passport and Walther on the table.

"A well-travelled man." He riffled through the passport pages, then put the passport back on the table. "I gather you did well at the tables tonight."

"I quit while I was ahead. I had some instinct that my luck was about to change."

Sanchez nodded gently. "A wise man. Only good gamblers know when their luck's run out." He reached forwards and picked up the pistol, examining it as though it were some precious piece of art. "Why bring this into my house?"

Bond's lips curled up at one side in a half-smile, though his mouth retained that hard and cruel look that he sometimes allowed to be seen. "In my business you prepare for the unexpected."

Sanchez laid himself back in the big leather chair, still examining the pistol. "And what business is that?" he asked.

Bond allowed his fingers to stroke his cheek, then drop down towards the cummerbund he wore around his waist. Thumb and forefinger found the

two tiny nodules tucked in separate little pockets.
He withdrew one. Nobody could possibly have seen
it. The movement attracted no attention, and the
lethal little bug was only the size of a match head.
He held it, covered by his thumb. "My business?
Oh, I help people with problems, Señor Sanchez."

"A problem solver." Sanchez nodded, as though
he knew all about problems and the best way to
solve them.

"No." Bond drew the word out. "No, I'm more
of a problem eliminator."

Very slowly, Sanchez moved forwards in his
chair and he replaced the Walther on the table. His
eyes lighted on Lupe.

"Lupe, go play. Leave us, eh?"

Lupe needed no reminders. She did not even
nod, but walked, straight and quickly, out of the
door. When she had gone, Sanchez spoke again.
This time, paradoxically, almost in a whisper.
"You're here on business?"

Bond gave a small sigh. "I fear that I'm tempo-
rarily unemployed. In fact, I thought I might find
work here. One of the reasons I came."

Slowly Sanchez shook his head. When he looked
up, his face seemed to reflect great sadness. "It is
very difficult to obtain work permits, here in Isthmus. You see, it is necessary for you to show some
special talent. A talent that people here don't
have."

Bond reflected that he would not like to play
poker with this man; he was a very good actor and

they both knew they were speaking a kind of
sub-text. The words bore little relation to the
meaning. He looked at Heller pointedly, then slowly turned to glance up at the man behind his chair.
"That shouldn't be difficult," he said, dropping his
right hand low under the chair arm. The tiny bug
between his fingers was quickly transferred from
hand to the underside of the chair arm. These bugs
were coated with a thin solution which allowed
them to remain easy to manipulate on skin or cloth,
but they adhered as though stuck by Superglue
when gently placed against wood, plastic, glass or
almost anything else.

Sanchez gave a short laugh. It sounded as though
he was genuinely amused. "Señor Bond, you have
big *conjones.*" He went on chuckling as he spoke.
"You come here, to my place, with no references.
You walk in carrying a piece. Throwing a lot of
money around. But you know something? Nobody
saw you come in. Nobody will remember you. So,
nobody has to see you go out."

"Señor Sanchez, I don't joke about my work.
Believe me, I could be quite useful to a man in your
position. I already know you have a reputation for
rewarding those who serve you well and remain
loyal. Sure, I carry a gun. It's a habit you don't get
out of easily. As for the money? Well, I got very
lucky with a hit. The people I was working for paid
me a great deal, but men in my line never hang on
to cash. Like life, it's easy come, easy go."

There was silence for a good forty seconds, and

in that time, Bond's thumb and forefinger had retrieved the second bug from his cummerbund. "You have a very nice setup here."

Sanchez rose: the same exaggerated slow motion. "It's okay. What do you think of this?" He pressed a stud in the side of his chair, and the wall to their right rolled back to display a long room, twice the size of the one in which they stood. There was a polished glass table at least twenty feet in length, and chairs were placed around it. Each place was set up for a meeting, with yellow legal scratch pads, sharpened pencils, pens and blotters.

"My boardroom." Sanchez smiled, gesturing for Bond to take a look. He did so, resting his hand on the edge of the long table, transferring a bug to the underside.

"Now." Sanchez picked up the passport and settled back into his chair, waving for Bond to come back into his room. "I think I'll keep this for a few days, then we'll talk again. As I said, you have big *conjones.* I like that in a man. We'll just have to see." He nodded towards the door, the lazy movement of his head signifying that the meeting was over.

Bond reached for the Walther, but Sanchez moved, fast as a snake's tongue. "No. No, Mr. Bond. You will not need this in Isthmus. We have a very safe city."

"I'm glad to hear it." He managed a smile as he walked towards the door. "If you need me, I'm at the Hotel El Presidente."

He paused, looking back at Sanchez, the door half-open.

"Yes, I know you are." Sanchez gave his lazy smile. "In the meantime, you're welcome to come to the casino and lose—or win—money anytime you like."

As he closed the door, Bond heard Sanchez snap at, he presumed, Heller. "Check him out!"

Riding down in the private elevator, Bond thought about the man he had just left, deciding he was probably one of the most callous people with whom he had ever met, and that, in a life filled with meeting villains and people of evil intent. On the surface, Sanchez was a calm, calculating man, with a penchant for the good things in life: behind that lazy charm lay complete indifference to suffering. Not only the suffering he saw with his own eyes, or knew of because he had ordered it, but the terrible cloak of despair, self-loathing, deceit and crime which he activated from afar by dealing in millions of dollars' worth of street drugs.

Now Bond had set himself firmly face-to-face with the baron of evil. It would only be a matter of time before Heller made telephone calls or tapped into his private sources. Then he would be exposed for what he was.

Now there was an urgency, and Bond realised that it was not just a matter of getting rid of Sanchez because of what he had done to Felix Leiter and his new wife: not simply revenge for that. Bond wanted to squash the man like an insect that carried some deadly disease. He was determined to smash Sanchez *and* his whole sordid empire.

The elevator doors opened. Plenty of people were still playing the tables in the Salon Privé. He even caught another glimpse of the big Chinese, Kwang, now seated at a roulette wheel.

He looked towards the blackjack table at which he had played. No dealer and no nearby pit boss. Just one person, Pam, sitting quietly, a drink in front of her. As he walked across the room, Bond realised another significant fact. The table was bare but for Pam's tiny sequined evening bag. Where his high pile of gaming plaques had been there was only green baize.

"Ready to go?" he asked, and Pam looked up past him at the manager who had given them this table. The man was hurrying over, carrying what looked suspiciously like a bank draft.

"The draft you required, Señorita Kennedy," he said, hand outstretched. But Bond intercepted the pass, snipping the piece of paper from the manager's fingers before Pam's hand could close over it.

The manager looked embarrassed for a moment, then bowed and left, almost walking backwards.

Pam shrugged. "Just the profits," she said, trying a lame smile. "I could use a little walking-around money."

Bond did not show his usual sense of humour. "You can walk one hell of a long way on a quarter of a million dollars."

"Okay. Only trying to help." She gave a little sad wave as he slipped the cheque into his pocket. Then, as they walked out of the Salon Privé into the lobby of the casino, she asked, "What did you manage to do with that hot tamale you disappeared with?"

Bond was so preoccupied that he did not even catch the jealous edge in her voice. "We went to see Sanchez."

"Oh, is that all? Jesus, James, I could hit you sometimes. Sanchez'll have you checked out quick as a buck rabbit with a doe. Then we'll both end up getting the deep six."

They had reached the doors now, and Bond was still distracted. He walked out onto the pavement and looked up at the big picture windows above him. There were flags flying above a piece of statuary, a lounging nude woman, graceful and surprisingly tasteful for Sanchez, he thought. The statue's arms were reaching up towards the flag.

The Rolls whispered to a stop by the kerb and the chauffeur held the door open. Bond glanced across the road towards the building under demolition.

As they drove away, he looked back and caught sight of the big Kwang and his fragile Japanese girlfriend, Loti. They were standing waiting for their car, but both looked back towards the Rolls.

"Did you find out anything?" Pam asked as they left the car and walked towards the doors of the hotel.

"I found out he lives behind windows made of

two-inch-thick armoured glass, and that there's a bodyguard with him almost twenty-four hours a day."

"You're not thinking of . . . ?" she began, but Bond held his hand up, a sign for her to stop talking as they entered the vast lobby of the hotel.

"Three-fourteen, please," he said to the night porter.

"There we are, Señor Bond." The porter gave a toothy and somewhat lecherous grin as he eyed Pam. "Oh, Señor Bond, you'll be happy to know that your uncle arrived."

"Really?" He did not show any surprise.

"Yes. I've put him in your suite. I hope that was correct."

"Of course. Thank you."

"What uncle?" Pam asked as they walked towards the elevators.

"You carrying?"

"Yes."

"Well, let me have it, then you stay down here until I send for you. I'd like to make this a proper family reunion."

"James." She sidestepped into a quiet vestibule, deserted but for a line of house phones. "James, what's going on?" Raising her skirt to show a very generous amount of leg, and more, she removed the small Beretta from its holster strapped to her thigh, handing it to Bond. "What's going on?" she repeated.

"Damned if I know. Wait, and I'll let you know."

He disappeared into the elevator, leaving Pam standing by the telephones looking concerned.

The third floor seemed to be empty and Bond made his way silently towards 314. He then flattened himself against the wall, outside the range of the peephole, and rang the bell.

The door opened almost at once, and, as it did so, Bond leaped at the figure in the doorway. One hand went for the man's throat, the other pushed the little pistol into his ear.

"Right, Uncle. Let's see who you're really related to," he whispered, pushing the figure back and kicking the door closed behind him.

— 10 —

Dear Uncle

BOND WAS LYING at a ninety-degree angle to the
intruder's body, well out of the way of flailing arms
and legs. His left arm pressed down across the
man's throat, while he literally screwed the muzzle
of the little Beretta into his ear.

"Right," he whispered, breathing hard, his voice
full of menace. "Who sent you? Heller? Or was it
Sanchez himself? Tell me now or I'll blow your
wretched little head off."

The victim struggled, making croaking sounds.
Bond relaxed pressure on his windpipe, so that the
sounds became words. Words from a voice he
recognised—

"Really, 007! For goodness sake! Let go!"

"Oh, my God!" The intruder wore sandals, baggy checked pants and a blinding floral shirt. He had taken that in, his mind telling him the fellow was dressed like a tourist which would be natural cover for his "uncle." He had not seen the face properly, but the voice was distinctive. "Good grief, what are you doing here?" He let go of the figure who had been struggling on the floor, standing up and helping him to his feet.

Standing in front of him, looking shaken, was Major Boothroyd, head of Q Branch, officially titled The Armourer, but more lovingly referred to by all at the London Headquarters as Q.

"I'm sorry, but you shouldn't go creeping in without being announced."

"Well, I couldn't have left a message at reception saying, 'Please tell Mr. Bond that Q's in his suite,' could I?"

"I suppose not. But what in heaven's name're you doing here? Sit down. Have a drink."

"Brandy, 007. Better make it a stiff one." Q made a clucking noise and walked towards the long table under the window. There had been a bowl of fruit on it; now, as Bond poured a liberal dose of Rémy Martin, he saw the fruit had been joined by one of Q's favourite briefcases: the type built on the bellows principle which gave you the impression that it would hold anything, like a bottomless pit.

Q lugged the bag over to a chair and sat down heavily. "You're certainly fast and fit, Bond." He massaged his neck. "Well, that's as it should be, I suppose. What am I doing here, you ask?"

Bond nodded, placing the brandy within Q's reach.

"I'm on leave. On vacation as they say in the States. This being the case, thought I'd pop by and see how you're getting along." Q's face had assumed a look of slightly overdone innocence.

Bond sat close to him. "How did you find me?"

Q drew a deep breath, as though he had been caught in one of his own pieces of trickery. "Damn it, Bond. Moneypenny. The woman's worried sick about you."

It was Bond's turn to sigh. "And how did she know?"

"Never mind about that."

"Q, listen to me. You're not a field man. This is a dangerous place, and you would be better off out of it. Why not slip off into the night, eh?"

For a moment Q looked quite angry. Then—

"No need to be coy with me, Bond. I know what you're up to; and frankly I believe you need my help . . ."

"But . . ."

"Face up to it man, if it wasn't for Q Branch you'd have been dead years ago."

Bond thought about it for a minute, then decided Q was quite right. He gave a small nod, but, by this time, Q was already opening the case, which sprang outwards, like a stage magician's trick.

"Everything for the man on holiday, eh?" Q actually chuckled, rubbing his hands together. "Just put a few things in. Travelling alarm clock." He pulled out the small digital timepiece no larger than a pack of cigarettes. "Stuffed with explosives. Set it for someone and poof!"

"Poof!" Bond repeated. "I really don't think I need a terrorist's weapon, Q."

"No, didn't think so, but . . ."

Bond saw a passport in the depths of the case. He put his hand out and grabbed it. It was in his street name, *James Boldman.* "You really have thought of everything. Just what I needed, they've taken mine." Q snatched the passport from him with a warning cry. "Don't open that. You might have activated it."

"Say again?"

"If you press hard on the centre of the crest, goat making advances to a lion, a little dot appears in the number window below." Q demonstrated. "Press twice and it deactivates."

"What, in fact, does it activate and deactivate?"

"Mace. If you don't really want your ID examined, you hand it over in the activated condition and it'll give a nice, wide-angled dose of Mace. Useful?"

"Quite possibly. Yes, I'll take a dozen of those."

"Cut the frivolity, Bond. We're into serious stuff here. Now, toothpaste," removing two king-sized tubes of a well-known brand.

"Don't tell me. Some terrorist tried palming one of these off on his girlfriend. What's in it?"

"What would you expect?"

"C-4?" Composition C-4 is an off-white putty-like substance, ninety percent of which is RDX, the other ten percent being a stabilising and binding agent. Nuclear weapons apart, RDX is the most powerful explosive on earth. In its C-4 form it converts to malleable *plastique.*

"Well done." Q looked pleased. "C-4." He pulled out a thick pen with a TV station's logo on the top. "And here, inside the tube, is a selection of detonators. The pen converts into a remote with a couple of triple-A batteries."

"Again, just what I wanted." Already a plan was starting to form in Bond's mind. "This will do very well."

"Oh, there's more. For instance . . . " Q stopped short, head turning and a look of alarm on his face as the door crashed open.

Bond's hand streaked out towards the Beretta lying on the table, stopping when he saw it was Pam, standing in the doorway, another automatic in her hand. "I thought there might be a mess to clear up, but I see it really is your uncle."

"Close the door, Pam. Uncle, I want you to meet Ms. Kennedy . . . my . . . er, my cousin."

"Really?" Q looked quite pleased at what he saw. "Are we related?"

"It's quite possible," Bond said grittily. "Ms.

Kennedy has a repertoire of tricks as well. I thought you only had one weapon." He looked at her with suspicion.

"All women have more than one weapon, my dear James." Her voice was as soothing as sandpaper on an open wound. "I keep this one in a much safer place."

"That I can believe. Uncle brought some toys."

"Nice toys?" she said in an overly artless manner. "Show me." She gave Q a devastating smile.

"Well, this is quite handy." Q pulled out a dull metal tube, about the size and thickness of a telescope. He stood up to demonstrate, holding the tube away from him and pulling a ring at the end in his hand. With a click, four curved steel hooks shot out of the far end. "A portable grappling iron, complete with a spring-loaded tough nylon rope. See." He demonstrated pulling out the rope from his end of the tube. "The spring allows you to wind, unwind, and stop at whatever height you want. A little practice and, once you've clipped it to a D-ring—I've brought a couple with me—on the front of your belt, you can descend, or ascend, to your heart's content. It'll take two men of your weight, James, and remain perfectly workable. Takes the strain out of abseil."

Bond tested the tension of the rope, impressed by what he saw. "This could be *very* useful for what I have in mind." He wandered up to the window, hooked the grapple over the brass rail from which the drapes hung, tested it for weight, then experimented with the rope. Q told him that if he merely hung on it, the rope would slowly unwind from the grapple. A sharp pull would lock it dead. Two short pulls would start up the descent again, three and the spring would lift you up. "Easy to control. No experience required," Q said smugly.

"What's this?" Pam had removed a long, slim tube, again in dull black metal.

"Ah." Q sounded proud. "Now, this you *will* like." From his case he took several other metal components. A flat box screwed onto the tube. Then two other shorter, curved tubes clicked to top and bottom of the box. In turn a skeleton shoulder piece fitted onto the curved tubes. A press here, and another one there, and it was quite obvious that Q had assembled a simple rifle.

"You've been reading *Day of the Jackal* again." Bond sounded viciously sarcastic.

"Have care, James." Q pulled out the trigger assembly and showed how the action worked. "The magazine takes five rounds. Glasers. Teflon. 9mm, of course. There's a simple telescopic sight, and it is accurate up to one thousand yards."

"But we've had things like this for years. What's so special?"

"There's something very special, in the box that houses mechanism, breech and trigger." Q tried to sound mysterious. "One microchip. Once I set the thing, with your palms and fingers, nobody else can use it. It can't be reprogrammed, so it's yours for life. The chip operates an optical skin reader. It's a signature gun. Even you would agree, I think, that it's safer to carry a weapon that nobody can turn on you."

"Okay, Uncle. You win. I have a plan—or at least the start of one. I need to sleep on it."

"Well, if you're going to bed, you'd better check your Jabberwocky first. It was rattling away like mad when I came in."

"What the hell's a Jabberwocky?" Pam scowled.

"I presume you were seeding W9 pickups wherever you had the meeting with Sanchez?"

Bond nodded and said he'd placed two of them.

"Well, you can hear yourself on tape, and a lot more. It's all very interesting."

"What . . . is . . . A . . . Jabberwocky?" Pam shouted.

"Your first question should be, 'What's a W9?' but we'll let that pass."

"James, you can be the most infuriating man."

"Okay." He held up his palms towards her, as though warding off the evil eye. "A W9 is one of my uncle's favourite listening devices. Tiny, and also intelligent. You can just about hide them anywhere. I've put a couple into Sanchez's rooms. They override electronic sweepers and also garble the signal, like a scrambler device. They're tuned to a very high frequency—the kind of high that only dogs can pick up. The Jabberwocky is a receiver. It's about the same size as your average Walkman and contains a small tape machine. The whole thing is voice-activated. It unscrambles the signals and they come out in clear, onto the tape and through a small speaker. You can cut the speaker out and use headphones. That's a Jabberwocky, my dear Pam."

"You came over rather well, I thought." Q sipped his brandy.

"Good. I hope you only heard bad things about me."

"As a matter of fact, the fellow called Sanchez rather likes you; which is more than can be said of the others. They seem to . . . what's the phrase . . .?"

"Hate my guts?"

"In three words, yes. Though Sanchez is still having you checked out. He's quite obviously paranoid about everyone. Oh, you'll hear it on the tape. Ingenious about the TV programme, though."

"What TV programme?" Pam looked puzzled.

"To be honest with you, I don't know. Do you think I could possibly have another brandy?" Q held out his glass.

"They were watching TV when I went in. Some fruitcake called Professor Joe. Drumming up cash for research into the Olimpatec Indian cultures—religion mainly. Meditation of some kind, though I gather he's also doing research on their life-styles, buildings and things."

"Yes." Q took his replenished glass. "They mentioned the Olimpatec Temple. Olimpatec Meditation Institute."

"Sanchez even sent them a donation." Bond helped himself to brandy. Pam shook her head and wandered over to the refrigerator set in an ornate panel under the TV to get champagne.

Q laughed aloud. "I should think he would send a donation."

"Why?"

"You'll have to listen yourself, but someone they called Bill came in after you left, James . . ."

"Truman-Lodge. He's Sanchez's money operator."

"So it appeared. Well, it was clear to me what they were doing. They've got this Professor Joe in their pockets. They work in some kind of code. Donations float in from all over the place, and certain key phrases give Sanchez's selling price for cocaine and heroin. Other donations denote buyers —big buyers. What they seem to be doing is running a kind of drug auction via this man Professor Joe's TV show. They were very pleased tonight. I can tell you that the price of heroin rose very steeply and they had acceptance from no less than six major dealers across the United States. It's all on the tape, James. Listen to it. As for me, I think it's time for bed. I've taken the spare room. That all right by you?"

"Yes. Yes." Bond was already heading for the bathroom with Pam at his heels.

"So that's why you were so long in here tonight." She looked at the little Walkman-like machine which he took down from on top of the cupboard.

Bond nodded and carried the machine back into the main room, ran back the tape and pressed the play button. The recording had started as he activated the first bug, under the chair arm, and it was only after he had actually left that the real talking began. As Q had said, Truman-Lodge returned and the conversation anchored onto Professor Joe's TV show.

"Ah, even New York accepted our price of twenty-two grand a kilo." Truman-Lodge sounded ecstatic. "Twenty-two grand and they ordered five hundred kilos. Lord, you have to laugh at old Prof Joe . . . " He seemed to be going into an imitation of the so-called Professor, "And we have a wonderful donation from New York City. Five hundred dollars."

Sanchez's voice butted in. "Yeah, one day Joe's going to slip up, though. He's going to get an order like that and he'll miss the word 'City' off New York, or the word 'beautiful' off Boston, or 'lovely' off L.A., and we'll be sitting here wondering what's gone wrong. I worry, William. I worry that the guy'll slip one day."

Ingenious was right, Bond thought. An auction with bids and orders, all done on coast-to-coast television. "The problem is, how do they get the stuff delivered?" he asked.

"Search me," Pam shrugged.

They listened some more, and there was talk of the Oriental group and the meeting to take place on the following night.

"That's when I do it. Lupe mentioned the meeting tomorrow," Bond said, glancing at his watch. "I really mean today, don't I? But that's the time to do it."

"When you do what?"

"Take out Sanchez."

"Don't be stupid, James. How in hell . . .?"

"Let me sleep on it."

"Oh, James, come on, tell me." Suddenly her short fuse showed again. "You going to get at him through that little Mexican broad?"

"Don't be silly, Pam. She's a means to an end."

"Okay, but what kind of end?"

"Wait. Tomorrow night. I'll have it fixed by tomorrow night."

"You won't tell me a damned thing, will you?"

"Not tonight." He followed her towards the bedroom.

Pam stepped inside, turned, and as he was about to follow her, she gave him a thin-lipped smile. "Okay, you can sleep on it, James. Happy dreams." The door closed in his face and there was that sickening sound of a deadbolt being slid into place.

Slowly Bond walked across the room towards the spare bedroom and tapped on the door. From inside came a cheery "Come in." Q was sitting up in one of the twin beds reading a spy thriller.

"I hope you don't snore, Q." James Bond looked distinctly unhappy.

— 11 —

Crystal Night

PAM APPEARED TO have recovered from her flaring bout of temper by the next morning, and by constant monitoring of the Jabberwocky they made certain the reception for the Oriental party was timed to begin with cocktails at eight-thirty in Sanchez's apartment, followed by the meeting, which Bond presumed would be in the boardroom, through the sliding doors. After the meeting there was to be what Q described—on listening to the arrangements and orders on the tape—as "a right good blowout."

Bond thought Q did not realise the accuracy of this last statement.

Pam was dispatched to the nearest establishment that hired out fancy dress, after taking Q's measurements. Bond telephoned reception saying he wanted the Rolls outside at eight, but he would not require the chauffeur tonight. He then stretched out on his bed to go over the finer points of his plan. Tonight, if luck was with him, they would see the end of Franz Sanchez. That would, at least, be revenge and a beginning to the collapse of the man's empire.

At exactly eight-twenty that night, the Rolls pulled up in front of the casino. Pam had bought a new gown for the occasion; Bond was in his tuxedo, the pieces of hardware he would need skilfully hidden. A spare automatic, the pocket version of an FN high-power 9mm with shortened butt and slide, was in an ankle holster; the telescope-like grappling iron and rope was attached to his left calf, while two innocuous tubes of toothpaste and the pen which concealed detonators and a remote control system were distributed around his inside pockets. Last of all, he had clipped the Jabberwocky to his belt and secured a slim pair of lightweight earphones around it. With the W9 bugs in place he could at least listen to part of the meeting.

Q was at the wheel of the Rolls, looking the part in the grey chauffeur's outfit rented by Pam that morning. Outside, the guards were there in force with the omnipresent pump-action shotguns. "Everyone know what to do?" Bond whispered the question. Pam said "Yes," and Q simply nodded.

Inside, there was obviously more security than usual; strangers were being checked out and beefy men in tuxedos tried to look inconspicuous. Pam and Bond were greeted by the manager they had seen the previous night who told them to collect whatever plaques they required.

Bond went over to the cashier, returning to Pam with a pile of $10,000 plaques. "Open your hands," he said with a smile, his ice-blue eyes melting as he counted ten of the plaques into her cupped palms. "Slight change of plan," he continued as they walked into the Salon Privé.

"What change?" Pam sounded distinctly concerned.

"That hundred K's for you, my dear. Extra bonus. Your job's over and done with. Contact Q once I've picked up the other item, and fly out of here, *now*—tonight. I'll make my own way back."

She curled her fingers around his arm. "James, I want to stay. I want to see it ended as well."

"Go!" It was a serious order. "Anyway, I work better alone." He turned on his heel and headed towards the bar. Armed guards stood at the bank of elevators, checking a steady stream of tuxedo-clad waiters who pushed trolleys of food from the direction of the pantry and kitchen which were behind the wall far away across the room, and to the right of the pillared alcove in which the elevators stood. Last night, as he had waited there with Lupe, Bond had already noticed there was an exit from the kitchen area, shielded from the Salon Privé by the alcove. Another door, leading to the kitchen, was set in the long wall which now faced him as he sat at the bar, sipping a virgin colada. He would take no chances tonight. There would be plenty of champagne later if the job was successful.

The room was more crowded than the previous evening with all the tables open and waiters scurrying from bar and kitchen. He saw one pair of the Oriental party head for the elevators, then bided his time, waiting for the right moment when everybody was almost distractedly busy.

Without any fuss, he slowly walked over to the kitchen door and went inside, casually picking up a napkin from a stack just inside the door. Nobody queried him as he collected a cart, replete with cocktail snacks, and pushed it out of the far door which led to the elevators.

A guard checked the cart before he was allowed to pass into the elevator. On the previous evening it had taken 1.5 minutes to reach Sanchez's apartment, so there was little time for niceties. It took thirty seconds to unhook the grappling iron; fifteen to spring open the grapples and release the rope and another fifteen to hurl it at the inspection hatch in the roof of the cage. Then a further fifteen seconds for Bond to shin up the rope through the inspection hatch and return things to normal.

Standing on the top of the cage, now collecting more waiters, who must have been surprised at a cartful of food standing unattended, Bond slipped the buttons on his tuxedo jacket, and folded away the grapples and rope. To either side of him were the huge girders of the elevator shaft. Above, he could see the square inspection hatch which had to lead to the building's roof. As the elevator began its journey downwards again, he leaped for the girders, clung on and began a steady climb. Near the top a metal ladder was set into the wall of the shaft, and it took only a couple of minutes to reach the trapdoor which, as he had thought, led to the roof.

There was a light warm breeze and the buzz of an air-conditioning plant. The flags, one with the casino logo, the other the presidential flag, only moved slightly in the dry air. Bond stood above them, looking down into the street below. Cars came and went. Lights stretched out over the city and he could see a jet climbing out after its takeoff from Isthmus City Airport.

Directly below the flagstaffs there was the sculpture of the reclining naked woman whose arms stretched upwards towards him. Below her, he knew, were the large armour-plated windows of Sanchez's apartment, the boardroom and Lord knew what else—offices, a dining room perhaps? He took out the Jabberwocky, clipped it onto his belt, put on the earphones and moved the switch to On. A babble filled his ears so that he had to adjust the volume. Obviously the cocktail party was going well. There was time to spare, as he wanted the whole crew—Sanchez, his various henchmen and the group of Orientals—in the boardroom before he started the first part of his work.

He moved the toothpaste tubes of RDX into the breast pocket of his now oil-streaked jacket, made certain the pen was within easy reach, then opened up the grappling iron again, this time clipping the rope onto the D-ring that Q had fixed to his belt, under the cummerbund.

Bond smiled to himself. The nylon rope was almost half an inch thick, and there was a lot of it. "How the devil do you get this much into the cylinder, *and* the grappling irons?" he had asked Q.

Briskly Q had replied, "All done by mirrors, 007. Surely you know I've been a member of the Magic Circle for a long time."

Now, poised between the mastheads on the roof of Sanchez's casino, Bond made fast the grapple to the stone surround, pulling, and testing to be certain that neither the grapple would slip nor the stonework give way.

The noise was dying down in his earphones as someone—he thought Heller—was calling the party to order and asking them to step into the boardroom. There was a gasp as Sanchez obviously did his trick of electronically sliding back the wall, then a change of sound as people moved through, a scraping of chairs, coughs, the whine of the wall moving back into place.

The moment had come, and Bond gently lowered himself over the edge. Through the headphones he heard Sanchez speak, calling the meeting to order.

"I wish to welcome you here. By now you will have met my trusted staff. Mr. Truman-Lodge, my financial manager, and Colonel Heller, head of security for all the Sanchez enterprises."

Slowly Bond allowed the nylon rope to unwind on its spring until he slid neatly into the outstretched arms of the statue.

Sanchez was still speaking—

"This is an historic moment. East meets West. Drug dealers of the world unite."

His audience chuckled as he continued. "Asia is a new market for us. Mr. Truman-Lodge, here, will tell you the simple way in which we can all become billionaires ten times over. But I have another message for you. In this business there is a lot of cash; therefore there are a lot of people standing around with their hands out . . ."

"In a word, bribery." Another voice, vaguely Chinese. It was followed by another laugh.

"You said it!" Sanchez again. "So you pay! Everyone and his brother is on the payroll . . ."

Bond stepped out of the statue's arms, letting the rope lower him to the darkened window of Sanchez's apartment. Light flooded from the next window, that of the boardroom where Sanchez was still speaking.

". . . So you buy a mayor, a police chief, a general, a president. The beauty of it is that one day you wake up and find you own the whole goddamned country. And that's good, because then you just take what you want: a bank, a gambling casino, an airline concession. Why? I tell you why. Because it's easier for a politician to take silver than lead." This, Bond thought, really brought the house down. He swallowed the bile in his mouth which came unbidden when he thought of the evil incarnate just a few feet from where he hung precariously on the long window ledge of Sanchez's apartment.

He had tugged at the rope and now swayed safely with his feet inches from the lower edge of the glass. From here, he could reach both the top and left-hand side of the window. Gingerly he removed the first of the family-sized toothpaste tubes, and began the arduous job of packing the pliable C-4 along the left downside of the window.

In his earphones, and in reality a few feet away, Sanchez still spoke—

"You see, we have an invisible empire, from Chile to Alaska. What I wish to do, amigos, is to make *you* part of that empire. I want the Pacific to be our little puddle. You all have good business deals going for you, but by joining with me, you will see that it can not only be safe, but also truly rewarding. You can double your take in a month. After that? Well, I'll let Mr. Truman-Lodge explain some of it to you."

It was an arm-wrenching job, squeezing out the C-4 in little snakes and running it, like putty, along the window's edge. This became even more difficult when Bond had to reach up and pack the stuff along the top of the window itself. Truman-Lodge was being not a little boring—

"Here is a demographic report which breaks down each territory by age and socioeconomic group. You will see there is a huge potential demand for our product, given the implementation of aggressive marketing programmes . . ."

Bond was around a quarter of the way along the top of the window, when, concentrating on packing the C-4, he did not notice a missing piece of masonry below his feet. He slipped, swung dizzily downwards, then had to manipulate the rope again to bring himself up. He said a quiet prayer of thanksgiving that he had managed to hold on to the tube, which was rapidly running out.

Manipulating the rope, he found himself rising too fast. He pulled to a stop, swung outwards and hit the window with an audible bump. Through the headphones he heard Truman-Lodge pause, then the scrape of a chair and the sound of footsteps coming to investigate. Heller, he thought to himself as he pushed himself away from the window again, swinging wide and hitting the stone to his left, dragging the rope out of sight, pushing his body close to the wall only a few inches away from the window.

Truman-Lodge droned on, "As in the United States, Señor Sanchez is prepared to sell exclusive franchises. The price is set, and there can be no haggling. One hundred million dollars for each territory. We supply first-rate merchandise exclusively to you. Ten tons a month. That's twenty thousand dollars a key Hong Kong, right. That works out at twenty million per metric ton, if you need that information. A fair price, I'm sure you'll agree." There were quiet murmurs of assent.

Bond held his breath. He could feel, if not see, a figure inside Sanchez's apartment. The seconds seemed like hours. Then he heard the footsteps returning, and the W9 bug planted in the board-room even picked up the whisper of Heller's voice. "Nothing around. All clear."

Bond swung back against the window again, finishing the first tube and unscrewing a second. He still had quite a way to go.

"We guarantee quality and price for five years," Truman-Lodge said. "Any questions?"

By this time, Bond had managed to cover the top of the window and the left and right sides; now he allowed the rope to lower him below the level of the window, where he worked hard at setting the C-4 along the bottom edge of the glass. Truman-Lodge's words came at the end of a lengthy speech, and there were general murmurs of acceptance. Then a heavily accented Chinese voice—

"Señor Sanchez, since our arrival here, we've eaten well, heard a lot of good stories and generally enjoyed ourselves. However, you are asking us to put up a great deal of money to receive first-class merchandise. I like the idea, but, so far, we have no evidence that you can meet the demand. In other words, I, for one, would like to see the hardware."

Bond finally came to the end of the lower section of window. He resealed the small amount of explosive in the tube, dropped it into his pocket, then felt for the pen.

Sanchez's voice came clear into the headphones—

"Mr. Kwang. You don't pay for hardware. You pay for my *personal guarantee and protection.*"

So, it was the big Hong Kong delegate who was turning difficult. Bond uncapped the pen and rolled one of the radio-controlled detonators into the palm of his hand. Recapping the pen, he pushed the detonator into the C-4, at the outer left-hand edge. It crossed his mind that very soon there would be a lot of flying glass. He could almost see the way the armoured thick glass would fragment and splinter, turning itself into a million crystals.

As Bond tugged at the rope to activate the spring mechanism which would take him to the top of the roof again, Kwang was still arguing with Sanchez—

"How do we *know* you have the capacity, Señor Sanchez?"

As Bond reached the top of the building there seemed to be a long pause before Sanchez spoke. As he allowed the rope to disappear into the grapple's cylinder, and threw out what remained of the C4 and the few spare detonators, Bond heard Sanchez do an amazing change of heart. Even his voice altered—

"Hey, amigos, you're right. We're partners, no? Give it a couple of days. Until your colleagues arrive. A couple of days and you'll all go to our main distribution centre. You'll need to pack overnight bags. Now, that's settled, yes? Okay, on the far side of this room we have yet another surprise. A little festivity I have arranged for you with food, wine, women and song. Enjoy yourselves." There was a whining sound and gasps of pleasure.

Bond, now making for the rear of the roof, reckoned that the far wall of the boardroom also had a sliding mechanism leading to another large room. Heaven knew what kind of an orgy Sanchez had prepared for them there.

He looked over the roof coping, down into the streets behind the casino. They appeared to be deserted. He knew the casino did not go right back to the end of the building, and that the exits were located in the sides.

For the second time that night, he fitted the grapple around the coping. Tested it, and began to allow the rope to pay out, gently taking him down into the empty street below. As he dropped, he heard another conversation. This time, he thought, in Sanchez's apartment. Truman-Lodge's voice said, "I don't like this. That damned Kwang spells trouble. Why show them the laboratories?"

As Bond's feet touched the pavement, Sanchez replied, "My dear William, would you put up a hundred million dollars without a little reassurance? Don't worry. Nobody's going to blow our operation."

Brave words, Bond thought as he twitched at the rope, unhooking the grapple from high above him, reeling it in and telescoping the whole thing. Moments later he was hurrying across the road, heading for the half-demolished building.

Q sat patiently in the Rolls, around the corner from the ruins. He said nothing as Bond returned the collapsible grapple and took, in exchange, the signature gun. Then he simply said, "Good luck, 007."

Bond looked at Q for a long time. It was true, without this man, and those who worked with him in Q Branch, he *would* have been dead years ago. "I take back what I said." He gave a hard smile. "You're one hell of a field agent, Q. Get out now, while you can. I'll see you back in London."

Q did not reply. He merely put the window up and drove off into the night world of Isthmus City, leaving Bond to complete his work.

As he climbed over the ruins, looking for the best firing position, as low as possible but with a clear view of the window, there was another short conversation, carried from the W9 under the chair arm in Sanchez's apartment across to the Jabberwocky, and from there into Bond's ears.

"President Lopez is here, chief." It was Heller's voice.

"Hector," Sanchez said. "Please come in."

"There's been a mistake with my money." This could only be President Hector Lopez. "Look at this, it's only half the usual amount."

A long pause, during which Bond found just the right place. An open space, with half a wall behind it, and rubble in front. He would be able to get a straight shot from the rubble, which he had begun to climb as he heard Sanchez's voice.

"My dear Hector. You were a little too quiet after I was arrested in the U.S.A. You must remember that you're only President for life, eh?" The voice sent a chill down the back of Bond's neck. He settled himself on the rubble and took out the pen into which he now slid two triple-A batteries. Clipping the pen back into place, he put it down with great care beside him. One press of the plunger and Sanchez's window would disintegrate. Then one shot, and the Sanchez empire would begin to crumble. He settled into a comfortable aiming position, squinting through the small, night-enhancing telescopic sight. He could see Sanchez clearly, and Truman-Lodge. Windows gleamed along the entire length of the building's top floor. Behind them figures moved. The Oriental mission was having a good time. Well, he would soon put an end to that.

He was just swinging the sights back onto

Sanchez' apartment when he thought he caught a glimpse of someone familiar, framed for a second in a small window on the edge of the building, far right.

Bond focused on the window and his heart gave a leap. Two people were talking, waving arms in animated conversation. One was Heller. The other, he saw clearly, was Pam Bouvier. She had been too good to be true. Playing both sides against the middle, he guessed. Depression swamped him for a second as he watched Pam hand an envelope to Heller and then move out of vision.

His mouth hardened as he swept the sights back to Sanchez' apartment. He had the cross hairs smack on the man's back, but knew that could change quickly once the window blew. Holding the rifle firmly in his left hand, he reached out for the pen. Held it for a second, then pressed the plunger.

It was more of a crack than an explosion, but spectacular nevertheless. The window first seemed to become a sheet of flame, then a giant handful of diamonds which flew out, glinting and sprinkling their way down into the street.

He resighted, caught Sanchez clean in the cross hairs and squeezed the trigger. As he did so, something landed on top of him, and the shot went wide and wild as Bond rolled to his right.

In a second he was on his feet, to find himself

confronted by two human forms, both dressed in the familiar grey costume of the Ninja. Bond stood his ground as the wail of police cars and fire engines came floating at them from several blocks away.

The Ninjas closed in.

— 12 —

Both Sides of the Street

BOND FELT A heavy kick in his ribs, while a hand, like steel, crushed down on his right shoulder. He lashed out, rolling again and springing into the standing position, the skeletal rifle held in both hands across his body. Whoever the Ninjas might be, he would only go for a kill if his life became truly endangered.

It was a wrong move, and he knew it almost immediately. This pair *was* deadly. One feinted to his right while the other leaped, in a high, hard kick which took the rifle straight out from between his hands.

Bond dived to catch the grey figure on his right,

using his own foot, stabbing his leg from the knee in short sharp blows. The second kick caught the Ninja in the groin knocking him off his feet, his body doubled in pain. As he went down, Bond turned on the other assailant, his eyes flicking this way and that, looking for an escape route.

But the Ninja on the ground had rolled, grabbing at the rifle which he now lifted, twisting his body and pointing the weapon directly at Bond. He pulled the tigger and nothing happened, so, for a moment, the attacker just lay there, fiddling with the weapon.

An old nursery rhyme, about he who runs away lives to fight another day, went through Bond's mind. Normally he would always stand his ground, but this pair was really dangerous. They wanted him dead. The Ninja who was still on his feet came at him, arm outstretched in a series of jabbing blows, but Bond sidestepped, chopping at the fig- ure's shoulder, then leaping for the comparative safety of the mound of rubble he had so recently used as a firing point.

As he leaped, the Ninja on the ground lifted his arm. There was a low whooshing sound and a fine-meshed net was projected from the Ninja's sleeve, spreading and covering Bond, bringing him down like a snared animal.

He was aware of one of his assailants coming close to his body writhing in the net. He saw the rifle being raised, held like a club. Then there was a violent flash of light, a brutal pain in his head, followed by thick darkness.

Sense of smell was the first sign of life. Musty dampness slid into his nostrils; then pain returned: a numbing ache where the rifle had caught the back of his neck. He tried to move, and, for a moment, feared that he was paralysed. The fog cleared from his eyes and at last Bond realised he was in a sitting position, strapped to a chair. A naked light bulb swung from a rough, plastered ceiling and he could make out that he was in some kind of cellar, with the grey-robed figures standing in front of him.

They both started to remove their head scarves, revealing themselves as a thin Asian on whom Bond had never yet set eyes, and Loti, the big Kwang's girlfriend. A second later Kwang came down a flight of open stone steps. He carried the rifle and walked straight across to stand directly in front of Bond.

"Now, who the hell are you?"

Say nothing, Bond thought, desperately trying to clear his head. Out of the corner of his eye he caught sight of the Jabberwocky, lying smashed to pieces. The climbing device lay next to it.

His mind began to work a little faster. Nowadays very few people could hold out under interrogation, for the methods were advanced and very sophisticated, be it simple drug-induced questioning, or the more terrifying experimental techniques which rely on complete disorientation so that the mind begins to believe that it has left the body entirely. These people would not have the equipment required for the latter skills. Their way would be pain, and, in the end, Bond knew that no man can hold out forever under constant agony.

As though matching his thoughts, the Japanese girl's arm swung back, her hand cracking down over his cheek in a blow so hard that he felt, in his present condition, that his head had been broken from body.

"Be polite, and answer the man," she hissed, raising her arm to strike again, but Kwang caught her wrist.

"Wait!" he said. Looking at the gun, he removed the rounds of ammunition and checked that the weapon was empty. "His right hand!" It was an order and Loti's companion took Bond's wrist, twisting it while Kwang forced the rifle into his hand, curling the forefinger around the trigger. He forced the finger back and there was a click as the firing pin shot forwards.

"An interesting device. But what kind of man would be equipped with such a thing?"

"James Bond!" The voice came from the stone steps. Bond did not know how long its owner had been standing there, but he recognised it immediately. Trying to put a name to it, attempting to fit inflections to a face.

The figure moved, coming down the steps and walking into the light to stand next to Kwang. Only then did Bond know him. They had been on courses together; run training exercises, and been paired off in the innumerable training games that Bond's Service deemed necessary to keep its few remaining field officers in peak condition.

"Nick Fallon," he breathed. "Our man in Isthmus, I presume. As I also presume you've gone to the bad."

"Not me!" Fallon said sharply, taking the rifle from Kwang. "This is experimental equipment. As far as I know, it hasn't been issued to anyone in the field as yet. Where did you get it, Bond?"

But Bond realised that he had already said enough. Too much even. He had disclosed that he was a member of the Service, as was Fallon.

Kwang's tone became more soft and coaxing. "James Bond, who ordered you to kill Sanchez?"

After a few seconds he replied, "It's not official."

"Damned right it's not bloody official!" Fallon snarled. "You've turned rogue agent. I have M's personal orders to get you out of here and back to London double quick."

Kwang made a melodramatic movement, slapping his forehead with the palm of his hand. "That's all we needed, some idiot professional deciding to go free-lance. You know what you've done, Bond?" He paused, taking a deep breath. He had not expected an answer. "You don't even know who we are, do you?"

"You came in with a posse of drug dealers. I can only presume you're one of them."

"Presume! Presume!" Kwang shouted. "We're Hong Kong Narcotics Agency, you bastard." His foot lashed out, kicking the chair over. The leather straps and restraining handcuffs did not give at all. Bond just lay there in considerable pain while Kwang ranted on.

"For years I've been trying to set this up. I've lived cover for years. You know what that's like, Bond? *Living* cover? Associating with evil? Having to handle drugs which you know might eventually end up in your own children's hands and kill them? I've lived it for years, and, at last, we've set Sanchez up for the final kill. In a couple of days, unless your folly has undone everything, he's taking me to the centre of his operation. When I get there I shall have the power to bust him once and for all. I'll bust the whole damned lot of them, and close the thing up for good." He went on cursing.

It was Fallon who spoke next. Quietly and in anger, "Killing Sanchez alone would change nothing, Bond. Not a thing. His empire would remain intact. The real secrets would stay secrets, and one of his lieutenants would simply take over. There are plenty of them. Heller, for instance, even the German he has here: fellow called Braun. But more likely his main distributing agent, a man called Krest." He walked forwards and pulled the chair upright again.

"My God, I hope your little stunt hasn't scared him off, or worse," Kwang sighed.

The full horror of his own folly was just starting to reach Bond. All he had thought of was revenge. Yes, he had wanted to smash Sanchez's evil empire, but in reality, he had thought no further than Sanchez himself. M really did deserve his resignation, and he wondered how he could face his old chief if he could not, somehow, put matters to rights. "Take the straps and chains off," he said quietly. "I'll work with you. Together we can . . ."

"Oh, no." Fallon's voice was loaded with suspicion. "No, Commander Bond, you're a loose cannon on the deck. I'm arranging to have you shipped straight back to London."

In the short pause that followed, there came the sound of soft footsteps hurrying down the stairs. It was the thin Asian Ninja. Bond had not even noticed he had left the cellar. The man was trying to say something, breathless and in panic—

"Militia . . . Security forces . . ."

"Damn it!" Fallon headed for the stairs, a pistol in his hand. As he did so, the chatter of a heavy machine gun sounded a long way off, though its results were nearer at hand, just above their heads.

The thin Asian was still gabbling. "They have armour . . . a tank . . . !"

A machine pistol materialised from somewhere. Kwang took it and headed after Fallon, but they had not reached the top of the grim grey blocks which made up the open staircase before there was a shattering explosion.

Bond's ears rang and the place was covered in a pall of dust. A direct hit from some medium artillery piece, he thought. Before the knowledge of what was happening had settled in his mind, a second explosion followed the first and the roof was coming in. He saw Fallon's body sundered by shrapnel; a beam broke almost above Bond's head, one half falling, crushing the Japanese woman, Loti, who struggled, groaning under its weight.

Kwang had also been blown off the steps. He lay on his back with blood pumping from a severed artery.

The second half of the beam gave way, landing close to Bond. Then the roof really came in; plaster, debris and bricks crashed down. He could hardly breathe for the dust and his body felt as though he had gone three rounds with Frank Bruno. He was aware of Loti pulling herself free of the beam; dragging herself over to the dying Kwang. He even thought Kwang spoke. "Don't let them take you alive," he seemed to say.

Then the dusty cellar was full of people. Sanchez screaming at Kwang, "Who sent you? Who are you?" and Heller shaking his head and saying the word "Cyanide."

Then some kind of soldier swam into Bond's vision. He heard a shout, and saw both Sanchez and Heller standing above him, but out of focus.

For the second time in a few hours, the thick blackness of oblivion covered him as he dropped into a silent world of monsters, demons and all kinds of horrors.

Light poured onto his closed eyelids, and the scent this time was of flowers. Bond even thought he could feel a gentle breeze on his face. In the distance there was music. Not his kind of music. Not the jazz he so enjoyed. This was something else. Mozart perhaps?

For a few moments he wondered if he was dead, and should that be so, then he had been wrong about life. At last he plucked up courage to open his eyes. The room was large and pleasant. He could see his tux on a hanger, looking torn, dirty and bedraggled. His trousers were in an electric press, while his shirt, neatly laundered, lay on a chair nearby with the rest of his clothes.

Gingerly he touched his body, running his hands all over it. He felt bruised, but everything appeared to be there. He moved arms and legs. Everything there and in working order. Gently he raised himself up. He lay between silk sheets and indeed there was a breeze, soft from the sea. A pair of French windows was open and the thin drapes stirred like dancers.

He put his feet on the floor, with no ill effects, just a little dizziness as he stood up and the memory of the last twenty-four hours returned. The smashing of Sanchez's window; the abortive assassination attempt. Kwang, Loti and Fallon. The truth. He had really screwed up badly. Once more he heard the crash of the shells hitting the building, saw the bodies and the blood.

A towelling robe lay across the foot of the bed. Bond put it on and noticed the initials *FS* embroidered on the pocket. Taking deep breaths to clear his head, he walked through the French windows, out onto a patio and stopped, looking in complete disbelief.

The patio ran along a wall until it almost disappeared, so that it seemed to merge into the horizon of the sea. The view almost glowed in white. White plaster camels knelt by concrete palm trees, while deep couches were set at intervals near great marble-slabbed tables. It was a relief to look over to the sea, deep blue, sparkling in sunlight.

Ahead, stone steps led into what appeared to be dense greenery. Still taking things gently, as his head had an illusory tendency to detach itself from his body, Bond went down the steps.

The dry stone walls on either side were covered in unbelievable blossom and flowers: flora that Bond had only seen in Kew Gardens. The steps went down a long way, the walls slowly disappearing with dense and beautiful bushes taking their place as the ground flattened out into a maze of paths and walks.

The garden was magnificent. Ferns and plants grew on either side of twisting paths, which led to open spaces, fringed by cypresses and other conifers. He passed through at least three of these open spaces, each sporting a water garden, large irregular pools, with great lily pads and huge flowers. Small turtles scurried away from the edge of the pools and there was the scent of jasmine mixed with the more subtle aroma of herbs.

At last, he reached a path hedged by fern and roses, great archways blossomed above his head, and nearby he could hear more water. Coming out of the rose garden, Bond found that he was standing on a mossy bank, looking up at a rocky rise of ground down which a man-made waterfall splashed into a bubbling stream. In the rocks more flowers bloomed and he wondered what kind of mind could create such a wonderful garden, yet also be responsible for the plaster camels and concrete palm trees.

Turning right, he came upon another wide, low flight of steps. Above the steps a house seemed to rise, grey-white reaching high up the side of another rocky slope. At the top of the steps he found himself in a huge, open room. Pillars supported a roof entwined with flowers, and there were sliding doors which could seal off and close the room which was decorated in a style that could only be dubbed Hollywood Moorish. A wide swimming pool snaked around the room, and could be crossed by small bridges.

At the centre, Lupe Lamora lounged on a white couch, a table beside her laid out for lunch. As she saw him, her eyes lit up and she beckoned: little agitated butterfly strokes of her fingers. He crossed one of the bridges and went towards her.

"There is not much time," she whispered, clutching at his arm. "You must know one thing. *Wavekrest* is due in tonight. Krest is coming here, to Sanchez's palace."

"Good," he said tersely, thinking, "Yes, a man like Sanchez could never have just a house, it *has* to be a palace."

Before Lupe could reply, he saw Sanchez, striding over one of the bridges towards him, smiling with arms outstretched to greet him in an embrace.

"Amigo. Thank heaven you're okay, but you shouldn't really be up and walking about. The security forces almost took you out with the guys who were holding you. Come, sit down." His arm swept in the direction of the couch. "You feel like a drink?"

"I feel like a complete wreck." Bond laughed. "But, yes, I could do with a glass of champagne."

"Champagne for our friend," Sanchez snapped at Lupe, as if to show her off as a performing dog. Mildly she rose and went over to a bar the size of a small aircraft carrier. "All this," Bond thought, "all this and no style." Well, that figured. Sanchez's palace was built on the bones of people who had died from drug addiction.

"It seems we both had close shaves last night."

"Your people were just in time. Things were turning very nasty. Another few minutes and . . . Well, I don't really know. I can tell you that some of last night's still a bit of a blur."

"That doesn't surprise me. You were not in a good state when we pulled you out." Lupe came over with champagne: two glasses poured and a bottle in an ice bucket. Then she sat down again in obedient silence.

"Now, you must tell me," Sanchez went on. "Who were those guys? They had you trussed like a turkey."

Bond smiled. "I was trying to do you a favour. I suppose trying to get that job I asked for the other night. The Chinese, Kwang, was their leader. They were a professional hit team. It seems they had accepted a contract on you."

"So what did they want with you, amigo?"

"First, I recognised one of them the other night. The Japanese woman, Loti. I kept an eye on them; managed to stop their first attempt on your life. But they were too good for me. The idea was to silence me. I got the feeling that they were a little upset. Also they were afraid I would warn you and spoil their other plans."

"Other plans? And you knew them. How?"

"I told you the other night, I wanted work. I've recently retired from British Government service. We kept dossiers on people like Loti. She's done one or two unpleasant things in Europe."

"And you've recently retired?" There was a slight, uneasy but sharp edge to his voice.

"Well." Bond looked at the floor. "Well, let's say I *was* recently retired. They didn't like some of the free-lance work I was doing. Couldn't pin anything on me, but . . . well, you know how it is?"

Sanchez smiled, showing a lot of gold in his mouth. "So? I wondered. A British agent. You've got class, amigo. You'll also have a job if you stick with me."

"I asked for a job the other night."

"I was checking you out, that's all." He lit a small cigar and sipped at the champagne. "Tell me. This hit team, they had a contract. Who'd put out a contract on *me?*"

Slowly Bond let the words come out, spacing and timing them for the best effect. "Someone *very* close to you."

"They told you his name?" The question spoke whole encyclopaedias of what Sanchez would do to anyone who took action against him.

"No. But they were well briefed. They knew all about you. Knew the layout of the casino, the armoured glass in your windows. They even mentioned this place. They called it your palace. There were things only someone close to you would know about."

Sanchez had become very still, like a snake, or some dangerous creature about to strike down a victim. "They mentioned a name?" he asked.

"Not a name, no. But there was a clue. They were going to get the job done before tonight. *Had* to get it done before tonight."

"Tonight?"

Bond nodded. "They expected the payoff tonight. They were to collect a great deal of money from someone close to you who is due in Isthmus tonight."

Sanchez's face tightened, then creased into a

smile, then a laugh. Both smile and laugh rang very false, as did his next words. "Every single person in my organisation is one hundred percent loyal."

Through the garden noises came the faraway chatter of a helicopter.

"Then, if *everyone* is loyal, you've got nothing to worry about. But I wouldn't bet on it, Señor Sanchez. Not after what I heard. I promise you."

Sanchez bit his lip, stood and turned away. "Listen. I got people to meet. Important. We'll talk more later on. In the meantime, you must get plenty of rest."

"I should really go back to my hotel. I have things there that . . . "

"Later. You should rest here! For a couple of days at least. Now, save your legs." He snapped his fingers at Lupe. "My dear, why don't you show our friend the quick way back to his quarters, eh?"

Lupe nodded obediently, and all three of them walked out into the gardens. Instead of going past the waterfall and through the rose garden, they turned right. Screened by trees was a small funicular staging point. Lupe pressed a button and the machinery began to rumble as the funicular rose towards them from below.

"Never walk when you can ride, eh?" Sanchez appeared to be relaxed and in a good humour now.

Lupe supplied the information about the funicular as it came to a stop: a large car, riding on rails, disappearing upwards. "There are four stops," she said. "This one and the guesthouse at the top of the hill. Below there is a staging stop, mainly for the gardeners, and then the bottom. It takes you right down to the little dock where we keep the boats."

"Vaya con Dios," Sanchez said as he shepherded them into the cage. As the doors shut and the funicular began to move, Bond saw that Sanchez had been joined by Heller. He would have paid a lot of cash to hear the conversation.

In fact, Heller was telling Sanchez that he had a report on the man Bond. "You'll never guess who he is?" he said with a smile.

"Oh, no? I know who he is. A former British agent, with a somewhat tarnished reputation."

"How . . . ? How do you know that? Sometimes I think you have powers beyond mortal men. How?"

"You'd be surprised. You don't think I know such things? Now, listen to me, Colonel. I personally want to meet Krest's boat when it comes in tonight. You'll bring a dozen reliable men. Armed, of course."

"We have a problem with Krest?"

"We'll find that out tonight. You bring Lupe as well. She was there when things went wrong on *Wavekrest,* so Milton Krest won't dare to lie in front of her. Come." With a hand on Heller's shoulder, Sanchez led him up concealed steps, which would take them to the helipad.

When Bond and Lupe arrived back at his room, Bond excused himself for a moment, grabbed his clothes from the press and chair and went into the bathroom. He was back a few minutes later, wearing the black tuxedo pants and buttoning the newly laundered formal shirt.

Lupe's eyes widened. "What you doing?"

"I've really had just about enough of your friend Sanchez. I do have to go back to my hotel."

"You're crazy. Don't you learn? He told you to stay and rest here. When Sanchez says something like that, he's not asking you, but commanding you. If you're not here when he comes later on, he'll go . . . How do you say it?"

"Berserk?"

"Yeah. Crazy. He'll do terrible things."

"Don't worry." Bond kissed her lightly on the cheek. "Just give me five minutes to get clear, then scream your head off. I don't want you involved."

"No. I have better idea." There was a glitter of guile in her eyes. "We take the funicular down to the boat dock. Now, listen to me for a change. Okay, I know how to get you out of here, but you must promise me to return before dark, okay? Is important that you're here when he comes looking. You promise, and I'll get you out."

"I'll try to get back, if you insist. I can't promise, though."

She thought for a moment. "Okay. I take big risk with you. Take your clothes off."

"You're a very forward young woman."

She stamped her foot, in mock fury. "You're a fool. In cupboard over there are bathing clothes. Your own clothes I put in bag to keep dry."

"I'm going for a swim?"

"You guessed? Clever man. Now, go and take clothes off."

The guard on the boat dock below Sanchez' palace had little to do. He was, in fact, smoking a cigarette as the funicular came down. He stood for a minute or so, expecting Sanchez or one of the security people. At the moment he was only guarding Sanchez's sailing boat, and the twenty-two-foot speedboat.

The guard took a long drag at his cigarette, threw the butt on the ground and carefully crushed it with the toe of his boot. When he looked up, there was Lupe, a tote bag over her shoulder, smiling at him as she jumped into the speedboat and started the motor. Suddenly the guard was galvanised into action. He took two slow steps towards the boat, and so failed to see another figure run behind him and slide noiselessly into the water.

"Señorita . . . !" the guard shouted above the noise of the speedboat's engine.

Lupe cupped a hand to her ear as she opened the throttle and began to move away.

The guard gave it a last try. "Señorita Lamora. Señor Sanchez said nobody . . ."

"I go shopping! Back in half hour!" she called out with a big smile, just for the insurance.

The guard sighed, and hoped she *would* be back in half an hour. If she was not, then his job could be on the line.

When they were out of view, around the bluff which shielded Sanchez's palace from the smart yachting marina near the port of Isthmus City, Lupe slowed down.

Bond, who had been hanging on to the bumper line on the starboard side of the speedboat, out of the guard's view, climbed aboard, spluttering from the bow spray she had put up. Once he was safely in the speedboat, Lupe gunned the engine and they shot away towards the marina.

It took twelve minutes, and by that time Bond was dressed in pants, shirt and shoes. She pulled the speedboat up to the mooring with a good deal of skill as Bond jumped onto the dock, taking the line to tie up. "Come on, then, hurry!" he called.

"Hurry, yourself. I go back," Lupe shouted at him.

"Going back to Sanchez? Do you love him?"

"No! I hate him. But is best if you come back soon also."

"Why the hell don't you come with me, then, if you don't love him?"

"Because you're crazier than he is!" She laughed, opened the throttle and turned the speedboat back in the direction of Sanchez's palace.

Half an hour later, James Bond walked into the lobby of the Hotel El Presidente and asked for the key to his suite.

"But, señor, your uncle and Ms. Kennedy are already up there." The receptionist looked uncertain. "Is that not correct, señor? Should I not have allowed them . . . ?"

"No. No, that's fine," Bond snapped, heading for the elevators.

At 314 he rapped sharply at the door. A second later it was hurriedly opened. Pam stood there. In the background Bond could see Q.

She opened her mouth to speak, but he grabbed her arm, twisted it and pushed her back towards the bedroom.

"You're still here, then." It was an accusation, not a question.

Q looked up in shock. Pam was grunting with pain. Bond continued to push her towards the bedroom door. At the door he turned to Q. "Pack up, we're leaving," he commanded, throwing Pam into the room and kicking the door closed behind them.

"James . . . ? What . . . ?" she blurted, but he had already spun her around, reached up under her skirt and removed her pistol.

"What's wrong, James?"

He held on to her arms, pressing the pistol to her head. "Kwang and his people were Hong Kong Narcotics. One of my own Service's men was around as well. Now they're all dead, and I know you've been working both sides of the street. I saw you with Heller, Pam Bouvier—if that's your real name. You're a double, and that's trouble I can't afford, so I'm giving you one chance only. You've got thirty seconds to give me the full strength of what's been going on. Thirty seconds and counting. Talk!"

— 13 —

The Blowout

PAM WAS WHITE and shaking as Bond continued to put the pressure on, doing a countdown and pressing the pistol harder into her temple.

"James! For God's sake, stop! I'm not a double, but I'll tell you the truth about Heller. The truth about everything!"

He relaxed his hold on her. "I promise you, Pam," he hissed, his mouth set in a cruel line. "I promise you that, if I don't get the truth, if I catch you in a lie at any time, I'll follow you to hell itself and you'll suffer. By heaven, you'll suffer. Now talk."

She took a deep breath. "I really couldn't tell you before. Do you remember the day of the wedding? Felix and Della?"

"Am I ever likely to forget it?"

"You came into Felix's study. He had just handed me a letter."

Bond nodded. "Look, don't start running into backwaters and making up stories about letters and things. Yes, I saw Felix give you a letter. But I also saw you with Heller and you looked pretty buddy-buddy to me. Pretty desperate as well."

Tears were running down her face. "James, I *am* telling you the truth. I told you Heller was an ex-Green Beret . . ."

"And that he was wanted by the U.S., yes."

"He's been trying to do a deal. I knew Heller back in the old days. He knew I was a friend of Felix and he came to me. Wanted me to be a go-between. Asked me to contact Leiter for him."

"What kind of a deal?" All the outward signs told him she was giving him the truth, but he had to be sure.

"Sanchez has managed to buy four hand-held missiles from the Contras. He paid well over the odds for them."

"What kind of missiles? Stingers? Blowpipes? SA-6s? Sa-8s? Chaparrals?"

"I know they're not Stingers. I heard him say Stingers were no good because they were cumbersome. Difficult to cart around, what with the electronics pack and all. These are prototypes of some new thing. I don't know if they even have a proper designation. *You* know what they're doing: letting the Contras field-test new stuff for them. These things can be used in one of two modes: either ground to air, or ground to ground."

"Uh-huh" He had heard they were testing new, highly portable, wholly self-contained, small weapons like this. Certainly the Stingers were out with the maze of electronic packs, conductance bars, and complex things like interrogation systems (the IFF which told the operator if an aircraft was friendly or not) that went with them. The United States had been working on all kinds of smaller, cheaper, more easily portable hand-held missiles.

"The point is"—Pam took another gulp of air—"Sanchez has already threatened to shoot down an unprotected airliner if the DEA doesn't lay off. The letter Felix gave me is from the Attorney General. Washington's promised Heller immunity if he gets the missiles back, without any incident."

Bond was as certain as he could be that she was telling the truth. "Did Heller go for the deal?" he asked.

"Originally, yes. But after Sanchez got away, Heller panicked. He sent a message back to me saying the deal was off and I was as good as dead if he ever saw me again."

He was just about convinced. "You know where they've got these missiles?"

Pam made a frustrated gesture, balling her fists and beating them on her thigh. "The whole thing's over now. We've missed our chance, James, we'll never get another shot at him."

He dropped the pistol onto the bed. "Oh, yes, we will." He gave her a brief outline of what had happened on the previous night, and through until morning. "I've no other option but to believe you, Pam. So, what we're going to do is finish Kwang's job for him. Kwang told me—come to that I heard it all through the *Jabberwocky* anyway—that Sanchez is taking the Orientals on a guided tour of his laboratories. I intend to be there. But we have one little problem. My old shipmate Krest is arriving tonight in *Wavekrest*. Sanchez is going to want his money, and we've still got some of it left. Also, I've rather put the boot in. I think Sanchez is ninety-nine percent convinced that Krest's been double-crossing him. To begin with, we have to convince him. Make it a one hundred percent certainty."

He opened the door. Q sat in one of the deep chairs, his face bleak with worry.

"You still got that chauffeur's uniform, Q?"

"Yes." A sudden new light in his eyes. "What's happening?"

"Sorry about all the rough stuff, but I had to make certain we were all on the same side."

"And are we?"

Bond glanced at Pam, her cheeks still streaked

with tears, her eyes red and puffy. He gave her his
Sunday smile. "I think so. Gather round, and I'll
tell you what I think we should do."

They sat in a conspiratorial huddle, and Bond
began, "Pam, I know you're a good pilot in the air,
but how would you be on water?"

"Spectacular."

"Ah, well, I want you to be spectacularly bad.
You see, Sanchez might well control his empire; he
might well rule in his organisation, but he doesn't
rule the waves. Anything of size going into his
private harbour has to have an official pilot."

"You don't mean . . . ?"

"I'll tell you what I mean, then my uncle and I
have to go and do one little chore at the bank." He
went on speaking for the best part of fifteen minutes, then they spent an hour fine-tuning the plan.

Wavekrest's lights were plainly visible miles
away. Q, Bond and Pam watched them draw closer.
They stood together in the wheelhouse of the little
pilot boat, discussing how easy it was to bribe
officials. "Only a couple of thousand for the pilot to
turn a blind eye. I can hardly believe it!" Q had still
not got used to the whole way of life in Isthmus.
Earlier, his eyes had almost popped out of his head
in the bank when Señor Montolongo, with a philo-
sophical shrug, watched Bond withdraw all the
cash.

Now the money hung in sacks disguised as
fenders over the starboard side of the pilot boat.

When they were within hailing distance of

Wavekrest Bond whispered that it was Pam's big chance. "Get ready, and do your worst." He smiled grimly in the darkness.

"If I do my worst, I'll still be doing my best." She hunched her shoulders in the warm night air.

"Ahoy there, *Wavekrest!*" Bond called through the megaphone. "Stand by to receive the pilot."

They got some garbled reply, but, as they came alongside, a Jacob's ladder came down from the larger vessel. Pam swarmed up it and mounted the rail to be met by a startled mate. In Spanish she asked to be taken to the bridge.

"You are the harbour pilot?" The mate's voice matched his look of amazement.

"No." Pam grinned at him. "No, I'm his secretary."

The sarcasm was lost on the mate.

Back on the pilot boat, Q and Bond watched the progress, staying close to *Wavekrest* as she entered the harbour.

"She's doing very well, really," Q said.

They both winced as *Wavekrest* hit a sandbar, going over it with a nasty crunch.

"Very well indeed." Bond was stripped to the waist. "She's now got to make that tricky turn towards the main dock. That should be fun. Look, Sanchez, Heller and some of his gentlemen are waiting for Krest."

"After what you've told me, I'd like to be a fly on the wall when they meet." Q was at the wheel and doing better than Pam.

"I intend to be a fly on the wall, ouch!" *Wavekrest*

came around in a half-circle, smashing an untended dory into matchwood. "I rather think she's going to take that ship right into the dock wall."

Certainly that was what it looked like from the bridge of *Wavekrest.* "Señorita, are we not coming in a little fast, and the angle is bad . . ." the captain began.

Pam looked at him blankly. "Okay," she shrugged. "I'm the pilot, but if you want to do the driving you'd better take the wheel."

The moment had been timed well, for Pam merely walked away, leaving the captain and navigation officer shouting orders. They struggled to put engines into reverse, but it was too late. *Wavekrest* made it into the side of the dock with a shuddering crunch which made Sanchez smile grimly.

Nobody saw Pam leave the bridge, but everyone heard Krest's cries of rage, even Bond, who was by this time in the stern of the pilot boat, slipping into the water, taking the disguised sacks of money from Q, who cut them adrift as Bond gave the order. With the bags around his neck he went deep, heading for the well in *Wavekrest's* stern where Pam had, by this time, opened the well doors.

She put a hand down and helped Bond up, past *Sentinel,* into the area near the decompression chamber.

"Well done." Bond squeezed her hand. "Come on, we won't have much time. The decompression chamber." They lugged the bags of money over to the door, with its thick glass panel and big lever of a lock, ripping the bags open and letting hundred-dollar bills loose in the chamber. When it was done they closed the door again and looked around for a good hiding place.

Already, above them on deck they could hear Krest greeting Sanchez—

"I didn't expect you to come aboard personally."

"And I didn't think you would, but I like surprises. You've been having a lot of surprises lately, Milton."

"We got some crazy woman harbour pilot . . ."

"Let's talk about the money, eh? That's what I came for. Does he have a safe?" The last question obviously directed at Lupe, for she answered—

"In the owner's stateroom. I show you."

The conversation died away.

"Trouble," Bond whispered. "Better than we hoped for." They had found that there was room to hide behind a bank of lockers which gave them seclusion, dark and a good view of the decompression chamber, now almost bloated with cash.

They waited for around fifteen minutes, then there was the sound of doors banging, footsteps and angry words. Sanchez was shouting. "Search the whole ship. We know he hasn't put in anywhere. Either the money's on board or he's got it wrapped in plastic at the bottom of the ocean. Search everywhere."

Krest's voice was shrill. "I swear, Franz. It happened like I said . . ."

"Oh, yeah, and pigs might fly." The footsteps overhead seemed to be getting nearer to the companionway, and the voices were more clear. "So, let's go over it again. Make sure I've got it right." Sanchez's voice was gritty, laced with a well-honed edge. "You say he water-skied behind the plane, then jumped onto it. What is this guy? A circus artist?"

"No, well, yes. He was kinda dragged into the air. Then, well, like I told you, he threw the pilots out and flew away . . ."

"Like a bird, flapping his wings, I suppose."

"I'm telling you the truth, Franz. He took every cent. Would I make up a story like that? You gotta believe me . . ."

"I gotta get my money back, Milton. I don't have to believe anybody. What's down here?" They were right above, standing at the top of the companionway ladder.

"Only the docking well for the probe. For *Sentinel.* Docking area, and the decompression chamber."

"Let's take a little look. Colonel Heller, you organise the search."

There were four of them: Sanchez, Krest, and the two hoodlums, Perez and Braun, and it took less than a minute for Sanchez to see the money in the decompression chamber. Bond and Pam pressed themselves against the metal bulkhead, glad of the darkness.

"So what in hell's this, Milton? A tax shelter?"

Krest gave a cry. A cross between a turkey being strangled and a man with severe digestive trouble. "Franz! I swear it! That's not my money. I've never seen it before. I . . ."

"Too damned right it's not your money, amigo. It's *my* money." Sanchez's hand went out to the door lever. The clunk of it opening seemed to echo right through the ship. *"My* money. You think I'm that stupid, Krest? I know all about it. The water-skiing, plane-riding expert already gave me the evidence. You rip me off, then plan to use my money to pay a hit team. You have the nerve to put a contract out on *me?"*

They could see everything: the open door to the chamber, Sanchez screaming, holding Krest by the collar as he propelled him towards the chamber.

"You want the money so much? Okay, Krest, take it!" With a kick he sent Krest flying into the chamber, slamming the door on him, then looking around.

Pam clung to Bond, and he put his hand up, trying to blot out the picture from her eyes. Already he had a fair idea of what Sanchez meant to do.

They could see Krest's face through the thick glass, his cries muffled and his banging fists making no impression on anyone. Meanwhile, Sanchez had turned up the pressure valve to maximum: the needle on the big round depth gauge indicated fifty feet.

Sanchez shook his head, like a boxer going in for the kill, then grabbed at a fire axe, smashing the glass around the fire-fighting equipment to get at it.

Already the depth gauge was showing five hundred feet below sea level and Krest was sprawled against the huge pile of money, fighting for breath.

"Let's bring him to the surface! Fast!" Sanchez shouted, raising the axe and grinding it through the pipe labelled *Vent* running from the chamber to the service area. There was a terrible *whoossssshhhhh!* as the pipe gave way, the pressure dropping in a fraction of a second.

Krest's eyes bulged, his face contorted and then his head quite simply exploded, as though a balloon filled with blood and offal had been burst. Bond turned away as the horrible mess spattered over the glass, and he put his hand firmly over Pam's face.

"Good." Sanchez did not seem to show any emotion. "Poor old Milton Krest just had a blowout." He moved back towards the ladder.

Perez, in a weak voice, asked what should be done with the money.

"What d'you think?" Sanchez snapped. "Launder it."

They heard his feet clumping as he ascended the ladder, then Braun, sounding sick, said, "Come on. We'll get some of the boys to clean up the mess."

"Now," Bond whispered. "Don't look, just follow me into the well."

Within minutes they were out through the well and open docking doors, swimming gently towards the pilot boat, which was moving very slowly away from *Wavekrest*.

Stripping off his shirt, James Bond stretched out on the bed and pulled the sheets over him. By the sound of voices in the corridor he reckoned that he had only just got back in time.

Pam had swum strongly, keeping pace with him, and Q was there, ready to help them on board. Bond knew now that he had to move quickly. He hurried away below, turning to Q and asking him to get the inflatable ready, and put his gear on board. Five minutes later he came back on deck, dried off and in slacks, shirt and a pair of his favourite moccasins.

"It's all ready, James." Q, the old devil, sounded almost emotional.

"I can't tell you how much you've both helped." Bond took in a deep breath of night air. "Right, we split up now. You, Pam, take my old uncle in the plane. We meet again in Miami when it's all over."

"Shouldn't we stick together?" For all her toughness, and the kind of life she had led, Pam had obviously been shaken by the manner of Krest's death.

"No. They could well be after me. Particularly if

I don't make it back in time. It'll be safer if I'm left alone."

Pam tried to protest again, but he stopped her words with a kiss, then was away, over the side, scrambling down the ladder to the bobbing inflatable which contained his briefcase and overnight bag. With a final wave he started the near-silent electric motor and headed the rubber raft towards the shoreline.

He beached on the seaward side of Sanchez's dock and began the long climb up the hill, using his built-in sense of direction, occasionally glimpsing the lighted funicular railway, and finally, muscles aching, reached the well-lit guest and living quarters with its hideous white patio, plaster camels, concrete palm trees and couches. Now he only had to hope Sanchez had not already discovered his absence. He did not risk the French windows, but went around the side of the building, into the brightly lit corridor, with its perfectly spaced doors to the guest rooms.

He left the luggage outside, and did not switch the lights on. He was just about to close the door when he heard the voices. Sanchez and Lupe walking up the corridor. He stood beside his door, one ear to the tiny gap, listening.

"Goodnight, Franz," Lupe said, and there was a pause during which, Bond presumed, they kissed.

"You look very tired, baby. You get a good rest." Another pause, then, "What in hell is that?" He had spotted the luggage, and Bond heard Lupe cough, gaining time before she spoke.

"Bond's clothes. He had the luggage sent over from the hotel this afternoon. He's been sleeping all day."

"Perez!" Sanchez called, and more footsteps came hurrying down the passage.

That was enough for Bond. In a moment he had stripped off his shirt and leaped into the bed.

A moment later, the door crashed open and the lights came on.

"Wha . . . Oh! . . . Where . . ." Bond sat up, bare-chested, rubbing imitation sleep from his eyes.

Sanchez came over to the bed and smiled at him. Once more the gold in his mouth glittered. "Amigo! Sorry to wake you. You need the rest. But you should know that the information you gave me paid off. I got the one who had the gall to put out a contract on me."

"Anytime I can be of service, as you well know."

"Good." Sanchez nodded. "You think you will be well enough to travel tomorrow?"

"Of course." Bond felt a churning of anticipation in his stomach. He tried to sound disinterested. "Where're we going?"

"That will be my surprise. But I promise you won't be disappointed. Now, get more rest. See you in the morning, okay?"

"Right."

Perez, who had been standing behind his master, holding Bond's cases, nodded, putting the bags on the floor.

As soon as they had left, Bond undressed down to his shorts and began making preparations to shower.

He was heading for the bathroom when he heard the door move behind him. He swung around, hands up, ready for anything. Lupe had slipped in. She had a finger to her lips and wore only a filmy robe over an elaborate basque.

She approached him slowly. "I thought I heard that bastard talking to you."

"I think he probably trusts me now."

She gave an exaggerated sigh. "You're impossible."

"He says we're going on a trip tomorrow. Where's he taking me?"

"I don't know. Truly I have no idea. There is a place he goes to often, but he's never taken me. It is his big secret that he shares with everybody else around here—except me." She took him by the hand, pulling him towards the bed, where they sat, side by side.

"Surely you must have heard something," Bond pressed.

"Well, I do know he's showing the Chinese around this special place of his. Some other Oriental people arrived today. Mr. Kwang and his friend left, I think. But there are more here now." Without warning, her eyes filled with tears. "Truly, James. I promise you, I don't know where he's taking you; I don't really know what he intends for me—not in the end. James." She now clung to his arm. "James, what's going to happen to us?"

She was a very beautiful woman, Bond thought. Sanchez did not know how lucky he was. At a snap of his fingers this lovely girl would follow him to hell, even though she hated him. "Don't worry," he tried to soothe her. "You'll be safe. When all this is over I'll see you get back to your family. Back home."

It was as though he had put a torch to a fuse. He saw her fingers curl, their long nails like claws, and her eyes lit up with loathing. "No! I spent the first fifteen years of my life trying to get away from my home. People like you have no idea what it's like, living in the shantytowns all over this country. I was one of ten children. Ten, with no food, no hope, no love!" A fine spray came from between her lips as she spat out her hatred. "Bad and evil though he is, Sanchez got me out of there." She turned her head, looking up at him, her eyes soft, a yearning in her face replacing the rage. "James, can't I stay with you?"

"I'm not sure that would work out, Lupe." He knew it sounded halfhearted. Why could he never resist a beautiful girl?

Lupe's arms came up around his neck. "How can we tell?" she whispered. "How can we tell . . . ? Unless we try."

Bond felt her cool lips on his, then her thrusting

tongue and the pressure of her body on his as they fell back onto the bed.

The first time they came up for air, Lupe said, "I think this is going to work out very well."

— 14 —

The Temple of Meditation

PAM AND Q were ready to leave the hotel at seven-thirty. Breakfast had been served, and their bags were already packed and waiting when the buzzer sounded.

It was Pam who opened the door, expecting a bellboy. She gave a little gasp when she saw the nubile Lupe Lamora standing there, breathless, with her face etched in concern.

When she spoke, the words tumbled over one another. "Ms. Kennedy? I saw you at the casino with James." She glanced over at Q, who had emerged from his bedroom. "I need to talk with you. In private."

Pam glanced at Q. "It's okay," she said, closing the door. "James' uncle is with me. You can speak in front of him."

"It's James . . ."

"What's happened?" not disguising her alarm.

"He's in great danger. Sanchez is no fool. He might act as though James is his friend, but I know he's still running very detailed checks on him."

In spite of the small lump of jealousy that was rapidly getting larger in her mind, Pam smiled in reassurance. "It's okay. James is well out of the country by now," she lied.

Lupe's eyes widened. "But he's not. Don't you know? Last night he stayed at Sanchez's place. In fact he stayed with me."

Pam turned towards Q, who saw she had gone pale, her mouth set in a hard line.

"You mean he *stayed* at Sanchez's place?" Q asked, trying to pour metaphorical oil on proverbial troubled waters. The waters were starting to show, springing to Pam's eyes.

"Sí! Yes. Franz is taking him on some trip, with the Chinese. They leave at ten. Please! Please! You must help him." She was also near tears. "I couldn't go on living if anything happened to him. Lord help me, I love James so much."

Q saw Pam's back stiffen and knew what might come. He hurried over and took Lupe by the arm, leading her towards the door. "My dear, you must go back to Sanchez's place before you're missed. Now, don't worry, we'll think of something." And with that he hustled her out of the door.

When he turned back to Pam, the situation was much worse than he expected. The anger had flooded scarlet to her face, "The lousy, two-timing, double-crossing, lying, male chauvinist son-of-a-bitch!" she exploded. "Oh, I love James so much." She imitated Lupe's voice with a fair degree of accuracy. "Well, damned if I'll help him. Self-centred, reptilian, ungrateful, fornicating, useless cretin. James bloody Bond can go to hell in a handbasket as far as I'm concerned. I wouldn't even help him to cross the road."

"I think I'd better go and organise some transport. A couple of clapped-out cars, I think. Vehicles people won't look at too closely." He put a fatherly arm around her shoulders. "Pam, my dear, don't judge him too harshly. Field operatives have to use every means at their disposal . . ."

"Bullshit!" she yelled. "I *know* all about bloody field agents . . . I've . . . I know . . ." The next moment she was weeping on Q's shoulder. "Oh, damn him, Uncle Q. Did he *have* to do this?"

"Quite probably. Let me go and get cars. Damn it, Pamela, the man's in danger."

Once he had gone, Pam Bouvier sat down and thought. She had, in fact, been feeling a shade guilty, having filched the cheque Bond had taken, for a quarter of a million dollars, at the casino. After all, it was made out to her. Only after cashing the thing had she felt guilt.

By ten that morning, she was seated in a small, uncomfortable mongrel motorcar, in the main parking lot of Isthmus City International Airport. She held a small two-way handset and was waiting for Q's instructions.

Q, in the disguise of a peasant gardener, loitered near the gates to the estate, his car, a little Deux Chevaux, was hidden a mile down the road, and he hacked at the verge near the gates with a hoe he had "borrowed" on the walk up from the car.

They left at ten o'clock, on the dot. First, a pickup truck driven by the man called Braun, with three armed guards making a show of weapons. Truman-Lodge was at the wheel of the first stretch limo, driving four of the Chinese, while the rest were in Sanchez's private limo, driven by his chauffeur. An open jeep brought up the rear. Perez drove, and Q saw that Bond was sitting next to him, but two more guards, openly displaying weapons, were in the rear. Sanchez himself was conspicuous by his absence, which, Q reflected, did not make the heart grow any fonder of him.

As the convoy disappeared, Q took out his little handset and quietly spoke into it. "They've just left. Pickup, two limos and a jeep. Turning north onto the main highway. Sanchez not with them. Repeat, Sanchez *not* present. Wait . . ." He heard a familiar stuttering noise. A moment later, he saw a helicopter rise from the middle of the estate. "Get airborne. Sanchez probably in helicopter."

Pam's voice came over very clearly. "I copy that, Q. Base out." In the car park she picked up her briefcase from the seat next to her—she was not going to leave the quarter of a million out of her sight—locked the vehicle and walked between the airport buildings towards the executive parking area where she had left the Beechcraft.

Neither of them was to know the small drama that had gone on, an hour before, at the helipad. Sanchez had told everybody that he would be travelling separately, by chopper, and the helicopter landed around nine, while Q was still making his way towards the estate.

Sanchez and Heller both waited for the machine as it put down gently. Next to the pilot sat another of Sanchez' henchmen, Dario, who climbed out, carrying a canister around five feet in length.

"Good." Sanchez smiled, reaching out for the canister and unlocking the plastic covering around the electronics pack, which fitted in a stubby T-shape about two feet from one end. Nobody could disguise the fact that it was some kind of hand-held portable missile. "Good," he repeated. "You have brought my insurance policy."

"I brought all four, as you instructed, patron." Dario gave a well-oiled smile.

"We can put them in the vault," Heller suggested.

Slowly Sanchez shook his head. "Oh, no, Colonel. They come with us. In the helicopter. From now on until all this is completed, I want them nearby."

The Beechcraft was there, exactly where Pam had left it. But now, as Pam approached, she saw that several mechanics surrounded it. The engines were laid out neatly, in pieces.

"What in hell's name're you doing to my airplane?" She caught one of the mechanics by the shoulder. He shrugged off her hand and reached out for a clipboard. "Overhaul." He pointed to the signature at the bottom of the list. "Ordered yesterday by Señor Sanchez."

"But I've got to have a plane . . ." She stopped, looking towards the gas pumps. A little Cessna Aggwagon, with its high-domed single-seat cockpit and crop-spraying canisters under the wing roots, tight in to the fuselage. Very manoeuvrable, she thought. Low stalling speed, plenty of visibility. Just the thing for crop-dusting—or Sanchez-dusting, come to that. There was nobody nearby, and the keys were in the right place when she climbed onto the wing and peeped into the cockpit. If she was to do it, then it had to be done very quickly indeed. As she switched on, Pam's eyes swung across the instrument panel. She had a full tank of gas, and could see the spraying canisters were also full.

By this time she was taxiing and doing up the seat belts. Nobody appeared to notice; nobody leaped up and down, though she reckoned the tower would already be shouting blue blazes at her. Deliberately she dumped the earphones out of the cockpit and pulled the high Plexiglas dome down, snapping it into the closed position which cut out a lot of external noise.

She remained alert. The little Cessna was a dream to taxi: very responsive. Twisting her head this way and that, watching for other aircraft on the ground or in the circuit, she saw that the taxiway turned onto the main runway, almost directly ahead. She turned, braked lightly to make sure, for the last time, that no other airplane was either inbound or outbound, then swerved the aircraft onto the runway and opened the throttle. As the speed rose she had to bang on the rudder bar to keep the nose straight. Ahead there was a yellow airfield truck, heading down the runway towards her. A man in uniform stood in the back waving for her to stop. The airspeed indicator read 60 and she had no idea of the speed at which the crop duster would unstick. But unstick it must, for the yellow truck was growing larger by the second. Fingers mentally crossed, Pam eased back on the stick, rotating the airplane which lifted into its natural element with ease.

At seven hundred feet, she took the power off and turned north. She thought to herself that the man in the back of the truck was probably changing his pants at this moment, and smiled as she climbed out of the turn, going up to a thousand feet.

Fifteen minutes later she spotted the convoy, just as they turned off the one decent four-lane highway within spitting distance of Isthmus City. On the horizon she saw trees, an unusual feature on the flat red earth of the local countryside. The convoy still moved at a steady pace along a wide dust road.

Pam felt like the fighter pilots she had read so much about, her head swivelling all the time, eyes going from instruments to mirror, then sweeping the ground in a 180° arc. The trees were growing clearer and she could see that they were specially planted conifers, quite close together to form a protective circle. There was no doubt the convoy was heading directly towards them, and, out of the corner of her eye, she saw a helicopter below her, also aiming for the trees.

Time for cover, she thought. Away to the right there was a cluster of farm buildings. Fields of some kind of crop spread out in an irregular circle. Well, she thought, no farmer would object to a little free crop-dusting.

Pam gave the airplane a little flap and nosed down, levelling out almost parallel with the helicopter but now below it at around a hundred feet. She let the Cessna drop a shade lower, her right hand going out to the button array below the main instruments. There were four buttons: two for the port dusting compound, and two for the starboard. At around twenty feet she punched one of the starboard buttons, knowing that a cloud of powder was being released behind the airplane. Whoever was in the helicopter would, she hoped fervently, take little notice of a pilot at work dusting the crops.

Finger off the button, she climbed, turning back as she did so to get a perfect picture of the convoy, trees and helicopter. What she saw made her almost stop flying the plane properly. In the middle of the trees stood a huge circular construction.

It seemed to have been built of great red blocks, inlaid with pieces of mosaic, the whole edifice rising almost to the height of the trees. The building had an almost hypnotic effect: one of serene calm so that she could not take her eyes from it.

Though the construction was of large blocks, it contrived to form a complete circle, the interior floor of which was one great mosaic, while at the top of the structure, at regular intervals, other shapes prodded upwards: cones of the same red stone, but glittering as though showered with gold dust.

She levelled out, turning again, not wanting anyone in the convoy or helicopter to think she was taking a peek at this incredible piece of architecture, and, as the airplane banked, Pam realised she had seen this place before, but could not think where. Then, as she got a new view, she realised. This place was a temple, and you could see it on television each week. Yes, now she had it. This was the Olimpatec Meditation Institute, a full-sized replica of one of the Olimpatec Indian temples. The Temple of Meditation. This was where the Professor—Professor Joe—did his programmes from. And not only the programmes, she remembered. No wonder Sanchez was heading in this direction, for this was where, unknown to the outside world, the buying, price-fixing, ordering and selling of drugs went on each week. Live on TV.

The convoy had stopped at some kind of barrier which security guards had begun to raise, while the helicopter was slowly dropping for a landing right on the vast mosaic floor in the centre of the circle. As the chopper came level with the top of the temple, to Pam's amazement the floor appeared to slide away, breaking into two halves, turning the temple into a deep and dark crater.

The helicopter dropped out of sight, and the floor slid back into place again. Pam stood the Cessna on one wing and headed at full throttle low towards the nearby farm buildings. Somehow she had to get into the amazing Olimpatec Meditation Institute.

She landed on a piece of rough land near to the adobe buildings, using full flap and a lot of brake after the flare: the flaps would be dragging on the ground to get the plane out again, she thought, opening the cockpit dome and springing down to meet a puzzled farmer who greeted her in Spanish, saying she had sprayed the wrong fields. "I have no money for this kind of treatment!" He was almost wailing until she told him it was on the house. All she wanted was a lift in the decrepit old pickup standing near the building.

"I want to go to the Temple," she said. "The Indian place. Olimpatec . . . know what I'm saying?"

The farmer knew what she was saying, but did

not like it. Many spirits of the Indians lived in these parts. It was ill luck to go near the place.

She convinced him by saying he just had to drop her off. She would make her own way back. If not, then there would be a big charge for the crop-spraying, and her bosses knew how to get money out of people who said they were poor. "Just like those who collect the taxes," she said.

Instantly the farmer walked to his pickup and started it with a toothy grin.

At the Olimpatec Meditation Institute, the convoy had gone through the checkpoint, driven on well-metalled road and suddenly broken through the circle of trees. Even Bond, used to shocks of one kind or another, was impressed by the towering red walls, the mosaics and glittering cone-shaped towers. The building loomed over them.

The convoy proceeded around the perimeter of the building, stopping in front of a great studded door. Bond realised that Professor Joe's TV programme never showed this side of the Temple, or Institute as he preferred to call it.

They were signalled to leave the cars, joining together like a group about to be shown around Westminster Abbey or the Senate House. Bond almost expected Truman-Lodge to be carrying an umbrella to act as a sign for the party to follow. Also, for the first time he really had a look at the members of the party. There were at least one Korean and possibly a Burmese. The rest were Hong-Kongese. All the Orientals carried briefcases.

The guards appeared to be very alert, but stayed in the background as Truman-Lodge gathered the visitors around him.

"We started this place strictly as a cover," he began. "But Professor Joe, who you all know from his TV shows, has managed to do some really beneficial work here, and has turned a tidy profit. Now, these doors lead to our main laboratory area, and, before we go in, I'm going to have to ask you to wear face masks. There's a lot of dust from our product, and it floats around. I wouldn't want any of you good people developing a bad habit. Now, just step this way."

A white-coated and masked laboratory assistant appeared from a small door set in the big studded gates and began to pass out gauze masks which covered their mouths and noses. Bond, wary of unknown objects coming anywhere near his mouth or nose, carefully sniffed the gauze before deciding it was safe to strap it on and file, with the others, into the laboratory.

Once inside the door, they found themselves in a tunnel, illuminated only by blue lamps, behind small grilles set into the wall. As they walked, Bond could feel they were going down at a slight angle. Then the floor flattened out again and ahead a brilliant light began to flood into the tunnel. Quite suddenly, with more than a touch of drama, they had passed into the main laboratory area, finding themselves standing on a gantry which stretched around a massive hall, divided into sections by solid walls. From this walkway you could see the top of each wall, and what lay in each division. This, Bond decided, was more of a factory than a laboratory.

The hall was, as Truman-Lodge had suggested, full of white dust, the motes floating and filling the great shafts of light which came from high up in the roof above them.

Directly below, white-coated assistants, wearing dust-filter masks, loaded blocks of solid cocaine onto a conveyor belt which, in turn, carried them through a wall. From the gantry you could see that the greyish-white blocks were falling from the conveyor belt into a huge pulverising plant.

Truman-Lodge eased them along so that they stood directly over this giant pulveriser. An automatic filter made certain that none of the cocaine left the pulveriser until it had turned completely into a white powder. The powder was being drawn off the pulveriser, through a large vacuum tube that, Bond considered, probably contained other filters which, through the air pressure, ground the powder to an even finer consistency.

They walked on, through a door set in the gantry, for the next stage showed the powder being sucked through its pipe and dumped into a blending vat, full of a yellowish liquid, and this area of the walkway was enclosed in glass. The last section of this great factory was what appeared to be a kind of garage. Large gasoline tankers stood in line, and, in turn, they were being filled with the resulting mixture of cocaine and liquid.

"Our product," Truman-Lodge said, his mask producing an odd muffling effect, "dissolves completely in quite ordinary gasoline. This process makes the cocaine completely undetectable. You see, gentlemen, we ship our product to the United States in the reserve fuel tanks of this Institute's aircraft. We have six altogether. The tankers being filled now will be on their way to the International Airport this very afternoon, to refuel the aircraft which are, even as we speak, arriving from various destinations."

Bond leaned forwards. It was almost too simple, and he wanted to hear a great deal more. As he shifted his position something caught his eye across the gantry. Standing opposite them on the far side were Sanchez, Heller and the man Dario, whom he had last seen on the night he met Pam at the Barrelhead Saloon on the West Island of Bimini.

At that moment, Sanchez was saying they should walk over and meet the group. He turned ready to move, when Dario plucked at his arm.

"Who's the guy leaning forwards, patron?" he asked. "The one with the grey windcheater."

"Oh, *him.* He's someone who can, I believe, be very useful to us."

"I hope so." Dario's eyes darted back across the wide gap, towards Bond, then back to Sanchez. "I *do* sincerely hope so."

"Why?" Like a whip crack as Sanchez detected something was wrong.

"Because the last time I saw that bastard was in Bimini. That night we went after the Bouvier woman."

"He was with Bouvier?"

"Sure. You remember, patron, you told us to check on her contact and get rid of them. Well, he was the contact."

"And you didn't get rid of them, Dario. Perhaps you'd better be a stalking horse. Cut him off from the others, then we can finish him off in a very spectacular manner, eh?"

The three men began to move along the gantry, turning left to cross the width of the plant. Dario casually put one hand into his pocket and curled his hand around the butt of an HK4 automatic.

The farmer dropped Pam at the main gates of the Institute and she walked the few paces to the little guardhouse, hanging on to the briefcase, almost holding it in front of her.

The guard was a middle-aged man in a blue uniform who smiled politely and called her ma'am.

"I have a special surprise here for Professor Joe," she said, trying to sound winsome.

"I'm sorry, ma'am, but it's no visitors this week. The Professor and his people are on a private meditation retreat."

"Oh, my Lord," she gasped, a regular country girl. "And I've hitched and hiked and all the rest of it all the way from Idaho. Y'see, sir, the folks back home are real fans of Professor Joe. They took a collection . . . see." She slowly opened the briefcase to show her walking-about money won by Bond in the casino, all $250,000 of it. "They're going to be that disappointed. Chose me, in particular, to bring it, with instructions to put it into nobody else's hands except the dear Professor. They're sure going to be mor'n a mite peeved . . ." She broke off, for the guard was already on the telephone whispering.

Within three minutes, another pair of guards had arrived with "Strict instructions to take you straight to Professor Joe himself, ma'am."

"Oh, my goodness." Pam smoothed her skirt and tagged along with the guards, right up to the towering Temple and in through a small door which led to an unexpectedly large reception area. There was a long smooth reflecting pool, into which a waterfall appeared to cascade from midair. Even in her "golly-gosh" persona, Pam had to admit it looked pretty spectacular. She would like Q to figure out the trick of having a waterfall coming out of midair.

"Truly magnificent sight, isn't it? Rebuilt, stone for stone, from thousand-year-old plans. Now restored to all its original glory."

She knew the unctuous voice of Professor Joe. When she turned, almost into his outstretched arms, there he was restored, but, unlike the Temple, by a little skin-toning and a moisturiser, not to mention the very well made rug that rested, looking almost lifelike, on his head.

Professor Joe wore what seemed to be a designer robe: gold and white and gorgeous, tied at the waist with a rope belt. Pam thought she would look quite attractive in the robe. It would be a great talking point at dinner parties: if she ever got to any more dinner parties!

"Oh," she gasped. "Oh, Professor Joe, it's really you. Oh, my goodness." Pam hopped from foot to foot like a child.

"Is that the gift you've brought for me, child?" His little sharp eyes dropped towards the briefcase.

"Oh, golly, yes. I brought it all the way. Hitched and hiked and all . . . From Boise, Idaho." You just followed the yellow brick road, didn't you, Dor'thy? she thought to herself.

"From Boise, Idaho, eh? That's interesting. I once knew a man who hailed from there. Come, child. Bring it with you. I'll show you our Institute and you can tell me about the folks back home who have been so generous." He led her off at almost a canter, down passages, through richly ornamented rooms, to a door which he carefully opened with a key, hanging from a chain attached to the belt around his robe.

He swung open the door. "This is my humble sanctuary, away from the cares of the world."

"Oh, wow! Your own private meditation chamber!" She stepped inside the luxurious room, with its big bed and a ceiling made entirely of mirrors.

"Yes, child," Professor Joe purred. "Built from the sacred rocks of the original temple. I've had it completely soundproofed, so that nothing can disturb *our* personal meditation."

She saw his hand move behind his back, and heard the lock click as he turned the key.

— 15 —

Into the Jaws of Death

Q HAD DONE his homework before leaving London on the assignment given to him by M, but passed on discreetly as a request from Miss Moneypenny.

His last hours before going out to Heathrow Airport were spent in the basement of Headquarters, reading every extant file concerning Franz Sanchez. The most useful documents came from Nick Fallon's regular reports. Fallon had been the Secret Intelligence Service's man in Isthmus City for nearly four years. His title was that of British Consul, for there was no British Embassy in Isthmus. Consuls exist the world over, particularly in specialised areas of large countries, and they are often plain ordinary private citizens who do an exacting job for very little money.

For instance, the British Consul in Nice, on the Côte d'Azure, was for many years a retired businesswoman who had no office, but operated from her own apartment. Rarely did the SIS use such people, but in Isthmus they had no alternative, and Nick Fallon had done them proud, updating information sometimes daily, but usually weekly.

His file on Sanchez was thick, containing all known Isthmus politicians, members of the police force, together with security and intelligence agencies, who were known to be on the drug baron's payroll. In his daily undercover work, Fallon had only recently discovered a cadre of police officers who had been initially trained in the United States and were now attempting to break out from the stranglehold Sanchez had on their colleagues, not to mention President Lopez and many high-ranking politicians.

The leader of this small group was a Captain Simon Rojas, and Q managed to catch him at his home, half an hour after the last radio contact with Pam. There had been complete silence from the girl since she had okayed his information that the convoy and helicopter were heading towards the main highway. Over the last few days, Q had felt himself becoming more and more of an uncle figure to the girl, and his initial worry was turned quickly into action.

On the roadside, near where he had left his car,

was a public telephone. Heaven knew if it worked, but Q ran all the way back to it in the hopes it had neither been vandalised nor cut off from the primitive system operating in this part of Central America.

So far, luck was on his side. The instrument worked, though he had to dial the memorised number six times before Rojas himself answered. The police captain was wary until Q used the code word, *Cobalt,* through which Fallon had made contact on several occasions. *"Cobalt* was killed two nights ago by security forces." The captain took no chances.

"But I've seen the file in London," Q persisted, and only after he revealed several points which could only be known to someone with access to the *Cosmic* files in London, did Rojas believe him. In quick, terse, uncomplicated language, Q put the man in the picture.

"I'll get some trusted people on the roads now," Rojas told him. "Give me your exact position and I'll come out and pick you up, with some of my men. Stay under cover until you see a police helicopter."

As Rojas was giving these instructions to Q, Professor Joe was turning the key in the lock of his private meditation chamber.

Pam put the briefcase down, walked slowly over to the bed, sat down on the edge and crossed her legs provocatively, thinking that it was Q who had suggested she wear a skirt. "People looking for trouble rarely suspect a woman to take violent action when she's dressed in a skirt," he had said. "Don't know why. But that's what the Service trickcyclists tell us."

At the time, Pam had snorted, "Usual reasons, it's obvious. Male bloody chauvinism. Women are women and should be dressed like women. That's your answer, Uncle Q. Whatever changes appear to have taken place, the male will always, even if it is subconscious, think of the female as the little woman." Now she realised Q had been right. But so had she. It made no difference to her argument, but she was pleased to be able to use her sex.

"Guess what?" She smiled at the revolting Professor, gradually pulling her skirt back to reveal her thigh. Professor Joe could not believe his luck.

"What a pretty sight to set before a Professor." He just stood there, slavering, eyes bugging. "Can I see all the way?" His voice had gone very throaty.

"Of course you can, darling Professor Joe." Pam slid her skirt up as far as the holster on her thigh. "Okay, Prof, the key! Now! And keep quiet or I'll blow your balls off!"

His jaw dropped as he looked into the unwelcome end of her automatic.

"Just the key," Pam said, "and don't try any movie tricks like tossing it to me. Take it off the chain, put it on the floor and kick it, very gently, into my hand. Anything hard—and I don't mean that to be a joke, Professor—and I'll do as I promised. Okay?"

He nodded and did just as she told him. "Now we change places." She stood, moving to one side. "You come over here and sit down, with your hands on your head."

He did as he was told, very nervously. Pam felt there was nothing either gutsy or courageous about Professor Joe. With her back to the door she inserted the key, then drew it out again, operating the handle, still with the pistol trained at where the Professor had most to lose. Quickly she peeped out of the door and, to her horror, saw a number of white-robed men and women walking quietly in the central mosaic-tiled circle she had seen from the air.

"Who are the folks in the white robes?" she asked, the pistol moving forwards a fraction.

"They're here because they wish to be. Members of my flock, if you like." His voice was still hoarse. "Believe me." He sounded desperate. "Believe me, young lady. There is good as well as evil in this place. I promise these people come to study the ways of the old Olimpatec culture. They come to learn, and to study the Olimpatec religion. You might find it hard to believe, but they gain benefit from the old Indian meditations."

"I believe you." Pam was relieved now that she spotted a plain white robe hanging near the door. She took it from its peg and managed to get into it without allowing the gun to waver.

"You look . . . " the Professor began.

"Like a girl in a white robe . . . " she supplied.

"I was going to say, 'You look like an angel.'"

"Oh, shucks, Professor, you're a real flatterer." She batted her eyelids, then said sharply, "You move from that bed; you bang on the door; you do anything, and I swear I'll finish what I promised."

Professor Joe gave a shrug. "What good would it do? This room really is soundproof. Nobody's going to hear."

"Good. Have a nice day, Prof." Pam was quickly out of the door, locking it from the outside and then walking slowly away, the pistol tucked into the sleeve of her robe, and her eyes downcast.

At the same moment, things were happening inside the so-called laboratory. Truman-Lodge had just completed his speech telling the assembled Oriental businessmen that the product would leave, mixed with gasoline, in the reserve fuel tanks of the Institute's aircraft. The tankers were now ready and waiting to go.

The Korean delegate coughed, raising a hand. "Ah, please to tell," he began. "How you get product back from gasoline?"

"Hey, you want us to give away all our secrets before we become full partners?" Sanchez had come up behind the group. He sounded full of good humour. "Okay, take them into room three, William." He waved to a door leading just off the gantry.

Bond had already seen Dario, but Sanchez's henchman was very close. 007 adjusted his mask high over his nose and tried to keep well away from

Dario, Sanchez and Heller, who had now joined the group.

"That's our chief chemist's laboratory," Sanchez said. "He there, William?"

"He's here, chief," Truman-Lodge called back from inside the room.

"Come on then, everyone. Let's get a good look at this." Sanchez began to shepherd the group into the room, which was a more conventional laboratory. A short man dressed in a white coat and the ubiquitous face mask worked behind a large array of glass retorts, beakers, flasks, funnels and tubing. It was an impressive setup, and from what Bond could see of the chief chemist's eyes and stance, he was an intense little man. Behind him, on a bench at the far end of the laboratory, a tall complex of retorts bubbled, sending liquid through glass tubes and filters. A couple of Bunsen burners provided heat. This was obviously some very advanced experiment.

"We've told you *what* we do," Sanchez said loudly. "We'll demonstrate exactly *how* we do it once the deal's completed, okay?"

Truman-Lodge raised his voice to make sure everyone heard him. "I must remind you again, gentlemen, that the terms of the deal were one hundred million, in negotiable bearer bonds."

The Oriental group began to mutter and look at one another. To his concern, Bond realised that Dario seemed to have disappeared. Then the Korean, taking the first decisive step, slapped his briefcase onto one of the tables, opened it and held his bonds towards Truman-Lodge. Quickly the others followed suit.

"Righ', now you tell process?" the Korean asked politely.

Truman-Lodge nodded to the chief chemist, who began to speak as though he had discovered the true nature of the universe. "It's elegant and simple." He held up a large glass beaker three-quarters full of the mixture from the vat on the factory floor, below them. "The ideal combination is eighteen percent cocaine or pure heroin dissolved in eighty-two percent gasoline." He took a second beaker, half-full. "Ammonium hydroxide." The chief chemist poured the second beaker's contents into the first. Immediately they saw the cocaine begin to re-form and precipitate on top of the gasoline. The chief chemist then recovered the powder by a simple filtering through a prepared funnel.

The group applauded, beginning to buzz with talk, and at that moment, Bond felt the muzzle of a pistol pushed hard against his side. "Just keep very quiet, and do as I say, gringo." Sanchez's henchman, Dario, smelled of garlic and oil. He patted Bond down, checking for weapons, still whispering. "We take care of you later. You wouldn't wish to cause trouble here."

Truman-Lodge had started to speak again. "Those five tanker trucks you saw in the filling bay contain your first shipment. Twenty tons of it."

Bond stood quite still, convinced that the laboratory display was not yet over. His chance might still come.

Truman-Lodge droned on, "Your monthly delivery will be by oceangoing tanker. But we'll use the airplanes from time to time. Especially when you require quick deliveries, like this first batch. I shall personally make certain that our chief chemist, here, will always be at hand at your end if you have problems with the reconversion."

Sanchez now moved up towards the chief chemist. They were only a couple of steps from Bond.

Sanchez smiled, looking at the group. Bond noticed the man was exceptionally sure of himself. Like a good actor taking applause, his eyes roved around the buyers, making contact with each in turn so that, as individuals, they had the impression that he was speaking to them personally. "And you get to keep the gas as a bonus," he said with a laugh. Then he held up a warning finger. "Also, if there's ever any problem with customs . . . " Sanchez took the gasoline-filled beaker from the chief chemist, placed it in the middle of the table, lit a match and dropped it into the beaker. There was a small *whoomp,* and the gasoline ignited inside the beaker. Another smile from Sanchez. "No evidence!"

The little bit of drama at the end of the demonstration pleased the buyers, who all reacted, giggling and applauding, as the flame shot out of the beaker.

The moment had come. Bond shifted his right

leg, bringing the instep of his shoe down Dario's shin, and crushing onto the man's foot. His arm came up, the elbow smashing the bridge of the hoodlum's nose, chopping down on his wrist, so that the gun fell to the floor.

Again, Bond turned, his hand grasping the burning beaker, which he threw hard at the bubbling retorts and complex of tubes at the far end of the laboratory. The largest retort shattered, and flame exploded into the room as though someone had released a grenade.

With luck, Bond thought, it could develop into a nice cheery fire. Even the whole place could be destroyed.

The group of Orientals were in panic, pushing at each other as they made for the door. Bond saw Truman-Lodge grab at the bearer bonds, throwing them into his empty briefcase, then joining in the rush from the flames, which were now covering the far wall.

Sanchez was yelling orders and, in the next moment, Bond felt arms around him. Dario and the big German, Braun, had him in an armlock, marching him out of the blazing room. As they pulled him out, he saw the chief chemist go down, his spotless white coat blazing.

They hustled Bond onto the gantry, pushing him to the right.

"Get him down to Section One!" Sanchez shouted as Heller came rattling up one of the many metal staircases, followed by men with fire-fighting gear.

"Okay! You come quietly," Dario said. His nose was bleeding, but he had the pistol back in his hand. *"Nobody* does this to me. I'm sure El Jefe, the patron, has something interesting in mind for you."

There was no point in trying to struggle. Bond had won with the fire, but failed to get clear. He knew that Sanchez was unlikely to show any mercy now.

The henchmen dragged him down the steps and Bond realised that Section One contained the conveyor belt leading to the pulveriser. On the factory floor, the area seemed much larger than it had from the gantry. There were also many more exits and entrances than Bond had realised.

Sanchez had beaten them to it. Now he stood by the conveyor belt, which was loaded with blocks of cocaine, moving inexorably down towards the great mashing steel teeth of the machine which literally chewed the cocaine before sharp whirling blades, like a giant kitchen mixer, sliced the raw product into powder.

Sanchez waited until they frog-marched Bond to within a pace from him. "Oh, you have disappointed me, my British agent." His eyes were cold as an iceberg. "You want to tell me who you're really working for?"

Bond stood his ground, saying nothing. From above, Heller's voice could be heard shouting instructions to the fire fighters—"In here! Quickly, if this spreads . . . !" The shouts were cut off by a massive explosion from the laboratory. Even here, in Section One, they could feel the heat as a huge fireball ran the breadth of the building. There were cries as two of the fire fighters were thrown from the gantry, their clothes blazing. They hit the mixing vat a second later and a mushroom cloud of smoke and flame rose in the worst explosion yet.

Sanchez seemed oblivious to the destruction. His arm moved quickly and he backhanded Bond across the face. "You don't want to talk. No matter, Mr. Bond." He nodded to Dario, who limped across to a small door in the wall, level with the conveyor belt. Beside the door was a boxed-in knife-switch which Dario operated. The conveyor belt stopped moving.

Arms lifted Bond and dumped him onto the conveyor belt. He looked down. Once the thing began to move again he would quickly be hemmed in by the metal walls which held the cocaine in place as it was propelled downwards towards the metal teeth and whirling blades. The long ride down the belt looked like a bobsleigh run, he thought. The name of a book came into his head: *Slay Ride:* a good title for this.

Heller came panting down the gantry steps shouting at Sanchez, "I got the loaded tankers out in time. They're waiting on the road. Franz, I don't think we're going to save this place!"

Sanchez gave a shrug of indifference. "Forget the

fire," he spoke with a terrifying coldness. "Just forget it. Bring the cars onto the road, we'll leave with the tankers." Then, almost as an afterthought, "If there's time you can bring the buses around for Professor Joe's people. But make sure we're safe first." Heller nodded and quickly left.

The two henchmen still held Bond on the conveyor belt. Neither of them would move until Sanchez gave the order.

"This place cost ten million bucks. We've *got* to save it!"

Sanchez turned and rasped out, "Do as I say! This was good cover for a long time. Now it's over." He pointed to Truman-Lodge's briefcase. "We've got *five hundred million in there,* so why gripe? There're also twenty tons of Colombian pure, mixed with the gas in those trucks, so who needs this?"

"But the deal with the Chinese?"

"Since when did you get moral about deals, William? We got their money, didn't we? Just go and help Heller. Get the place cleared out, get the cars ready."

Lying on the conveyor belt, Bond caught sight of Heller again. A long way off now, and out of Sanchez's vision, for he headed towards a main exit across the room, behind Sanchez's back. The colonel, unnoticed by anyone in the chaos, was driving a forklift truck. On it were four unmistakable shapes. He had been right: they were not Stingers, or even Blowpipes. These little missiles were more

the size of the old, now outmoded—and unstable
—Redeyes. Even from where he lay, Bond could
see there were differences: more streamlining, neat-
er hand-packs. They looked like prototypes of
something brand-new. Small had become beautiful
on the present-day electronic battlefield, and these
missiles would almost certainly be activated and
guided by the new generation of microchip technology. To Bond their size had little to do with things.
The quartet of missiles looked dangerous as they
lay on the forklift, the sharp metal points of the
forks sticking out from their deadly cargo.

Bond detected the anxiety flowing from Dario
and Braun, who still held him down, hard, seem-
ingly oblivious to the raging fire, smoke or people
coming and going in panic. Then Sanchez bent
closer. "You want to do this the hard way, or the
easy way, Bond? You see I've still got a very large
business to run, so I have to know who you've been
working for. Understand?"

Bond took a deep breath and told Sanchez that
he was the least of the drug baron's problems. "If
you couldn't trust your old buddy Krest, who can
you trust, Franz? Truman-Lodge has gone off with
all that money in his case. He going to give that
back to you? And what of the missiles? Who's in
charge of those? Your precious Colonel Heller? He
could use them on you with ease. Did you know
he already almost sold you out to the Bouvier
girl?"

"What do you know about the missiles?" For the
first time, doubt clouded into Sanchez's eyes.

Smoke began to eddy into Section One as one of the other henchmen, Perez, came coughing through the door.

"Patron, we gotta go soon. This whole place's gonna blow." There were tears streaming from his eyes, and the smoke was getting thicker.

"Where's Heller?" Sanchez snapped back at him.

"He went to get the missiles, patron. We didn't want them near the fire."

"That's the last you'll see of the gallant colonel," Bond said loudly.

"Find Heller. Don't let him out of your sight! Get him, you understand?" Perez was out of sight before Sanchez had completed his orders.

"Thank you, Mr. Bond, for your advice." Sanchez's arm came up, a closed fist crashing into Bond's jaw as he moved away.

Bond saw the raised fist, felt a flash of pain, then the grey clouds of half-consciousness. Through the fog and mist he realised that he was moving, and a voice somewhere in the back of his head was telling him to do something: to rouse himself. His mind sent out orders to his limbs, but they refused all commands. The voice became louder and louder, more urgent, and with a massive effort, Bond began scrabbling with his legs, and the movement helped clear the grey film that surrounded him.

He looked down to see that he was being relentlessly carried along the chute leading to the pulveriser. There were three blocks of cocaine ahead of him, and he rammed his feet down in the nearest block in an attempt to give him purchase.

The block held for a second, and he was able to make a grab at the steel guiding wall on the right of the belt. His hands slipped and burned as he clung on, using every ounce of strength to pull himself to the top of the wall. He managed to slow down the movement, but his hands still slipped, and his body still moved. Inch by inch he saw the block of cocaine on which his feet rested being drawn closer and closer to the gnashing steel teeth of the pulveriser.

Then, with a final effort he hauled himself upwards, so that his shoulders now rested on the metal wall. But he was still slipping. He pulled again, then saw a movement, by the door, near the knife-switch that operated the conveyor belt. Smoke and flame seemed to be close and the figure took on a strange, almost warped shape. It was coming towards him, and, in another moment, Dario stood close to the wall of the conveyor belt.

"I came to make sure. I'm glad I am not too late," he hissed, climbing up so that his paunchy stomach pressed onto Bond's slipping hands. Above him, Bond saw Dario's arm raised, and the long knife in the man's right hand flashing, reflecting the flames.

"You're a dead man, Bond!" The knife began to descend. Bond tensed, waiting for the pain that would send him to oblivion and the steadily chewing jaws of death, already chomping down on the block of cocaine under his feet.

— 16 —

Goodbye, James Bond

"YOU'RE A DEAD man, Bond!" As Dario yelled, something else completed the words like a violent exclamation mark. The hand remained poised for the strike, but Dario's eyes widened with shock.

It took a second for Bond to realise that the exclamation mark was a shot. Then someone spoke, and the voice seemed to come from far away.

"You took the words right out of my mouth," the voice said, and Bond could not believe his ears.

Dario's hand opened and the knife clattered down the chute and through the crunching teeth. There was not much blood, just a little around the man's right shoulder, and as he pitched forwards he was still very much alive, if not in control. He made one terrifying sound, half-scream, half-cry for help as he went straight down and into the steel teeth of the pulveriser.

The scream hung on the air like some bad odour. Bond looked down, still clinging to the side of the chute. The powdered cocaine had turned from white to red. He blinked twice, not believing what he saw by the door, a vision in a long billowing white robe with a gun in her hand. For a fraction in time he wondered if he was indeed dead. Then the woman in white stretched out to her right, closing the knife-switch to Off, and the conveyor belt ground to a stop.

"You're an angel, Pam," Bond said quietly as he came towards her, still a little unsteady. "You're an absolute angel."

"Somebody else told me that, quite recently." She grinned at him. Then, nodding at the machinery, asked, "Did I . . .?"

"Let's say you chewed him out." Bond went back and looked over the side of the metal, once more thinking that the conveyor belt looked like a bobsleigh run. *Slay Ride,* he said to himself, must tell Sanchez. "Sanchez?" he said aloud as he walked back to Pam.

"You okay, James?"

"Will be in a minute. But what about Sanchez?"

"Well, your uncle arrived with the local law . . ."

"And they got him?"

"I don't think so. Not yet. They're in the Institute parking lot, dealing with Professor Joe's disciples."

"They didn't stop the convoy? The tankers?"

"What tankers?"

Bond was already moving towards the door. "There're five tankers and all Sanchez's people, heading away from here. I suspect towards the airport. You mean, the police didn't . . . ?" He saw the look on Pam's face and knew the answer. "You got transport?"

"Only the little crop duster."

"Let's go, then . . ."

"James, you've done enough. Let the police handle this."

"Oh, no!" He was up and running. "I want Sanchez for myself. Come on." He passed through the door, dragging at Pam, who was hampered by the robe, and just as they got through the exit, an explosion caved in the factory roof.

They went back the way Pam had come, down wide corridors and walled mazes. Behind them the heat and smoke became worse, and occasionally they passed people in the white Olimpatec robes, running in panic.

Just before they reached the final exit they turned sharp right. Pam stopped in a skid, hand to her mouth, eyes wide with fright. A forklift truck stood facing a brick wall, its sharp jutting forks skewering into a body crushed against the wall. It was Heller.

"My God, what . . . ?" Pam began.

"Looks like he came to a dead end." Bond knew two things. First, his bluff with Sanchez had worked; second, that Sanchez had the missiles and would undoubtedly use them if any problem arose. It made action against the tanker convoy even more hazardous. "Where's the plane?" he asked.

"A mile, mile and a half away."

"We have to get transport before that." People were still running about, there were cries of panic everywhere, white robes flapped and, behind, the awesome sound of fire increased as though someone had turned up a volume control.

Around the next corner they found themselves at an archway, and outside the Temple; the great red-blocked walls seemed to rear up above them. It had to be a side entrance, for Bond could only see dusty dry grass, with the trees some four hundred yards away. Near the archway stood a little electric golf cart. "There," he shouted, but Pam beat him to the driving seat, starting the motor. "I only hope this is fully charged. I always . . . " They were moving and she stopped speaking suddenly, slewing the steering wheel over the dry ground, sending up a spray of dust.

All Bond saw was a figure in white and gold robes, panting along at a steady trot. "You're going to take that gut out, Pam. Careful . . . " The cart hit the figure sideways on, throwing him into the dust, and Bond was aware of Pam reaching down and pulling a briefcase into the cart. "Good luck, Professor Joe!" she yelled as they moved off, her foot down hard on the accelerator so that they must have been doing almost twenty-five miles an hour.

"What the hell's that?" Bond shouted, making a grab for the briefcase.

"What d'you think it is? Money, of course. I lent it to the Prof."

"What money?"

"The walking-around money from the casino. The cheque was made out to me, remember?"

Bond smiled. "We'll talk about it later," he said. "Just put your foot down!"

"What d'you think I'm doing? Both my feet are *through* the floor."

"Look at her go!" Bond raised his voice in what sounded like a yell of triumph, though he knew triumph had yet to be earned.

Captain Rojas had been very efficient, arriving with two helicopters within twenty minutes of Q's call. "My people are shadowing Sanchez and his party. He has Orientals with him, Chinese, yes?"

Q nodded. "Chinese, Koreans, you name it, he has them. The major drug dealers of the Orient."

"Then I think they will be heading to the so-called Olimpatec Meditation Institute. The locals call it the Temple. My own colleagues have suspected the place for some time, but nobody has ever been there. It is difficult to take action like that when the really big brass are on the take, you understand?"

"Only too well." Q was itching to get going, for

he really was very worried about James and Pam now.

"It is sensible first to make a small detour." Rojas was a man who knew exactly what to do, and Q could see there was no way he could be deflected from whatever he had decided. "So first, back to the helicopters. We're going to do a little mopping up at the Sanchez estate. If the big man is away, there will not be many of the criminal element there."

As the police chopper moved away, Q shouted at the captain that they should at least take Sanchez's mistress with them.

"The Lamora woman?" Rojas sneered. "Why bother with her? Her kind are two a penny."

"I think not," Q howled in his ear, telling him of the way she had shielded Bond from suspicion, and even come to the hotel that morning, putting herself at risk.

Rojas' attitude changed slightly. "We'll see. You realise this is probably the only chance I'll ever get to deal with Franz Sanchez and his people. Even if we get them all, I cannot vouch for any fair trial. Or any trial at all, come to that. Maybe it would be best if we just did away with them. We'll see."

There were only seven people left at Sanchez's estate. Two gardeners, three chefs, one bodyguard and Lupe. The bodyguard made no fuss. The others seemed quite pleased to see the police doing their job properly. Lupe insisted on being taken with them. She was so insistent that even Rojas could not persuade her to stay. Oddly she also made considerable fuss about taking Sanchez's iguana with them. "Me? I don't like the beast." She gave a prima donna performance, both voice and gestures in a high key. "But I want it to be there to see Sanchez's end."

When the two helicopters arrived over the Temple, the chaos was already mounting. They landed near the main entrance where Rojas' other police had closed off the exit road with cars. Smoke and flame were rising from the rear of the building, but the police were busy checking queues of white-robed disciples. Buses belonging to the Institute were lined up, and the disciples had been sorted out, while the police helped them on board.

"They look like some big choir, eh?" Rojas said. "We'll interrogate them later."

Q was more concerned about Bond and Pam. "Find them and you'll find Sanchez I'll be bound," he said, suddenly pointing towards one of the buses. "Better take a look at that little lot." He was pointing to a group of Orientals whose robes seemed to fit badly; some of them were swamped by the garments, others completely overwhelmed by them.

Rojas strode over to the bus, unholstering his pistol. "Okay, you people." They stopped, looking for a way of escape and, when finding none, slowly raised their hands. "You ready to sing, boys?" Rojas asked with a chuckle.

The Oriental drug dealers were handcuffed and

removed from the bus, then Rojas turned to Q. "I've instructed my men to get into the Temple and look for Sanchez and your people." He clasped Q's shoulder. "However, my friend, I have told them they must take no risks. To me it looks as though this building's done for. It'll take over an hour to get the fire department out here, and by that time . . . well."

Sanchez, his remaining lieutenants and the tankers were by this time long gone. As were James Bond and Pamela Bouvier.

It took them twenty minutes to reach the crop duster, and another fifteen, once airborne, to spot Sanchez. Bond was crammed in behind Pam, his legs resting on her shoulders, and his body crouched, head down just below the cockpit dome.

Bond had done the navigating, taking a chance on Sanchez and his convoy not going by any direct route. He had been right. From nearly two thousand feet they plainly saw Sanchez's car first, just beginning to climb through the foothills.

The road looked perilously narrow, and higher, when it reached the mountains; it snaked and climbed upwards, doubling back on itself, so that, at times, one part of the road twisted directly above another section. The convoy of tankers, led by the jeep, was spread out over two miles of roadway, the jeep about a mile ahead of the first tanker. Sanchez's car and the pickup followed, far behind.

"Keep well above Sanchez's car," Bond shouted.

"I'm opening the canopy and I want you to put me slap on top of the last tanker in line."

Pam nodded, concentrating on flying. They passed over the limousine. Bond slid the canopy back, and with a struggle, climbed out of the cockpit. The wind was so strong that his extra weight slewed the aircraft, making Pam readjust constantly by kicking the rudder bar, while it took Bond all his skill and concentration to stay on the wing.

Gently he grabbed the foothold in the fuselage below the cockpit, and, by stages, climbed down through the wing struts until he reached the undercarriage.

During the whole procedure the wind forced his body back, so that the least mistake, one wrong move, and his body would be thrown from the plane like a piece of torn paper.

Pam had started to descend, and Bond could see the big tanker ahead of him, getting larger with every second. He tucked his legs around the strut between the wheels of the undercarriage, waiting for Pam to level off, match her speed with that of the tanker and drop to within inches of the curved top.

The noise of the wind, and that of the tanker below, pounding over the primitive road, was almost unbearable. Dust flew up into Bond's face so that he could hardly see what he was doing. Then, quite suddenly, everything changed for a tiny moment. The airplane seemed to float motionless over

the tanker, and the wind dropped. He was within
feet of the curved metal container. He dropped,
scrabbling for a second on the slippery surface,
then hanging on as he adjusted to the new mode of
transport, the tanker bumping and jolting over the
road's bad surface.

The crop duster lifted and climbed away, leaving
him with only the smooth metal and juddering
tanker. Slowly Bond inched his way along the top of
the tank, heading precariously towards the cab—
the four-wheel detachable prime mover unit—
which seemed to be bounding over the road with
ease, almost oblivious to the heavy load it pulled.

As he reached the end of the tank, Bond looked
down into the space between it and the cab. He
could clearly see the couplings and hydraulic tubes
passing between the tank and the big prime mover
unit. Just as he was about to attempt the jump into
the small area between the two parts of the vehicle,
he heard the bullets whining and chipping around
his head.

He looked back over the long tank and saw that
Sanchez's car was coming up fast behind them. He
thought he could see Sanchez's chauffeur at the
wheel and Truman-Lodge in the back. He could
certainly see Sanchez himself, for the man was
leaning out of the front passenger window, firing an
Uzi.

Bond had no time to hesitate now. He dropped,
and with a jarring crash found himself clinging on

to part of the cab, his legs dangling, feet only inches from the road.

The fall winded him, and he hung on tightly until he had control of his breathing, then began to pull himself up among the couplings and tubes. The prime mover hit several potholes in the road and, three times, Bond was in danger of being hurled to his death under the wheels.

It seemed to take an eternity to drag himself to the passenger side, and at first his brain refused to work out the moves that would carry him to the door of the cab. He could afford no delay. Already Sanchez's car must be getting very close.

Then order returned to his mind. In four carefully judged movements, Bond swung from behind the cab to the passenger side, reaching for the door handle and conscious of bullets thwacking into the door under his arm as he pulled it open and swung into the cab.

The driver turned towards him with a shriek of rage, as though he was an animal who must at all costs protect his territory. As Bond turned slightly to pull the door closed, the driver lunged out and downwards with his right hand, drawing a lethal-looking machete from a scabbard under the dash. His arm came up, then down in a heavy blow, the machete aimed straight at Bond's head.

Bond's arm instinctively came up and blocked the blow. Out of the corner of his eye he saw the prime mover's fire extinguisher clipped in front of him. His hand moved like a striking snake, and before the driver had a chance to aim a second blow, Bond banged down on the plunger, spraying the man's face with foam.

With a cry, the driver dropped the machete and let go of the wheel, blinded by the foam. Bond caught hold of the wheel, leaning over the driver, who was screaming in a mixture of pain, fear and frustration. As he took the wheel, Bond glimpsed Sanchez's car in the big wing mirror, coming up on their left-hand side, almost level with the cab. In a reflex action, his hand went right across the driver, pulled down on the door handle, unclipped the man's safety harness, and with a final burst of strength, pushed the driver from the vehicle.

The body stayed half in and half out of the cab, so he finally had to lift a foot and kick the man out into space. He went with much screaming, and above the noise of both man and engine, Bond heard the nasty thump as the driver landed smack in the middle of the pursuing car's bonnet.

By the time Bond had got into the driver's seat, and hauled the heavy vehicle back onto course, the car was overtaking him. He saw the tanker driver's body being thrown from the bonnet by a swerve, then ducked as Sanchez emptied an entire clip of bullets into the cab. The machine kept going. In front of him, Bond saw the next tanker, and Sanchez's car, at full power, riding alongside to overtake it.

There was some panic and fury in Sanchez' car.

Truman-Lodge was reading from a map, breathlessly giving map references to Sanchez, while Sanchez himself was operating the window, in order to shout instructions. As they came alongside the tanker, Sanchez, half leaning out of the car, ordered his chauffeur to get the tanker driver's attention, which he did by a perpetual honking of the horn.

"That mad gringo stole the tanker behind you," Sanchez roared above the noise. "Don't let him pass you. If you do . . . " He drew his hand over his throat in a gesture that left no doubts. The tanker driver nodded, allowing Sanchez's car to surge ahead.

As it did so, Sanchez prepared for Bond's final destruction. Grabbing a walkie-talkie, tuned to the frequency of a similar device in the jeep ahead of the convoy, he gave fast instructions. "Perez! Listen to me. Do you read? Over."

In the jeep, which had been making steady, contented progress until now, Perez pressed the button on his walkie-talkie. "I read, strength five. Over."

"Bond has escaped," Sanchez told him, gesticulating to urge his own driver on. "Wait for us at Demon's Cross. You'll have the honour of finishing him once and for all."

In the jeep, Perez smiled and passed the news on to the three heavily built thugs who rode with him.

Just over seven minutes later, Sanchez reached that part of the road which climbed in a series of loops and S-bends, up the most treacherous part of the mountain pass. Perez waited there, the men with him each carrying an Uzi at the ready.

Sanchez gave quick orders to his driver, who went to the rear of the car and opened the boot. In it, Sanchez had stored the four missiles Dario had taken from Heller after skewering him to the wall with the forklift.

"If this doesn't stop him, nothing will." Sanchez showed Perez how to aim and fire the missile. "Easy as shooting fish in a barrel," he said.

"And this is one fish that will not escape, patron. That I promise you." Perez was confident that he could use the missile with no problem. Once the thing was switched on and sighted, all you had to do was press the trigger.

Truman-Lodge was less happy. "Each of these tankers is worth forty million bucks, chief . . . " he began.

"Then that's a cheap price to pay for us to be rid of this bastard. I worry about him. He's the kind that doesn't give up until he's dead."

"In a few minutes he'll give up, patron." Perez leaned the missile against the jeep's bonnet and pointed it directly up the road, as Sanchez and Truman-Lodge returned to their car, the chauffeur gunning the engine in a racing start, leaving a cloud of dust and the smell of rubber in their wake.

Bond was fighting it out with the other tanker. The first time he had tried to pass, a country bus, loaded with people inside and crates of chickens and assorted livestock on top, had almost ploughed straight into him, head-on.

At the second attempt, the tanker swerved violently, cutting off Bond so that he had to brake hard. But at the third attempt, Bond brought his vehicle almost abreast of the other rig's cab, before yanking at the wheel. The two great road monsters crunched together, showering sparks as they hit, parted and then hit again. At each hit, Bond brought his juggernaut a little further ahead. Finally the other rig was forced to give way, sliding onto the verge as Bond lumbered past him.

The second tanker driver shouted into his walkie-talkie, hoping someone would pick up his calls of distress. "He's passed me! The gringo's ahead!"

Hearing it, a mile further on, Perez pushed on the transmit button. "Don't worry," he almost whispered. "This one won't trouble you any further."

The driver of the tanker that had just been overtaken was not convinced. He had racing instincts and was on the road again, right behind Bond, drawing out to pass him. The loᴦ ʰard bend ahead came nearer. Now there was another distraction, for the crop duster had caught up with them. Pam flew almost level with the tankers, giving the aircraft little bursts of speed as she came up on Bond's wing. For a moment Bond's concentration went and the other tanker, with a burst of speed, came up and passed him.

Bond pulled out, determined to overtake the other rig again. The long bend came up, and both Bond and the other driver saw the immediate dangers. There was a steep drop off the left side of the road. The lead driver began to brake as he went into the turn, and Bond put his foot down, coming abreast of him once more just as they rolled out of the turn and saw, three hundred yards ahead, a jeep at an angle across the road.

Through the sights of the missile, Perez saw two targets, then only one as Bond's tanker passed and moved ahead of the other.

In the cab, Bond glanced over to Pam's airplane and saw her gesticulating violently. He could not understand what was wrong, looking from her to the road ahead. Only then did he see a figure crouched behind the jeep. A picture of the small missiles sprang into his head.

The tanker was right in the sights now. "Goodbye, James Bond!" Perez whispered as he squeezed the trigger.

— 17 —

Man of Fire

A WHOLE SERIES of images went through Bond's mind in that split second. He heard Pam first telling him about the attempted deal with Heller over the missiles, and the colonel's final rejection of the plan; his sight of Heller with the deadly things on the forklift truck; then Heller stapled to the wall in the Temple, the missiles gone . . .

Missile gone . . . ! Missile gone . . . ! He saw the flash just as the full horror imprinted itself on his mind.

Bond wrenched the wheel over and felt the tanker hit a large mound on the verge. One moment he was travelling in a straight line, the next the whole vehicle was rolling over, two of the cab's wheels still holding the road, the other two angled high in the air, pulling the tanker with it so that the entire rig was tilted to one side.

Later, he swore that he actually heard the thing pass underneath the cab and the tanker, but in his heart he knew this might be an exaggeration, and that he only thought he heard it. It mattered little because that was what happened. For some obscure reason—the Pentagon never would provide the full facts—these hand-held missiles had no target-lock, nor were they heat-seeking. The big dart-shaped projectile just followed the track on which Perez had set it as he squeezed the trigger. It shot under the cab and tank, scorching the road in its fiery wake, and hit the following tanker head-on.

Bond *did* feel the heat in his cab. There was no doubt about that. Behind him the other tanker simply turned into molten metal and a great fireball from the explosives and the cocaine-spiked gasoline. Even Pam's crop duster was lifted on the thermal produced by the explosion.

For Bond it did not end there. He was desperately trying to control his rig, which still travelled, tilted to one side. The jeep lay in his path and he gave the wheel a slight touch, accompanied by a short jab at the brakes. Perez leaped clear and the other three men flung themselves to one side. With a merciless grinding sound the entire tanker rig righted itself—on top of the jeep.

It had been slowed to almost a crawl, which gave Perez and the other three their last opportunity.

Uzis performed a choral chattering requiem and Bond felt the bullets hitting the metal, then three of the tanker's tyres. They blew one after another, the tanker itself going out of control.

The rig swung violently across the road, swerving first one way and then the next. To Bond it was like being on some demoniac roller-coaster ride. The road tilted and the tyres squealed, and his stomach turned over. Maybe it was reaction following the missile shot. Bond knew he would have to stop. This hunk of metal just would not go on with three of the tanker's tyres blown out. Any moment it would jackknife, and with the road twisting and turning, beginning a downward sweep, he just could not hold it.

Bond braked, glancing in the mirror to see the four men begin moving as though to chase after him. There was one chance in a million: try to blow this tanker in their faces. He braked again and drew the rig onto the side of the road, where the verge ended in a steep drop.

His hand was on the door lever when he saw something else in the long mirror. Way behind the men was the silhouette of the crop duster, edging down, lower and lower, like a fighter plane about to machine-gun a road: which, in a manner, Pam was about to do.

As the crop duster came in over the group's heads, she fired off another canister of chemical spray, dumping what must have been a nauseating cloud on the entire group. All four dropped their weapons, and went down, clutching their faces and rolling around in pain as though they had received a truckload of Mace full on the face.

Silently Bond thanked her for good common sense. He was out of the cab by now, groping underneath and uncoupling the tanker. He went to the edge of the road and looked down. Below him the road corkscrewed in a series of S-bends as it wound down the far side of the mountains.

The other tankers would only be a short distance in front of him; in fact, he could see the lead rig already approaching the road below. He ran back to the cab, turned on the engine, slammed the cab into reverse and started to back up, gently pushing the tanker towards the edge of the cliff, which was the road's verge. One final touch on the accelerator and he heard the grind and crunch as the tanker went over. Banging the cab into neutral and cutting the engine, Bond was out and looking over the edge again.

Below he saw the first two tankers pass harmlessly, but his tank was falling, hitting an outcrop of rock, turning like a rogue satellite coming out of orbit, before plummeting down, smack onto the third tanker in line.

The reaction was even worse than the missile hit. The two big cylinders, full of gasoline, made a spectacular fireball which shot outwards and upwards, so high that Bond had to step back to avoid being singed.

"Three down," he said. "Two to go." He ran back

to the cab and went screaming off in pursuit of the last two tankers and the revenge, which he now knew he would achieve.

Below, on the flaming road, it looked like a battlefield. Sanchez's car had pulled up just in time and he was still feeling a little unsteady at the near miss. Beyond the fire he could see that the first two tankers had stopped as though awaiting instructions.

"Okay. We'll ride in the other two. Have to go around this." Sanchez was taut with frustration and something he had never felt before, so could not recognise—fear.

Truman-Lodge had a tight hold on the briefcase, and Sanchez, holding the Uzi, ordered the chauffeur to get the three remaining missiles from the boot. As the man went to carry out the order, Truman-Lodge gave an officious grunt. "Well, you've certainly messed this up, Franz. Another eighty-million write-off."

In his current humour, it was the last straw. Sanchez turned on his Wall Street wizard. His eyes turned into tiny slits filled with lapis lazuli. "Then I'd best start cutting down on overheads," he said. He only pulled the trigger twice to cut away the best part of Truman-Lodge's chest.

The driver acted as though nothing had happened, for he was a man who had seen much worse than this, having fought for one side or another in all the trouble spots of Central America. "Got the missiles, boss."

Sanchez walked over to the body of Truman-Lodge and prized the briefcase from his hand. He noticed that the young man hung on to it even in death. When he dragged it clear, Sanchez wiped the blood off with some earth, muttering something about this having been an expensive case—"Oxblood Gucci."

He signalled to the driver and they skirted the fire and walked quickly towards the two last waiting tankers.

Sanchez nodded at the driver of the lead rig. "Missiles in your cab," he said, then turned to his chauffeur, "You go in the second one, and take the Uzi with you."

The chauffeur did as he was told, checking the Uzi as he climbed into the second cab and waited until his chief, holding on to the briefcase, had settled himself into the first tanker's cab.

They slowly moved out.

Above them the pickup truck, being driven by Braun as the rear guard of the convoy, came to a halt, after having gone straight through the debris and flames that littered the road. He had been going at speed and only braked when he saw Perez and his men trying to get themselves together, wiping their eyes and coughing.

The pickup stopped right by Perez. The two men merely looked at each other, their faces heavy with anger. The three other men, who had been under Perez's command, did not look at anyone. Braun gunned the engine and they went hurtling down the road. They were not far behind Bond, who got his first glimpse of the pickup as he approached the wreckage and pool of fire across the road. There was no time to stop. Bond slewed the wheel to avoid Sanchez's car, then went straight through the fire, putting his foot down. He could just make out the two tankers ahead as they came to straighter roads and the terrain began to flatten out.

The two tankers were taking it easy, doing a steady sixty-five. Soon they would reach towns and villages, before turning back towards Isthmus and the airport. He pressed the accelerator harder, and saw the pickup, minus Perez's three men, who had not found the stomach to go through the flames and gasoline in such a comparatively open and slower vehicle. Even from the mirror, Bond could see that the pickup's tyres were smoking badly. He was still looking in the mirror when the first burst of fire, from Sanchez's chauffeur's Uzi, rattled across the bonnet of the cab.

A moment later, as Bond was going for broke in an attempt to overtake the tanker now in front of him, another burst shattered the windshield. He punched out a hole with his fist, and made up his mind quickly. Setting the cab's cruise control to 70 mph, Bond smashed the remainder of the windshield and steered so that it faced immediately behind the rear of the tanker in front of him.

This was no time to hang around. He pulled himself out of the cab onto the bonnet, crawling forward until the radiator was only feet from the growing circle which was the rear of the tanker. A short inspection ladder went up the back, at the bottom of which was the main valve. Twice, Bond almost had the valve in his hand. Then again, but this time he grasped the lower rung of the inspection ladder. As he did so, the tanker went into a turn, accelerating as its driver took it around.

Bond found himself stretched between cab and the tanker. It was the tanker that won, picking up Bond and pulling him from the bonnet. The tanker continued around the bend, and the cab went in a straight line, off the road and across the stretch of parched earth on the far side of the verge.

Two bullets clanged into the back of the tanker, inches from Bond's head. The pickup with Perez and Braun was gaining. He reached out and finally got a grasp on the main valve. It turned easily, and gasoline started to flood out onto the road.

Bond continued up the ladder just in time to see the pickup, its tyres still smoking from the pass it had made through the earlier wreckage, hit the gas on the road.

Flames lit up all around the pickup. It stayed on a straight course for around thirty seconds, the two occupants screaming and struggling to get out. Then the fire took hold and appeared to turn in on the pickup, which disappeared for a fraction of a second in a red bloom of flame before it left the road.

By now, Bond was atop the tanker and realising the situation in which he had placed himself. As the tanker moved forwards, more gasoline pumped out of the valve, and the flames, begun by the pickup, were now racing towards the tanker.

Pam, who had been wheeling and banking in an attempt to find Bond, saw the cab leave the road, and then felt the airplane rock to the next fireball. She turned in its direction and took in the situation in a second.

There was practically no time, she realised, as she lowered her flaps and began to make an approach above the running flames. She was beating the flames by less than seconds now, cutting her engine and gliding down to less than four feet above the tanker, holding her line of flight until she felt Bond's weight on the undercarriage. She opened the throttle and put the nose up, turning hard left as soon as there was enough airspeed. The plane was starting to bank when the tanker exploded.

"One to go." Pam said it aloud, and knew instinctively what Bond would want. It was not her idea of Saturday afternoon fun, but she wanted vengeance as well. She opened the throttle, turning back, low towards the road and the last tanker. Flaps down again and approaching from the rear, Pam kept the airplane level, losing height slowly.

Underneath, watching and waiting as he hung from the undercarriage strut, Bond saw movement in the cab. It was Sanchez himself and they were now only fifty yards from the tanker, and around a hundred feet up.

Forty feet, and fifty up. Bond's heart missed a beat. He could clearly see Sanchez now, half in and half out of the cab, another missile balanced on his shoulder as he took careful aim at the light airplane. Down, Pam, fast, Bond willed her.

Ten feet away and about fifteen above the tanker. Sanchez leaning further out to make certain of his shot. Over the tanker now, and at almost the same moment, Bond dropped, Pam raised the airplane's nose and Sanchez squeezed the trigger.

Bond landed feet-first, slipping and almost sliding right down the side of the tanker. He slapped his hands hard against the metal and, almost by sheer willpower, hauled himself up again.

Pam had climbed away when the missile struck, missing the fuselage but clipping the tailplane so that she lost all directional control. Bond could not bear to watch, and in any case he had other things to do. Pulling himself to the back of the tanker, he swung onto the inspection ladder, once more heading for the valve and its precious gasoline. He was quite prepared to go as well if it meant ending Sanchez's life.

He got to the valve as the rig slowed, obviously coming to a stop: he turned the valve and the gasoline spurted out. At the same moment he heard Pam's aircraft slam into the ground a mile or so away.

As the tanker came to a skidding stop, Bond climbed back onto the top of the tank as he heard the cab doors slam. He moved as quietly as possible along the gleaming metal surface, while below him Sanchez was screaming, "Get that valve! No, leave it, I'll do it myself." Bond reached the end of the tank and was standing above the gap between it and the cab. He had been here before, he thought, but this was not the same.

He dropped, landing reasonably, and started to uncouple the tank from the cab. Once it was clear, he thought, the tank would roll back, for they were on a slight incline.

He uncoupled and started to reach out for the hydraulics lines, which were the only things keeping the tank held to the cab. As he reached, he heard a roar of rage. Sanchez, a huge machete in his hand, stood beside the coupling.

"Now, James Bond." He was breathing heavily. "Now I'll have your head." He leaped up into the space between the tank and cab, bringing the machete down in a fast hard chop which was deflected by the hydraulic lines. Both men stood on the tiny ledge of the tank, which began to roll away from the cab, the final umbilical cord severed.

The tank gathered speed as it went backwards and neither man could move as they clung to pieces of the ruptured lines. They felt the first bumps as it left the road and began to roll in Sanchez's direction.

Bond jumped, pushing himself away and landing well clear as the tank turned over twice, its main seam ripping open and spilling gasoline onto the dusty dry ground.

After the noise came an eerie silence. Sanchez, Bond thought, could never have survived. He skirted the great pools of gasoline, keeping well away in case the whole thing blew. No sign of life anywhere. Taking no chances, he completed the circle, ending up where he had landed after his leap.

There was no sign of the driver, but he was the last of Bond's worries. If Sanchez was dead . . . The hand caught his hair, strong and unexpected. Bond dropped to his knees. The stench of gasoline on Sanchez's clothing was strong as he hauled Bond's head back, the machete raised.

"This really is the end, Bond. And I don't even care why you did it anymore." The machete flashed in the sunlight, and Bond's last hope lay in his hand stealing towards his pocket.

"Do you really want to know? I'll tell you, then." Bond's fingers closed over the lighter given to him at the wedding, which now seemed a million years ago.

"Quickly!" The machete hovered.

"Felix Leiter," said Bond, flicking the cigarette lighter against Sanchez's gasoline-soaked clothes.

He let go of Bond's hair in a reflex action. Bond leaped away as Sanchez shrieked and cried out. He wanted to put a lot of distance between himself and this blundering, moving man of fire.

But he need not have worried. Sanchez, screaming and flapping, was completely disorientated. Even Bond felt a cringe of horror. From behind the wreckage and into the pools of gasoline came the driver. He saw Sanchez, a horrible walking torch, coming straight towards the spreading gasoline. He reached it long before the driver could move away. Bond dropped to the ground, burying his face as he felt the flames. When he looked up at the broiling landscape, he thought he could still hear the screaming.

A few minutes later, feeling no sense of either victory or vengeance, he began to stagger along the road, back the way he had come, in the hope that he might find some kind of transport. He heard the engine of the cab before the two police helicopters.

It was the one he had ridden in. The one with the windscreen shot out. Someone was driving it slowly along the road, as though searching. Overhead the helicopters turned and began to drift downwards.

Bond reached the door of the cab. "Look what I found." Pam Bouvier, white and not a little shaken, looked down at him.

"Want a lift, mister?" she said.

— 18 —

Special Friends

PAM TOLD HIM about the crop duster as they waited for the helicopters. "The missile clipped the stabiliser," she said with a nervous laugh. "So I had no rudder. I had pitch but couldn't yaw the damned thing. And you need that for landing, James."

"I know. I fly as well." Bond was simply relieved that she had walked away from what had happened.

"It was quite funny, really," she prattled on. "I got her into a glide, found a nice flat piece of ground, but when I touched down it wasn't flat. It was a kind of gorge. I ripped the wings off. Want to buy a good crop duster fuselage? Those missiles didn't really do Sanchez much good, did they?"

"I've a feeling," Bond said, "that he picked them

up cheaply. I don't suppose we'll ever know, but my guess is they're training aids. To acclimatise troops in the handling of portable missiles."

"Thank heaven he didn't have Stingers or Blowpipes." Pam raised her eyes upwards. "We'd have been clobbered."

Bond gave a wry smile. "So would Sanchez. Things like Stingers are portable, but you have to know the hell of a lot about them. The early ones, which just had infrared, were not good, and the latest designs are just too technical for the kind of people he had around him. Anyway, if he'd had Stingers he couldn't have made the shot that clipped your rudder. You have to carry around a terrible lot of gubbins with a Stinger."

Rojas and Q arrived with the helicopters. On the way there had been exceptional news. "We have had what is called a bloodless coup." Rojas gave them a big beam.

"It wasn't so bloodless out here," Bond muttered.

"President Lopez has resigned, and most of his government with him. Four of our senior military people have come from the closet, and declared themselves with us. At last, I think maybe the corruption will end."

"What will you do with Hector Lopez?" Bond asked.

"Probably nothing." Rojas did not seem to wish any ill on the politicians who had been in Sanchez's thrall. "You know, old Hector Lopez's heart was in the wrong place for a few years, that's all. Before he tried politics he was a pretty fair lawyer. He was a greedy man, rich in his own right. He just wanted more. The sin of avarice . . . " He cut himself short, conscious that he was about to make a lot of boring statements. "I fear I shall have to ask you to stay in Isthmus until we have held the enquiry into Sanchez's demise, and other matters." He looked from Bond to Pam, and then Q.

"Naturally." Bond answered for all of them. "How long will that take?"

"Oh, twenty-four, maybe forty-eight hours. I don't think we want to go into it too deeply."

They all laughed. Anywhere but Isthmus, the enquiry would have gone on for months, even years.

Two nights later, when everyone was rested and statements had been made to the authorities, Lupe, who had assumed control of Sanchez's palatial estate, invited what she called "a few very special friends" to a celebration of the new regime.

Two hundred guests ate, drank and generally enjoyed themselves. "A few special friends?" Pam said with a quizzically raised eyebrow. "I always thought that about Lupe. Nice girl, has no enemies."

"Well, I like to think of her as a special friend." Bond knew, as he said it, that he was, as they say, in deep yogurt with Pam, who flounced away.

Early in the evening, Bond placed a person-to-person call to the hospital in Key West. The Isthmus telephone company, true to form, managed to get the call through around midnight. At the time, Bond was sitting alone at the bar, occasionally feeding Sanchez's iguana with cocktail nibbles.

"Good of you to call, James." Felix sounded down but not out. "They're giving me a lot of therapy."

"The pain goes with time, Felix." Bond was not talking about physical pain, and he knew all the hurt his old friend was suffering from Della's death. "I've been there, old buddy. Never leaves you, but it does get easier. Look, I'll be over to see you in a week or two."

There was a silence at the distant end, then Leiter said, "Great. I might even be on new feet by then. Oh, did you know M's been nosing around? Says he wants to see you in London. PDQ."

"He'll wait."

"Yeah, there are other things to life than the crazy business we're in."

"You're right there, my friend. I was just going to find another thing. See you soon." He closed the line, and looked up to see Lupe stroking the iguana.

"I thought you didn't like this beast."

Lupe raised her elegant right hand. The iguana's diamond-studded collar was around her wrist. "Iguanas, James, are a girl's best friend."

"So I see."

"Can you come into the garden with me, James? I've got something to talk about. I need your advice."

They went out and stood near the waterfall.

"Hector Lopez, our former President, has asked me to marry him," she said quickly, not meeting his eyes.

"And?"

"And I wanted to know what you thought about it."

"You love him?"

"No. But that could happen. He has much money. I would be safe. Before I say yes, I had to ask if I'd be safer with you?"

"Nobody's ever really safe with me." Bond did not smile. "I think you'd make a beautiful couple. Go in peace, Lupe. Go and say yes."

She nodded, then reached up, twining her arms around his neck, and kissed him hard. At last, she pulled away, whispered "Goodbye" and walked off towards the house, the night and the music. Bond turned away from the waterfall. Pam stood there, her eyes brimming with tears. "If that's how you want it, James."

He went to her. "You're wrong. Lupe's going to marry Lopez. That was just a goodbye. I was about to come looking for you to say hallo." He pulled her, almost roughly, into his arms, and kissed her with passion.

After several minutes, she pushed him away. "Why don't you wait till you're asked?" There was a sparkle in her eyes.

"Then ask me," Bond said, reaching for her again.

NOBODY DOES IT BETTER THAN

IAN FLEMING'S
JAMES BOND

230